GHOST
PARACHUTE
105 FLASH FICTION STORIES

Published by Ghost Parachute Press
ISBN 978-0-578-90274-6

Editors:
Brett Pribble (Editor-in Chief)
Genevieve Anna Tyrrell (Assistant Editor)
Marelize Roets (Assistant Editor)

Artists:
Geneveive Anna Tyrrell: Cover Illustration, & "The Big Place"
Brett J. Barr: "Parable of the Wasp", "Road Kill", "Smoking in the City"
Kaylan Stedman: "Tell Them a Pretty Story", "Beehive", "The Distractions"
Katiana Robles: "The White Witch of Ghetto Lane", "Let's Get Loud",
"Two Moons and a Hummingbird"
Paulaidan Minerva "Starry Night", "When We Feng-shuied Sebastian", "Overripe"

Graphic Designer:
Helen Henny

Printed in the United States of America

CONTENTS

—

Tell Them a Pretty Story by Terry Ann Thaxton (February 2017) 9

Bone Wars by Laura Citino (June 2017) 11

First Mars, then the Moon by Ciera Horton McElroy (May 2018) 13

The River Before Dawn by Evan James Sheldon (February 2020) 15

Brothers by Benjamin Reed (March 2017) 17

Those Who Grow Horns by Miranda Williams (September 2020) 19

Malibu Lacey by Tara Campbell (October 2019) 23

Root Baby by Laura Lee Bahr (April 2019) 27

Parable of the Wasp by David James Poissant (March 2018) 31

Arnie Upstairs by Audrey Lindemann (May 2019) 35

All Our Heads in a Row by Abby Burns (June 2018) 37

Disneyland by Robert Vaughn (September 2018) 41

Polite by Kelle Schillaci Clarke (August 2019) 43

July, 1944 by Shaemus Spencer (May 2020) 47

Last Seen by Shinelle Espaillat (March 2017) 51

Little Will by Patricia Q. Bidar (August 2019) 53

Road Kill by MFC Feeley (December 2016) 55

Yala Ela by Christopher James (August 2018) 57

Violations by Shasta Grant (May 2017) 61

An Old War Hog by Desmond White (February 2018) 65

Common North American Lifestyle Predators and How to Evade Them
by Jane Ridgeway (September 2018) 67

Camp Potomac by Brendan Stephens (May 2017) 71

Cold as Charity by Rob Metcalf (December 2017) 75

The Dandelions by Lilian Vercauteren (December 2017) 79

The White Witch of Ghetto Lane
by Tamra Artelia Martin (October 2020) 83

Drink by William R. Soldan (October 2018)...................................87

The Art Room by Susan Lilley (October 2018) 89

Buddy Holly is Dead by Sarah Viren (July 2018).........................93

My Visit to the Psychic by Pat Rushin (May 2017)........................95

In Defense of Killing Betsy Ross by Ryan Little (February 2020) 97

N n' N by Rosa Boshier (July 2018)...101

Collateral Damage by Nancy Hightower (April 2018)................... 103

Starry Night by David Morgan O'Connor (July 2018).................. 107

Human Interest by Ron Burch (February 2018)............................ 111

In the Headlights by Brittany Terwilliger (September 2019)...............115

Hummingbirds and Things Like That
by Epiphany Ferrell (November 2016)..117

Tony and the Breeders by Sean Patrick Mulroy (March 2018) 121

Class Reunion or I'll Use Your Entrails to Bind Our Legs for the Sack Race
by Michael Grant Smith (October 2017) 125

Out of Season by Michele Finn Johnson (February 2021)................ 127

Pieces by Chuck Augello (July 2017)...129

Let's Get Loud by V.G. Anderson (June 2018) 133

Between the Liking and the Pretending
by Cathy Ulrich (February 2019)..137

12 and Counting by Scott Paul Hallam (August 2017) 139

New Price by Scott Garson (March 2020)......................................141

Broken Keys by Jennifer Fliss (January 2021).. 143

Oaks Fall by Christopher Ramsey (October 2020).. 145

Jaded by Wilson Koewing (May 2020) 149

The Art of Cutting by Joshua Begley (December 2016)................................153

Two Moons and a Hummingbird by Jo Varnish (March 2020) 157

Distance by Justin Brozanski (February 2021) 159

Forest of Friends by Claire Polders (August 2019)...................................... 163

Fairytales by Kieron Walquist (September 2017) 165

Nurture by J. Bradley (April 2017) 169

It's a Long Way from Here to There and Back Again
by Rachel Smith (September 2019) 171

The Swan Maiden's Children by Bethany DuVall (June 2020)....................173

Surrender by Kevin Hogg (April 2017).. 177

The Distractions by Liza Monroy (May 2017)..181

The Girl in Jake's Red Hoodie by Maura Yzmore (September 2018) 183

Bridgetown by James R. Gapinski (May 2019) 185

The Spell by Meg Pokrass (August 2020)...187

Holiday of the Flies by Erik Deckers (November 2020) 189

Through the Reeds by Maria Pinto (January 2017)...................................... 193

Reluctant Orpheus by Teege Braune (October 2016)................................... 195

Putting One's Affairs in Order by John King (November 2019)................... 197

Beehive by Karen Gonzalez-Videla (May 2020) 201

Inpatient by Philip Elliott (November 2017) 203

Every Reachable Feather by Gary Fincke (June 2020) 205

The Art of Being Industrious by Len Kuntz (July 2019)..............................207

The Death Trip by Rachel Kolman (January 2017) 209

Stress Cardiomyopathy by Sheldon Lee Compton (October 2017)...............213

The Siren by Alyssa Pearl Fusek (September 2018).....................................215

Different by Francine Witte (January 2021) 217

When We Feng-Shuied Sebastian by Christopher Allen (May 2019) 219

End in Sight by Paul Nevin (September, 2020) 221

Leapers by Joe Baumann (March 2017) 225

First Date by Rose Andersen (September 2017) 227

Yalobusha by Tristan Durst (November 2017) 229

Pentagram by Mike Lee (August 2018) 233

1985 by Cheryl Pappas (September 2020) 235

Sparta by Ryler Dustin (December 2016) 237

The Big Place by Kimberly Lojewski (April 2019) 241

Dog Sitting by Kim Magowan (September 2018) 245

Outline for a Lyric Essay about Cavemen
by Nicole Oquendo (March 2018) 247

Lost Going Home by Bradley Sides (January 2017) 251

Mrs. Bee by Sara Comito (June 2019) 253

The Most Metal Band You've Ever Heard
by Patrick Cooper (July 2017) 255

Freaky Phalanges by Tom Lucas (March 2017) 261

Hostages by Michelle Ross (March 2020) 265

Overripe by Leslie Salas (July, 2020) 269

Andrea's Senses by Paul Beckman (April, 2019) 273

Breath and Blood by Juli C. Lasselle (December 2017)..................................275

Death Every 3 Seconds by Meg Tuite (May 2018) 277

The Shed by Dominic Lim (December 2017) 279

The Rats by Jared Silvia (October 2019)..283

Even as an Airplane by Amanda Chiado (November 2017) 115

We Were Waiting for Big Polly to Bring Us Our Cocaine
by Ephraim Scott Sommers (July 2017) 287

Smoking in the City by Jennifer Todhunter (June 2020) 291

It's Natural by Curtis Ippolito (June 2020) 293

You'll Never Leave by Steve Gergley (March 2020) 297

flippin, arkansas by Lauren Suchenski (November 2017) 299

Half White, Half Charred by Tara Isabel Zambrano (October 2019) 301

Insomnia by Dan Kennedy (November 2017) 303

Funeral Arrangements by Racquel Henry (February 2018) 305

The Good Book by Lynn Mundell (September 2017) 309

The Magic of Hanging Upside Down
by Gabrielle Griffis (March 2020) 311

Artist: Kaylan Stedman

TELL THEM A PRETTY STORY

Terry Ann Thaxton

—

Tell it in second person or pretend you don't exist. Climb inside a wicker box, glue the lid to your head, and don't ever come out. Don't tell them about the three knobs on the dresser across the room or the dried flowers and rat trap you slipped inside. Tell them something pretty: an Adirondack chair at the edge of the ocean, breeze blowing the towel tossed across its back. Don't tell them about your bruised face, the gunshots behind your head to keep you in line. Don't tell them about the lies chained to your lips.

*

Don't worry about me, I disappeared long ago, in childhood after I beat my brothers with sticks, threw rocks at cars, and cried to go home from church camp. I disappeared when church service began, my father standing in the choir (top row, center), after my mother slapped my face for singing different words to the hymns, after I counted the number of flies inside the church building. Don't worry about me. I'm not a pretty story. I disappeared years ago, after I caught my brothers smoking in the woods. Don't worry about me. Here's my story: I failed to sit on men's laps when my boss asked me to, I failed at smoking pot, failed at watching my mother die, failed at getting off caffeine, failed at raising a child. Don't worry about me. I'm not here.

*

She drops dirt like a child blinded by broken bottles. The story is in the floorboards, or is dust, or is a flower above her window.

Chains of ash from the red hotel sink spread across her dream of a blast that was once the soft ground where she sat, and now she refuses to be quiet. Find her in the woods, tied to the cypress trees. Fourteen times the solstice opened her eyes, conjured her up like words dripping from a throat before she found a way to say things like, "No, get out of my life."

Her fingers are on the trigger of her past. Her fingers are careful in the garden of sand. *Our father who art in heaven? Give me a bouquet of dogs, give me a pack of storm-whipped sticks, give me a mandible, lips that fit on the curtain's wistful breath, give me police reports, give me a bonfire, my first husband's rifle. Give me my enemies.*

*

I was never a pretty story, and now my entire body has become bone. I simply wish to become a mummy filled with rocks, with straw, with bangles of cartilage and teeth. I wish to make my life a junkyard that holds my hungry, pointless sins.

BONE WARS

Laura Citino

—

This kid is trying to tell me that Brontosaurus didn't really exist. He wears a black T-shirt halfway to his knees, skinny like they all are. These kids get bussed in from tri-county or the group homes because a day at Suffolk City Dino Park is a cheap way to occupy restless eyes and destructive little hands. Most of them get right to vandalizing. Some of the park people hate these kids, but I like them. They're easy, really, so easy to help.

"I don't know, buddy," I say. "We got one right here." I gesture like I've been taught to the animatronic sauropod creaking its head back and forth above us. From where I stand, I can see the bolts in its neck, green and yellow paint rusting. I'm supposed to be doing rounds to make sure the tri-county kids aren't clogging toilets or scrawling DICK on the flat boulders along the walking path. This job is low stakes. No flashing lights or emergency tracheotomies, no rollovers in cornfields. *A positive step forward*, was what I wrote on my application.

"Brontosaurus was a mistake," the kid says. His nose runs and he keeps slinging the back of his hand across his face. Snot doesn't freak me out. In EMT school, I always had the strongest stomach. Blood, vomit, the strange clarity of viscera, no problem. "They thought they discovered another species but they didn't," he says. "It's just an Apatosaurus with a funny head."

My first day, José quizzed me on dinosaur knowledge in the breakroom while he sorted through OSHA videos. Velociraptor means *Swift Seizer*. Dimetrodon means Two-Sized Tooth. José can't wait for me to see the Dino Park in the fall, how the flaming leaves enliven the machinery. I like his faith in my future here.

I say, "Did you know that Brontosaurus means *Thunder Lizard*?"

He looks at me with suspicion, caught off guard by how much of a dweeb I am. These kids are hard to impress. Even the dumbest ones just know things, but I'm trying to get into the habit of automatic good will toward others, the belief that someone, somewhere, is having a worse day than I am. The potted ferns rustle and I pull José from his hiding place, pluck the joint from his lips. José loves kids. He places his long fingers on the back of my neck. "Oh, Carlotta," he says. "These are the most majestic creatures to ever walk the planet. We have to help him. This could save his life."

I flinch. "He's right here."

The kid says hi. He says his name is Carter.

José pinches his eyebrows together, rearranges his face into one of deep concern. "Carter, are you telling my beautiful friend here that Mr. Brontosaurus isn't actually real?" He winks at me. The kids always ask if the adults here are dating or married, as if that'd be the most natural thing.

Carter stomps his foot. "Brontosaurus just isn't the right name of that thing. Somebody switched the skulls." He has the face of someone who has never been told, I believe you.

José says that the admittance of failure is not my strong suit.

Carter says, "Well, she stinks."

Kid, I can admit failure anytime. The ease with which I admit failure would blow your fucking mind. The history of prehistoric discovery in America is fraught with lies and deception, one-of-a-kind fossils destroyed out of hand simply for the pleasure of undercutting another man's work. How's that? And I knew the guy was dead. The car was crushed in like a pop can, this guy hung by his seatbelt, bleeding out at a speed that seemed impossible to me. His femur was white and clean. But I thought maybe he needed to breathe. That's why I jammed my little knife into his throat. That's why I did it, even though I didn't need to, because I was surprised by all that white.

José grabs my hand and holds it tight.

Here's another. When I was a kid, I visited a park just like this one. I screamed the whole drive home because I thought the dinosaurs were alive. Carter says that we create and destroy in equal measure and José says, Babe, he's got a point, but I knew all their names. I knew they would follow me home. We found the bones. Even when we are wrong, the bones will still be real.

FIRST MARS, THEN THE MOON

Ciera Horton McElroy

—

I knew I would go to Mars when they told me my baby's heart was no longer beating. They scheduled me for a 36-hour delivery to excavate my dead baby girl from my body. This body that buoyed her to new life for the past eight months. I took the anesthesia, couldn't bear the thought of her silent entry to the world. After the procedure, when they whisked away my small purple girl, they led me to a secret shower and washed the blood and shit, then wrapped me in towels, handed me and my husband pamphlets about Maternal Grief and Recovery, and the chaplain sang Psalm 23, and a nurse asked if I wanted pictures of my baby girl from *Now I Lay Me Down To Sleep* photography. Then they wheeled me out the door without a birth certificate. Stillborn babies don't get birth certificates, just a memory box with a snip of infant hair, and the promise to receive her ashes.

#

It didn't have to be Mars. It had to be anywhere away from my second story apartment, decked with bassinets and swing sets and Fisher Price Zoom 'n Crawls. Away from my husband who loved me too much to cry when I was watching—who locked the bathroom door and sobbed in the shower, as if I wouldn't hear.

It could have been hang-gliding in Croatia, like a bird over the Dalmatian coast.

It could have been an expedition to Machu Pichu, hiking along the vertiginous peaks in alpaca wraps of crimson, saffron, gold. I could have collected postcards of llamas, the sprawling, mountainous jungles, brought them back to paste on our fridge, cover the ultrasound pictures we left there, the announcement already printed with her name. *Annabeth.*

It could have been a volcanic exploration in Reykjavík, followed by a bout of salmon fishing. Then, I could have descended to those milky pools, succumbed to the geothermal waters, serpentine amid the snowbanks.

It could have been a cruise to the far reaches of the Pacific, where the wide-hipped women could show me how to dance, how to move my thighs, reclaim my body.

I might have gone diving with great whites, hiking with penguins, spent every equinox and solstice in some place holy, mythic, impossibly far.

But then again—what was farther than space?

I registered as one of those Mars tourists, submitted the down payment, the paperwork, the healthcare proof. There was a NASA-sponsored online course about what to expect in regards to g-force and dried food and peeing in space, that sort of thing. I packed a small bag, imagined its contents floating inside the space chamber when I unzipped it. My hair brush, wrinkle cream, nail file, wedding ring. Her memory box.

We leave Cape Canaveral on a bright November morning. I wave goodbye to my husband who has come to see me off—whisper to him through the glass, "I'll see you next year."

She is in the wooden box, which is in the second pocket of my packed bag, which is in our cargo room at the back of the shuttle. The pilot tells us we will hyper sleep—me and the other Mars tourists, a divorced man and an old hippie woman. As we depart our galaxy, sleep is descending and I will dream of her as we tumble through the dark. And when I awake after six months, I will strap on my suit, leave the shuttle, hover over the blood-red planet, and sprinkle her ashes in space. She will never be buried, never tossed into a river bed somewhere. She'll float among the stars, become space dust.

THE RIVER BEFORE DAWN

Evan James Sheldon

—

I'm in the boat, a small two-seat wooden affair without oars but one long pole, and I'm leaving for the opposite shore when I hear a whistle. People who whistle for the attention of others are almost always terrible, and I know I should push down into the mucky bottom and be done for the night. It's late and nothing good ever happens after midnight, as my mother would say, but it's only one person and I'm heading for the other side, for home, anyway.

I turn around and wait as the person clumsily climbs into the boat, shaking it from side to side. I'm standing and I almost rock it a bit harder to see if the person will topple into the water. I don't do it. Restraint is the better part of valor, as my mother would say.

It's my father. He has a long cloak on that he's rummaging around in awkwardly. He flips a couple of coins in my direction that clatter on the bottom of the boat, the sound echoing out across the river. I turn and begin pushing us toward home without saying anything.

I hear a soft, wet sound. My father is holding something and quietly weeping. I can't make out what's in his hands, but he shifts ,and it lolls like a dead thing.

Tough night? I ask, trying to deepen my voice to an unrecognizable basso. I'm not quite sure why I do this, perhaps for the same reason I didn't announce myself when I recognized him. Something in me says that he is up to no good. Plus, I don't want him to know I've been ferrying people across the river at night. My father is nothing if not protective. I don't want to defend my choices, but maybe I want him to defend his own, whatever they are.

He cradles the dead thing with one arm and pulls out an old cream-colored handkerchief, wipes his eyes and nose. He laughs a dark laugh, a sound I've never heard from him before. *You could say that. But then, that would be correct on almost any night in this town.* As we draw nearer to the far shore, the pine trees shift from a dark wall to individual stark shapes, a different texture of black against the night sky.

Most nights are tough nights? It almost sounds like an aphorism, something my mother would say, but there's something about the way he said it, a weariness to his tone that made it ring true. I wonder what he's up to at night, who this person is who sneaks out and returns crying over small dead things. All he's ever been before is my father, steadfast if quiet, a bit boring really. The kind of father you don't realize is good until you meet other fathers. Now, I think back through my sixteen years and find hundreds of moments to question his behavior.

So, do you cross the river often? I ask. Even as I say it, it sounds like a bad pickup line, something I never thought I would mutter to my father.

Not often enough, he says. He kisses whatever it is he is holding and lets it slide gently into the water. It drops without a sound, without anyone but the two of us to see.

We coast the rest of the way in, and even though I've landed this boat dozens of times, the shore is jarring. I hop out and drag the boat all the way up onto the beach. My father steps past me. I plan to wait a while before sneaking home, give him some time to get there and get in bed, *if* he even heads home, and I realize how little I know of him, maybe all the people in my life.

My father stops and turns. *Come now, Son. Your mother can never sleep when we both are out at night.*

It takes me several moments before I can collect myself enough to follow him into the trees.

BROTHERS

Benjamin Reed

—

When Jerry got sick, I didn't know what to do. And then suddenly there he was in hospice, dying. His oncologist said he had weeks, maybe a month. I knew Jerry's parents were both dead, but he also had a bunch of siblings and cousins in different places. I went through his phone and emailed everyone, but it was the weirdest thing: no one wanted to come make their final goodbyes. They all had some excuse, or they didn't reply. Except for his youngest brother, Devin, even though he was on the other side of the world. He was a lance corporal with the Marines, in Afghanistan, but he emailed right back to say that he'd already been granted emergency leave, and that he'd be here as soon as he could. Four days later he showed up at Jerry's bedside, sunburnt, in his camouflage uniform, his tan-colored combat boots still dusty from Kandahar or somewhere. Jerry couldn't talk by this point, but I saw in his eyes that he recognized his little brother. Devin sat next to Jerry and took his dying brother's hand in his. Then he made Jerry slap his own face. *Smack.* "Stop hitting yourself, Jerry," Devin said. Then he made Jerry slap himself again. *Smack.* "Stop hitting yourself." And then again—*smack.* "Jerry, I mean it—stop hitting yourself."

THOSE WHO GROW HORNS

Miranda Williams

—

In eighth grade, Juno takes my hand—the prosthetic one—and tells me a secret. I can help you with this, she says. I feel her weight on the plastic, but not her skin. I imagine her fingertips are cool and soft like a salamander. The bathroom we're in seeps grey—uneven paint, metallic sinks, muted light—and tastes of perfume.

Juno steps closer and whispers, I can tell it bothers you. It doesn't have to anymore.

A ring loops through her left nostril. Her lips are thin and pale. Dirty-blonde locks sprout and fall from her head like wilting flowers. She is beautiful. The type of beautiful that doesn't hurt to look at.

When she was younger, Juno was adopted by a Neo-Pagan couple. My parents would be skeptical of them. Would probably talk shit about them at dinner. Sweat bites my hairline. Slithers where my prosthetic melds to my forearm. I meet Juno's gaze and say okay. Her eyes become shiny, filled with tears, and she nods.

#

We walk to Juno's house, and the hanging sun turns our cheeks ruby. She tells me I have Aquarius energy. I say I'm a Libra. We don't speak much after that. Yard after yard embraced by white fences, cut grass, sparkling wind chimes swim past. I consider turning around when Juno strolls up the walkway of one. My house is just like it.

Juno opens the front door for me. I fold myself, holding my damaged arm with the normal one, before entering. Her living room is hazy and sanded with objects: smooth seashells, animal figurines lacquered with gleam, jars and soup cans stuffed with lively, sprung plants. Everything gathers on polished wood shelves, congregates in corners, drips off untouched walls. Lemon-scented Lysol licks my nose.

She is waiting for me to speak. I hear it in the way she sucks in air—heavy and long, muffling the silence. A painting is pinned to the wall. It's washed in browns, yellows, and greens. Vomit colors. In the middle is a satyr. His beard is clean and sculpted. Horns burst from his forehead. He acknowledges us with kind, round eyes and a tilted smile.

Who's the goat guy? I ask.

He's a god. Can't you tell?

Juno's balmy breath kisses my ears. She trails her hand from my shoulder to elbow and her jagged nails summon goosebumps.

He splintered from vines and bone. Defied darkness. Conquered the labyrinth, Juno says.

I step onto the carpet. It's buoyant and speckled. The kind of carpet that would leave red imprints on your arms if you lay on it for long.

I didn't expect you to live in a house like this.

Why wouldn't I live in a house like this?

I turn to face her. Juno smiles, small and close-lipped. Quiet simmers between us. She nods, encouraging me to answer. My jaw is twisted shut. I want to ask her why plants can still grow without sun. Why seashells tether to dirt despite cracking waves?

Juno takes my hand—the real one. Follow me, she says, pulling us to center, a crevice between leather couches. It's all looking at me, staring with eyes of leaves and canvas.

We sit on the floor, knees touching. Legs prickle with hair. Lie down, she says. Her voice is Playdough. Both pliant and firm. Her gaze—that of a deer to another deer—glides down my throat and sits on my lungs.

Are you sure?

I don't know what provokes me to ask. She bobs her head, so I spread myself on the ground, stretching my legs to either side. My limbs cradle her. The prosthetic cowers in the cave of my stomach.

One moment, Juno says, standing up.

I close my eyes until the carpet shifts and skin touches mine. Crystals the size of perfectly sliced carrots fill her palms. They are jagged and sparkling. For a second, I hate her.

Why'd you bring those? I ask as she spills the crystals at my sides. They glitter so bright they could line wedding rings or my mother's necklaces. Juno exhales, picking an apple-colored garnet and rolling it in her fingers.

Why're you upset by it? she says, soothing. Eyes throb. Words fall into the chasm between us. Reaching to caress my plastic hand, she speaks again. Crystals heal us. Show us who we are. They grow by hardening. Like people.

I want to tell her it's all bullshit, but that would make me feel like my parents, so I don't. I bite my lip. Halt the tears. Juno moves my hand to the floor and I'm starfished. It reminds me of how I stood to be fitted for a bridesmaid dress. We'd like a nice pair of matching gloves for her, my mother told them.

Juno places the garnet by my arm and plucks the rest from the carpet, clustering them along my skin until I'm outlined in shiny flecks of rock.

You're all the energy of the earth, Juno says. She runs a finger from the top of my forehead down the bridge of my nose. Do you feel it?

Maybe her lunacy blankets me. I imagine the vibrancy of the crystals dripping from their bodies. It erodes the ground, melts magma until there's only a single pillar of earth and it belongs to me. The room is warm. Juno kneels behind my head. It makes my breath heavy, and the sharp edges of the crystals needle my flesh to remind me they are there. They are there.

Juno touches her forehead to mine, mixing her sweat with my sweat. It belongs to you, she says. There's the sound of static—shifting carpet, raveling hair, buzzing heat—like an old TV losing grip.

The crystals crawl again. This time, they embrace every crevice of plastic—where screws meet rounded caves, the slip of space where it meets my arm, the small indents of knuckle. I let the tears go.

MALIBU LACEY

Tara Campbell

—

Malibu Lacey wears cutoffs and tank tops, or wraparound sarongs and tiny scrunchies to hold up her hair.

Malibu Lacey goes pretend swimming and lies on her blanket under the sun. She's not the kind that gets tan, though. She didn't come with stickers that leave behind pale shapes on her skin. She remains unmarked.

Malibu Lacey drinks piña coladas made of air and air. She sips them from tiny pink wineglasses because Girl lost the bigger glasses, which is fine because she's trying to cut back anyway.

Malibu Lacey is trying to cut back on a lot of things, mostly things that involve Girl's brother. Malibu Lacey hasn't been quite the same since the first time he ripped off her head.

Girl was at a sleepover at a friend's house, and had left Malibu Lacey at home, and must have said something to her brother to make him mad. This is what Malibu Lacey tells herself to justify what came next: the boy's clammy fist clenched her torso, pinning her arms to her side. Then his other palm covered her face and his fingers curled around the back of her head. And then she felt a *snap* and both halves tingled—she felt each half—before she slammed against the wall.

From where she lay, Malibu Lacey could see her shoulder sticking up from the folds of the bedcover. She'd never seen her own shoulder before.

Girl's mother found her and tsked, and popped her head back onto her body and went to yell at the boy. Then all Malibu Lacey could see was the ceiling, dull cream with flocking. She counted the peaks and valleys until Girl came back home, and forgot how high she'd counted as soon as Girl picked her up.

It still makes her tingle, thinking about the curve of herself. Until then, all she could see was her forearms, and her legs up to her knees.

The second time the brother popped her head off, he hid it in a different room of the house, face down in the carpet, which wasn't exciting. But the third time, he threw it into the yard. She watched a line of ants trek across the lawn, their shiny black bodies flowing like water between blades of grass. A few of them tickled her cheeks with their twitching feelers, but once they realized she wasn't food, they went back to carrying bits of grain much larger than themselves.

Things were just getting good when Girl found her and plucked her head out of the grass. To this day Malibu Lacey wonders if the team of ants was able to lift that giant dead bumblebee and get it back to their nest.

Girl cried because Malibu Lacey's head didn't sit the way it had before. It kept tipping, she said, and her mother yelled at the boy again and said she'd use his allowance to buy Girl a new doll. But Malibu Lacey didn't mind so much, because at least now she could look down even further and see her legs up to her thighs.

Then the boy got so mad, he took one of her legs off and threw it into the woods. So Malibu Lacey focused all of her admiration on the one leg she had left.

And Girl didn't care, because she had a new doll, so the boy took off Malibu Lacey's remaining leg and threw it on the floor, then did the same with her arms and torso and head. He left everything in Girl's bedroom so she would see it.

While she waited for Girl to come home, Malibu Lacey took in the whole of herself: her broad shoulders, tiny waist and trim ass, her shapely arms and impossibly long legs. She began to tingle again with the beauty of herself.

Girl only put her back together again because she wanted a friend for her new doll.

Now Malibu Lacey and the new doll drink piña coladas and lie on the beach and gossip. Malibu Lacey feels like she's supposed to tell the new doll how beautiful she is. Girl didn't say it outright, but Malibu Lacey knows what's expected of her, knows the price for being put back together.

And yes, the new doll is beautiful, and she's the kind that gets pale reverse tans when you put stickers on her skin. But that means Malibu Lacey is beautiful too, because they're basically the same, except for the leg, which is living its best life out in the woods.

Sometimes Malibu Lacey feels things in her hip socket. She senses when her leg is frightened or excited, or when it feels like laughing. And happy things happen to the leg more often than bad things, so on balance, thinks Malibu Lacey, it's a success.

And sometimes she purposely doesn't tell the new doll how pretty she is, and the new doll gets cross and is mean to Girl, and Girl is then mean to her brother, who gets angry and goes into her room and rips Malibu Lacey's head off again. Then Malibu Lacey gets to admire herself: from her dainty, permanently pointed toes, up her single shapely leg that stretches for days, to her wasp-like waist, and her breasts surging like impossible missiles out of her torso, up the curve of her shoulders, ending with the fleshy dull spike that slips into her head. She tingles then, imagining that spike slipping back into her head once more.

Sometimes the brother leaves one of her arms aloft, tipping a tiny piña colada directly down her neck. This is her favorite kind of afternoon. Her head feels like sparkles. She's flying.

ROOT BABY

Laura Lee Bahr

—

First, he gave me this rock.

We stood on a pile of dirt that had once been a garden that the elementary school kids had used, but now it was just nothing but where bits of trash got stuck. He'd asked me to meet him there after school, saying he had something for me. And then there we were, both of us staring at our feet, and he handed me this rock he said he'd found. He said it was shaped like a heart. I thought it looked more like a kidney bean, but I got what he meant.

Meanwhile my heart beat like a fish suffocating on land before someone smashes its head so it stops flopping. I thought I could maybe hit it with the rock, but I knew the logistics were too messy. I'd have to, like, cut myself open and get through the rib cage and...

He put his lips on mine.

I had never really kissed anyone before and my guess was he hadn't either, because it was like neither of us knew what to do. Our lips were touching like people in old movies when they couldn't open their mouths and when we pressed in harder our teeth bumped beneath our closed lips.

I could smell that behind his ears he smelled like salt and vinegar potato chips, and I wanted to lick him there and see if he tasted like he smelled. Instead, I asked him if I could bite him. I guess it seemed too weird to ask if I could lick behind his ear and biting him seemed less so?

But he said "Sure," like that wasn't weird at all.

And I bit him, kind of soft, like a puppy does when it's playing, and he pulled me closer and he took this deep breath like the sound you make when you are home after a long day.

So, I guess we were in love.

And that patch of dirt was ours. We stared at it enough, both of us looking at the ground until we found a way to push through the force field that separated us and collapse into the other.

We'd meet there when we could, and we'd see things like where the garden refused to die. We saw some lettuce putting its head through some clumps of plastic bottle-cap riddled grass like it didn't care about trash. It was just gonna grow. And every once in a while, there would be a root vegetable — a carrot or a potato. We never thought of eating them. They didn't seem edible, to be honest, they always looked pretty sad.

Once he was kicking some clots of dirt and you could see the top of this root — honestly, I'm not sure what it was. We pulled it out of the ground. It didn't look like a carrot or a potato or anything else I knew. It was about the size of two fists, and it had this indent in it that made it look like it had a shriveled little face with an open crying mouth.

"It's our baby!" I said.

And he didn't even laugh. He just kissed it and got dirt on his lips and then he kissed me. We were both better at kissing by then.

And then we buried it again, our hands working together to cover our root-baby with the dirt like a blanket, so he could sleep until he grew big and strong, we said, and then we would dig him up again and each of us would take turns taking care of him. And we laughed a lot about that.

That was the last time I saw him. I won't get into the whole thing but there was an issue at school, and he had been kind of homeless for a while with his family and well — he just never showed up again.

And all I had was that rock which looked more and more like a bean every time I looked at it.

And then it rained.

It rained like it would never stop.

They even cancelled school because of the rain, because things were flooding. Trees were falling over, and there were mudslides.

And I was in my room listening to the thunder and the rain and wondering where he was and if he was dry.

When the rain stopped and I got back to school, that patch of dirt had new trash in it, but the root-baby was gone. I thought of it floating down some storm drain, or washing into some street and getting smashed by tires.

I thought of its mouth open and crying — and I thought how no one would care about it — they wouldn't even know if it was something they could eat or just trash or that it had ever been something we had kissed and claimed as something we had made in the way that we made love.

And I still have this dream: the water is rising and rising in my room, and our root-baby, which has floated so far and been in so much peril, has finally made its way back to me. It floats right on to my bed, crying with a wail. It sounds so much like a real baby it breaks my heart. I lift up my shirt and put my nipple in the open mouth indent, and the mouth closes and softly suckles. Root-baby drinks my milk. I marvel. How big and strong it will grow! The water rises all around us.

But we don't drown. We never drown. My bed is a boat, and we float like that for as long as I can stay asleep.

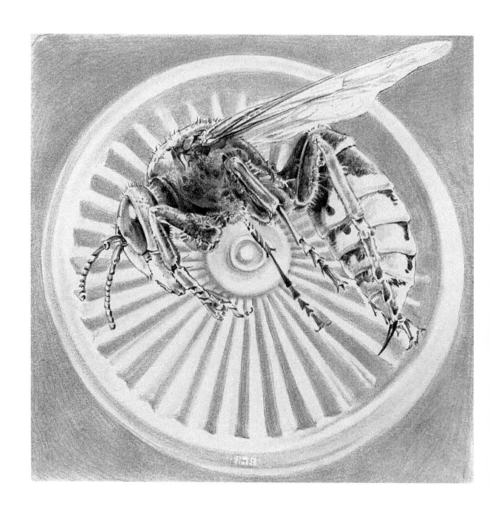

Artist: Brett J. Barr

PARABLE OF THE WASP

David James Poissant

—

The husband stands at the window with a wasp trapped in Tupperware while, in the kitchen, a teakettle screams.

How he'd gotten himself into this predicament was this:

The husband had spied a wasp circling the house. He wasn't allergic, but his wife was. Stung, she'd have thirty seconds to get the EpiPen into her leg before her throat swelled shut.

Luckily, his wife was not home. The husband sat at the kitchen table, a book in his lap, waiting for water to boil for tea. The wasp buzzed from kitchen to family room to kitchen again. The husband stood, book in hand, and the wasp flew to the family room, charging the windows and bumping the walls.

In time, the wasp landed on a window. The house was old, the windowpanes thin. To swat the wasp might break the glass. The husband waited for the wasp to lift off, to settle on a surface the husband could smack with the book. Wasp crushed, the husband would dispose of the body, the stinger. In this way, he would save his wife. Except that the wasp would not budge.

The clock struck four in the afternoon. Soon the wife would be home from the elementary school where all day she helped children become better human beings than they were, or, at the very least, she kept them from becoming worse. But, what if, right then, his wife came through the door? What if the wasp lifted off and landed on her?

The wasp had to be stopped, but the wasp would not leave the windowpane. The water on the stove was not yet at a boil.

The husband waited.

Waiting, the husband had an ingenious idea. He moved to the cupboard and extracted a Tupperware bowl—not the largest, not the smallest. The bowl was a two-quart bowl, clear plastic, and, carrying the bowl to the family room, the husband watched the wasp. The wasp clung to the glass. It did not fly at the husband's approach. It did not fly as the husband's shadow darkened the windowpane. It did not fly until the instant the Tupperware was thrust, flat to the glass, the wasp trapped inside, at which point the wasp flew quite a lot, thrashing and banging the bowl's plastic sides, so that the husband could almost feel the wasp on his fingertips.

The bowl buzzed in his hands like a vibrating phone.

Then the kettle began to sing.

The kettle's song was pleasant. At first. After five minutes, the sound had grown less pleasant. But the husband tolerated it. He had to. After all, he was trapped.

For, you see, the husband had not thought to bring the lid. He'd not thought to prepare a sheet of paper or cardboard strip he might slip in the seam between window and wasp, and, in this way, trap the venom inside of the bowl. To release the Tupperware from the window, now, was to release an angry wasp into the house.

And, once released, if he could not find the wasp, what then?

What if the wasp went into hiding, only to emerge with a stinger for his wife once she'd gone off to bed?

What if the wasp waited beneath a bar of soap, ready to sting when she washed her face?

What if the wasp waited in the shower? His wife would not have her EpiPen with her in the shower. Did epinephrine auto-injectors even work in the shower? The husband didn't know much about the devices, but he was reasonably sure they did not.

No, the husband could not release the wasp from the bowl. This would be unwise, unsafe. Soon his wife would walk through the door. Soon she would pull the kettle from the stove and the lid from the cupboard's Tupperware pile. Soon the purgatory of wasp buzz and teakettle cry would be complete.

Unless.

It was only once the clock on the wall read quarter past four, once he'd endured fifteen minutes of the teakettle's screams, that the husband began to wonder whether the parent-teacher conference his wife had mentioned—a conference with the parents of a student working, perhaps, less diligently than most on becoming a better human being—whether that meeting was tomorrow, as the husband thought he remembered, or whether the meeting was, in fact, that day.

Were it today, the husband had a dilemma. The conference might go another hour. The husband's back was cramping. His fingers hurt. But the real problem was not the husband's discomfort (mild) or the ringing in his ears (at this point, severe).

No, the real problem was that the kettle was literally losing steam. As in, much of the water, by now, must have boiled off. Then there would be only sizzle, followed by the scent of a kettle bottom burning. Then the house would fill not with steam, but with smoke.

How long could he stand there, after all, the husband, Tupperware in hand? For, while the wasp might sting his wife walking through the door, were the odds not better, and growing better by the second, that their house might soon be consumed by flames? That, should he choose not to drop the bowl and remove the kettle from the stove, there might be no doorway for his wife to step through, no home for her to come home to?

Say his wife was saved from the wasp's sting. Would she love him for letting their home burn?

Say the husband saved the house but lost his wife to the wasp. Would he ever forgive himself for her death?

No.

The husband would stand, *will* stand, at the window as long as it takes, even as the house burns around him and the Tupperware fuses to the palm of his hand.

The kettle screams.

The wasp rattles the bowl.

And, right then, mercifully, in the driveway, the chirp of car doors being locked. A homecoming. His wife's key in the door.

There are tears in his eyes.

Soon, in the entranceway, his wife will set down her things. Soon she will see him. Soon she will take in the sight of this man who for only a couple of years now she's loved. Soon she will stand, a foot in either room, and see the kettle, the wasp, and, just seeing, she'll know.

She will understand. Or she won't.

And, understanding, or not, she will love him. Or laugh.

Knowing which makes all the difference.

What happens next means he must love her forever, or forever doubt her love.

So, he waits. The husband waits for the open door. Waits for rescue. Waits to see whether his wife's love, as he sees it, will pass this test, and whether he, in turn, will love her back.

ARNIE UPSTAIRS

Audrey Lindemann

—

Arnie's smelled like woman for ten months come yesterday. In that time, she hasn't come downstairs. I bring Arnie her food four times a day, five since Charlie's emergence, who's oily like a Vaseline covered piglet. But before oily Charlie, there was only Arnie in a state of perpetual prostration, in the bed she drips across and bleeds on.

I had told Arnie I couldn't do it anymore, that as of a few weeks ago I had my own hemoglobic suicide to attend to, my first, and that it was gushing from me in clumps and pulling itself out of my cracks. I looked down at my body, because Arnie doesn't believe in mirrors, and I touched my little chest and little smooth legs and pet them slow like a pussy, terrified at the un-sewable ruptures intersticing what used to be porcelain, and I put the cream of wheat on a tray. I set it next to Arnie and told her it was the last time she should expect me, that I needed fresh air which didn't reek of her, but she rolled toward me and I saw her belly and I saw that belly and when I saw it, I knew I couldn't run.

When I closed my eyes at night, Arnie's sweaty figure on the sheets gurgled around my pupils like she was circling my drain, and I still believe this is what infected me. That the constant exposure was conditioning my mind to condition my body to morph, perverting me with its terminal bloatation. I put the heels of my hands into my eye sockets until it was painful, smothered myself in pillow, trying to think of anything else besides her oceanic caverns, her massive breasts straining toward the ground, the lightning bolts rupturing her overworked skin, her fur, ache, curve, resignation, and I cried out in terror, waking the baby.

When I pulled Charlie out of Arnie, he stayed connected to her from what appeared to be a portion of Arnie's intestine, and dripped with her insides. She asked me to cut the tie, and put the baby into her droop. She shined at me like a sun, and I screamed at her that if she looked in just one single mirror, she would see that she needed help, that she is becoming a beast with some parasite or cancer, but she serened at me like glass, and told me that this is how I came from her, and this is where I was going.

Before I cut the tie, before the eruption, I would rub Arnie's tumid ankles, prop a pillow under her engorged neck, spray air freshener around the room, and spackle itamin E salve over her chinks. I would brush her hair, wipe her sheen, lather her folds, and when I left my duties, I'd lick my own wounds downstairs— the stomach heaves and double-overings, vacuum up my blood, not expecting help because Arnie was too busy being submissive to her own anatomy.

The worst part about Arnie was how she went down with her legs spread open and without a fighting chance. The second worst part was the size, the way she oozed over the side of the bed like a hopeless goop, like a balloon how she swelled and grew and bulged. But no, the worst was the complicity, I hated that, her on her back, the passivity, like a cog in some subservient sacrificial cycle, bellying, excreting, ecstatic moaning and painful yipping, it made me cringe to the bottom of my toes. I hated her tears of joy, most of all, on a face that looked like mine. And all of her sluice.

ALL OUR HEADS IN A ROW

Abby Burns

—

P E changed the day a woman named Doctor interrupted our game of badminton. She said, *Today, we're going to learn how to inhabit the body.* She looked at me, then over my shoulder. *I need all the girls to follow me.* We lined up in alphabetical order by our first names while the boys took turns lobbing shuttlecocks at our backs. For the most part, these birdies torpedoed off our shirts and onto the floor, but some we would catch, some we would steal away to crush their feathers within our pockets. I fingered the two I'd stuffed in my jeans until Doctor noticed and took them away. *It looks like you're touching yourself,* she said.

She led us to an empty classroom. Someone had shoved all the desks against the right wall and left in their place large blue mats, the kind that stick to your skin when you sweat or the kind that make you sweat when they stick to your skin. We sat crisscross keeping as much space between our knees as we could without anyone falling to the floor. Doctor surveilled us one at a time, running her hands along our head to discern the shape of our skull—its divots, bumps, and bald spots. She told us to stand and measured ratios of hips to waists to thighs to knees, then stepped on our feet to determine our resilience. Grace yelped and squirmed the loudest. I did my best to stay silent when Doctor approached, but my shoes were thin and she was tall and muscular. I felt the full brunt of her body and I let out a squeal.

Doctor told us we would spend the next ten minutes concentrating on the sting of our feet, locating with precision the exact place it hurt. *Close your eyes and follow the shooting pain back to the tops of your feet,* she said in the voice of a hypnotist. I no longer felt anything, so I searched out the memory. Wisps of pain swirled up my calves and my right leg spasmed. When time ran out, Doctor had us go around the room and share where we ended up. Every girl said ankles or feet or toes. When it was my turn, I hesitated before pointing to my right knee. The room giggled. *And why do you feel pain there?* Doctor asked after the room had settled and I whispered a story of how the first time I rode a bike, I fell and shattered my kneecap against the blacktop, how my brother was forced to stop playing tetherball and carry me home, how he complained the whole way and I was forced to reassure him through my tears. *That pain has yet to leave you,* Doctor said and turned away before I could nod in agreement.

Class continued and we stretched and breathed, circled our arms around each other's waists and held on. My body tingled every time Doctor spoke. Before the close of the hour, Doctor interrupted our unilateral hamstring stretch. *For our last activity of the day, I want you all to place your hands on either side of your head,* she said and we complied. *Now, twist your head first to the right, then to the left. Continue this motion until you feel your neck muscles loosen.* My muscles gave almost immediately and euphoria buzzed through me. Calm had turned me to liquid, fluid and strong. *Stay here in this space,* she said, *keep your grip and reach up to the ceiling.* The room filled with the sound of vacuum burps as we pulled our heads from our bodies in a haunting procession.

Air stung the gape of my neck. I clutched my hair tightly in fear of dropping my head to that sweaty mat. My chest heaved, mimicking breath while Doctor pleaded with us to retain our senses. As we murmured our dread and pinched our cheeks, she walked around the room and collected our heads, pulling hair from our careful fingers. She then lined all our heads in a row beneath the blackboard. Here, I could see only knees and feet and the blue of the mats. Dust the custodians had neglected to sweep. I wished for long hair to keep from witnessing the moment our bodies rose and stumbled forward.

The lesson is complete when you find and reattach your head. Then and only then, you can leave. The moment grew chaotic as bodies scrambled to reach the front first. The ordered line we had formed earlier gave way to desperation, pushing and scratching. Legs passed in front of my eyes and I squinted in search of my jeans. To my right, Lindsay's head disappeared from my peripheral. Maggie's flower-print leggings tripped as they stepped from the mat and her arms pinwheeled to keep her chest from crushing the head on the far end. In their rush to leave, some girls took each other's heads. Jessica-Grace skipped out first, followed by Hanna-Arielle. The muscles of my throat swept up chalk dust as it clenched, once, twice, three times. A panic settled behind my eyes like a migraine. Pulsing. I felt certain my eyes would soon pop from their sockets and my assemblage would take on new dimensions. My body came last. *You'll get better*, Doctor said from where she stood by the door. *Set yourself right.*

I approached myself on my knees.

DISNEYLAND

Robert Vaughn

—

I came into the office and she was doing a Suzanne Sommers video. Air chopping step-ups, her flesh moving like a summer lake on a hot day. She said, "Wanna play?" but I pretended I'd misheard her and jetted toward the kitchen. She followed me.

"Hey, what's the rush?" I heard behind me. I cracked the top off a Bud with my teeth. Drained half of it while she stretched in the doorway, arms reaching toward the molding above her head, her sweaty upper lip quivering.

"They called again." Her voice had that familiar spooky sound like a guest on a Jon Walsh program.

"Who?" I sat at the counter on a stool I've always hated because my feet can't find the floor.

"The police. They have a new lead-"

"I don't want to hear it..." As soon as I'd blurted, I felt shitty because I knew in some way it was all she had. All we had. Memories. The past. "I'm sorry," I mumbled. "What'd they say?" Downed the other half of the Bud.

"Inspector Stevens thinks he might have a match- some kid in Letchworth, New York."

Happened over ten years ago. That's a lifetime when it's your only kid. Disneyland. Easier for me to assume he's dead- and in some ways, I suppose he is. Maybe we all are, going through the motions, muddling through another day?

Easy to blame each other, even though it happened so fast.

How does the sky reconcile a lost cloud?

The sun a spot that no longer exists?

A shadow crept over the room like it had always been there.

Milk cartons.

Wanted lists.

Missing Children support groups.

I was done. I walked to the fridge and opened a second Bud.

"What's for dinner," I asked.

POLITE

Kelle Schillaci Clarke

—

Everyone was so concerned with the counting of fingers and toes and the soft slapping of bottoms, they didn't notice her reaction, a rush of relief at first glance, knowing everything was going to be okay. Her heart felt all the right things —love, adoration, respect — as his wrinkly purple fingers reached for her nipple and politely moved it toward his mouth. From that moment, he was easily the most polite baby anyone had ever met. He let her and her husband sleep, preferred formula to breastmilk, and learned about the birds and bees from schoolmates, rather than embarrassing his parents for details.

He wasn't the easiest baby, but he was always well-mannered. *Pardon me,* he seemed to say when he first started crawling and clumsily bumped into things. *Excuse me,* read his expression as he addressed the furniture, the dog, the hardwood floor, once he'd started walking and fell face first. *So very sorry,* his face said, its lip split open, a moment before the tears and blood arrived. She scooped him into her arms and whispered, *it's not your fault, it's not your fault,* rubbing his arched back as he screamed.

Diaper changing was embarrassing for them both. He'd look away. She'd hurry about the business and be done.

He held doors for strangers and never picked his nose or ears like other kids. Once he could talk, he called strangers and parents of friends "Ma'am" and "Sir" without being taught or told to do so, which was cute only for a short time. *He must be getting it from somewhere,* the other parents gossiped. Other kids didn't particularly want to be around him, though they didn't hate him or tease him or bully him.

His dad became impatient when the boy got stuck holding doors for parades of strangers. *I don't know where he gets this from*, his dad barked, stomping and gritting teeth.

I'm sorry, said his mom. *I don't either*, she claimed.

Concerned by his suspicions, she encouraged her boy to try out for team sports. His developing height made basketball the obvious choice, though her husband was more rugby-built, both physically and mentally.

Go watch him play, she pleaded, when the boy made the team and quickly became the team leader in assists.

"Shoot the damn ball!" his dad barked from the stands, as his son passed the ball to the scrawny point guard who sunk shot after shot.

"Take a *seat*," his dad barked at him, when they boarded the bus after the game. But his son stood politely holding the rail, impervious to his dad's demands.

Never prone to eating much, the boy's slim body grew so tall he developed a bend in his spine from hunching over, too polite to take up space that could be used by others.

"It's good manners to eat what someone makes for you," his mom would say at mealtimes, using his politeness against him; if only to provide for him.

"There's no way he's my son," her husband barked at her after dinner, once the boy excused himself and began clearing the table. She pointed out the shape of his lips, the shade of his hair, but avoided his extraordinary height and polite nature. She knew these traits had nothing to do with her husband, and that the heart-shape slope of his lips also mirrored her own.

The next time she and her son took the bus, she pulled at his hand, forcing him to sit beside her.

"I prefer to stand," he said, but she insisted it was impolite to leave his mother seated by herself. He sat, politely crossing his long limbs to make room for hers.

"No," she said, pushing his legs apart so they created a wide 'V' of space, crossing her own to offer him more. They both looked at the floor, embarrassed.

"But now there's no room for you," he said, his knees bouncing anxiously beneath her palms. "I'd rather stand."

She gripped at his oversized fingers and pulled him back into the seat. She hated herself for what she was creating—even more for what she was destroying—but what choice did she have? He was too polite for his own good, and hers, too.

"Claim your space," she whispered, as the bus filled up.

Slowly, he stretched out his long legs — expanding, unfurling, savoring the newness of the sensation.

Then he released a sigh so full of relief that it shook her to her core.

JULY, 1944

Shaemus Spencer

—

MAIN ENTRANCE
Under the big top the tightrope act is introduced, and he knows the show is almost over. In an hour he'll be drunk, shoveling elephant shit and carcass scraps that the big cats leave behind. The smells cling to him: days-old sewage, bodies that haven't showered in a week, the singed wick of the fire breather's tools. The stench is comforting in a way, because it is familiar, constant. Elephant shit means he's getting paid. Getting paid means he's getting drunk.

He leans. The fabric of the big top resists, holds him almost upright. Tonight he smells something else under the usual circus funk, something that cuts through his whisky buzz and makes him restless. Gasoline. He drops his cigarette and stumbles to the tent mouth to watch the finale.

BANDSTAND
This is probably the worst band he has ever conducted. The trumpets are late and sharp. After the show they'll blame it on the summer heat. The entire woodwind section is dwarfed by two sousaphones, and the sousaphones spend half the night fucking with the trombonists. Ten more shows and he can leave. Ten more shows, and he'll have enough money to take his girl to Chicago and try out for the orchestra. He doubts their trumpets ever miss a cue.

Glancing over his shoulder, across the sea of guests and wild animals and performers, he sees something that turns his legs to jelly. He signals for the music they play only in emergencies. The Sousa song builds slowly as the band realizes what's happening. Behind him the noise of the crowd rises as the entrance to the big top fills with smoke.

100 FEET ABOVE RING THREE

Deep breath in. Tight Core. Steady legs. She glides her feet along the tightrope, toe-to-heel, toe-to-heel. Her arms flex against the weight of the balancing pole. She is aware of her surroundings in the way a fish is aware of its brook. The babbling crowd below gasps as her right foot slides forward and she falls into a full split. Deep breath in. Toes pointed. She makes a million imperceptible movements and prepares to stand when the band starts to play the last song she wants to hear while 100 feet in the air.

On the platform fifty feet ahead of her is her father. He motions to the entrance, where a small patch of flames licks its way up a panel of the tent. Her father climbs down the ladder, leaving her alone on the tightrope. There is no net.

CENTER RING

A clown is useless in most situations, but never more useless than in the midst of pandemonium. He knows this, and so he runs.

RING ONE

The tiger circles the edge of its cage, low to the ground, afraid. The tiger hears fire, smells death. The ringleader plays this off as just part of the routine, folks, and tries to hide the nerves that make his voice waver. Smoke finds its way up the tiger's flared nostrils, tendrils winding into his lungs, choking him. He bolts toward the long tunnel they brought him in through, back to the train car. The crowd laughs at him, this massive beast suddenly and inexplicably hunkered and weak. At the end of the tunnel a gate blocks the exit. The tiger sees the train car ahead of him, smells the danger behind him. He has never felt more trapped.

SIDESHOW TENT

The sword swallower and the bearded lady (who really doesn't mind the beard thanks for asking) stand next to the sideshow tent watching the fire. For a moment, the bearded lady considers offering help however she can. Then she remembers the woman who called her a freak and tugged on her beard so hard she clacked her teeth. She remembers the man who groped her and how the crowd laughed at him, at her. She decides the world would be better off without them. The sword swallower wraps an arm around her waist and offers his flask, the most romance he will ever show her outside their shared train car.

The clown runs out from behind the big top. As he runs, the toes of his bloated shoes pull up patches of grass and dust. He passes the bearded lady and the sword swallower and cackles. When he makes it to the street, he does not stop.

SOUTH GRANDSTAND J

The woman watches the big top burn, enthralled. Her child clings to her dress, screaming. Tiny stars of fire poke holes in the canopy, blooming into swaths of dark smoke and blazing light. People leap over seats and stampede toward the only exit not yet engulfed. The captivated woman does not notice when her child is torn from her. She barely feels the weight of the bodies against her as she is pushed to the ground, her head smacking the concrete hard. The last thing she sees, staring up through the crushing hoard of bodies, is the sky in flames. It is the most beautiful thing.

LAST SEEN

Shinelle Espaillat

—

Surrounded by crowds that swell with anger and purpose, the woman feels her stomach roil. She had hoped that a Wednesday afternoon would mean a lull in holiday shoppers. She wishes to stop, to sit, to go outside for a gust of crisp air. She swelters and itches inside her wool coat, and her left arm aches with the weight of her purchases. Her body forms a taut angle with her right arm, at the end of which the child pulls, running hard at nothing.

One gift more, she thinks, wading toward a rack of pullovers. "Just one more and we're done. Just a present for Grandma. Do you want to help me pick a nice sweater for Grandma?"

"No! Nononononononononono! Get off me!" The child jumps and twists, trying to wrest itself free. The woman presses her lips against another wave of nausea and tightens her grip on the sweaty little palm. She had tried letting the child roam a little, and the child had sent a mannequin clattering to the floor and ripped several blouses off a rack, one of which floated and settled over her so that she looked like a baby ghost as she scampered out of the store, setting off the security alarms, before the woman could catch her. "No! Get off! No touch!" The woman feels the will of the crowd press against her in rumbling waves.

"Hmph. If that were *my* child . . ."

"Leave it at home if you can't control it."

"Just let her stretch her legs."

"Does the mother know you pull on her like that?"

If only the child had inherited a little of the woman's color. The woman doesn't bother looking for or responding to the speakers. She ignores the objections and lifts the child, who becomes leaden, then becomes a hurricane. She carries the struggling child toward jewelry, but then a flailing fist catches her throat. Gagging, she drops the child, who promptly runs headfirst into a glass table. The woman feels rather than hears the resulting thunk; even her filings tremble. The child gasps, pauses, gasps and screams. And screams. Already, a purpling knot adorns the pale forehead.

The woman waves away offers of help and lugs the child through tightly-packed displays to the bathroom. They are both crying. The woman wets a wad of paper towels in cold water and gently presses them against the lump. The child presses her face against the woman's neck and winds her fingers through the woman's hair. Slowly, her sobs become whimpers, then murmurs, then occasional sniffles. They begin to breathe in sync.

"Okay my love." The woman remembers the first time she held the child, how they were exhausted then as well. She nestles into the scent of baby shampoo and thinks about the plum-sized person inside her. *It'll be alright,* she decides, *I can do this again.*

She sets the child on her feet, holding the small hand as they walk back into the store. Just as they reach the first rack, the child wrenches away and runs, giggling, through the displays. The woman does not follow. Hot blood rushes through her body, threatening to erupt from her eyes, mouth and fingertips. She closes her eyes against the spinning melee of shoppers and fluorescent lights. She inhales, 1, 2, 3, and exhales, 1, 2, 3. Fine. She will let the child learn what it means to be lost. She will search for the last gift and wait to hear the overhead announcement about a lost little girl.

This is what she tells store security, after the announcement doesn't come. This is what she tells the police, and then her husband, and then the reporter, and then herself, over and over.

LITTLE WILL

Patricia Q. Bidar

—

W ill was born as a little friend for his mother. His scorched hometown was the sight of an oil boom, and the murder capital of the country.

His sisters had married and been carried off to make homes in Houston, in St. Louis, in Knoxville, Tennessee with the earnest and citrus-smelling men they'd ensnared.

The wildcatter's kids would bully Will for his blonde curls, his soft life. To make it up to him, his doctor father bought him a Shetland pony. He wasn't allowed to tell.

His father turned away a silver miner and his family because they couldn't pay. The family staged a protest where they walked on their knees to Will's dad's practice. The local paper sent a pimpled high school student who'd been hounding them for an assignment. The receptionist had cried and been fired.

In the mornings after his father strode down the walk with his leather satchel, Will would cry to stay home, and his mother would give in. He wasn't allowed to tell.

A handful of ladies would arrive for luncheon, taking in the interior of the doctor's house for later gossip and speculation. They all knew what his mother didn't: little Will was curled under the table with a fistful of lemon cookies. Filled by the women's most intimate scents—the sight of their restless legs. Spectator pumps lined up alongside stockinged feet.

One wore bracelets that tinkled prettily. Another had dabbed bitter orange behind her knees. A transporting sight: the metal clip that secured a stocking to a flesh-tone panty girdle. Will experienced his first erections there, gnawing on sweetness. His whole life, he'd have a thing for older women.

Artist: Brett J. Barr

ROAD KILL

MFC Feeley

—

The raccoon's fur left a pattern in dried blood when Sylvia peeled him off the asphalt. She held him by the front paw. He was stiff.

"Mommy loved your bandit face."

Sylvia named him Brady. She knew that whichever neighbor had hit Brady would never tell and would go on living like everything was normal.

Sylvia put her doll in the bed where Mommy's head should be and tucked Brady under the pink coverlet in her doll cradle. She sprinkled Brady with Shalimar and promised God to never tell anyone if he let Brady come back alive. She would love him and feed him and give him garbage cans to play with.

"And if you can't do that, God, please make Mrs. McGowan go away, not get hit by a car, just go away and send Brady to heaven to be with mommy. I can take care of myself." Sylvia pulled all the roses off her mother's bush and laid them over Brady.

In the morning, Sylvia woke holding her doll. Scattered toys ringed the empty space where Brady's doll cradle belonged. She heard the scrape of a shovel. Her mom's rosebush lay sideways on the grass, muddy roots like fingers reaching toward her father as he dug. Daddy had tears. He said he'd thought she was too little for funerals.

Together, Daddy and Sylvia lowered Brady into the hole, planted the rosebush on top, and twisted their fingers up with each other's while Sylvia sang Brady up to heaven.

Mrs. McGowan would come again, but Sylvia hugged her father and thanked God that Mommy wasn't alone anymore.

YALA ELA

Christopher James

—

E very year, on her birthday, Ela did something she'd never done before. She's lived a good life, run her own business, never had children, saved up some money, likes to enjoy herself. Sixty-one, she stepped out of a perfectly good airplane. Sixty-two, she took acid. Sixty-three, she took acid *and* stepped out of a perfectly good airplane. No, she didn't. I made that one up. Sixty-four, she bungee-jumped.

Joining her, awaiting our turn on top of the bridge, I asked her, you see that story about that woman whose cord broke and she got herself dragged a mile through crocodile-infested white water rapids? She broke every other bone in her body, but survived.

I'm glad you're here, Ela said. Before, I was feeling nervous, but you're a regular ray of sunshine, Joe.

She survived, I pointed out again. And the next year she went back to the same place and bungee jumped again.

The bungee people said next victim, and pointed at us.

I'm up, dear, said Ela. Or down, I suppose.

Her cord didn't break, she didn't brave crocs or rapids, but she did do something to her ankle when they rowed out in their little boat to gather her dangling body. It called for an ambulance. In the hospital, she happened to mention this lump she had, probably no big deal and the docs said cancer. They told her not to watch any long movies. She asked me to bring her the longest film I could find, and could I pick up her bits and bobs too. Hey, I said, at least your ankle's fine.

The neighbors had found out already about Ela's c-news, were waiting either side of her door for me to arrive.

Just goes to show, said one, you can have all the money in the world, it can't save you from cancer.

I could have money if I didn't have kids too, said the other. She thinks because she doesn't have kids, does all these things, she's better than us?

She doesn't think that, I said.

Well, who's got cancer, said the other.

Just goes to show, said the one.

Inside her house, I found more neighbors. They were searching through her things, deciding ahead of time what they'd take if Ela died.

She's always smiling, they told me. Gives me the creeps, they said. Something not right about people always smiling.

It takes more muscles to frown than it does to smile, I said.

Quality, not quantity, they insisted. Look, we like Ela, we do. She didn't have kids, fine, we respect that. She goes off and does all these things, holidays, sports, adventures, fine, it's rude if you ask me, but we respect that. She's saved up money, bully for us, we respect that. Always smiling, though? It's not on.

Not on?

Not on. You can smile all you want, they said, but it's going to catch up with you in the end.

You think if she'd smiled less she'd not have cancer?

Can't have hurt, can it? they said. They called dibs on Ela's library, on her TV, on her record player, on her records. You don't even like records, they argued with each other. I don't care, they said. I already called them.

In my car, heading back to the hospital, I found more neighbors.

She thinks her shit smells like strawberries, they told me. She thinks she hung the moon and stars, they told me. She thinks she can leap tall buildings in a single bound, they told me. She thinks she's missing a cape, they told me. She thinks she craps lottery balls. She thinks her knees her elbows. She thinks down is up. She thinks *cancer* gets *her*. The fact of the matter is, they told me, if she'd settled down, had kids, not tried to be young again at her age, she'd still be with us.

She is still with us, I reminded them. They smiled like they knew better. Sure you are, dear.

Back in the hospital, a beautiful giant of a woman was fluffing Ela's pillow and jabbing a finger in her face. I don't *hate* you, she said. You *baffle* me. And she spat out *hate* the same way she spat out *baffle*. We have one job on this earth, and you've *eschewed* it. Other beautiful giants were in Ela's room. You're missing out on so much, they told her, pulling out the hair from her head one follicle by follicle.

That hurts, said Ela. Ouch! OUCH! MOTHERHUBBARD!

The most beautiful giant of all climbed in through the window of her room and said You know what hurts the most? It's fearing for the safety of your child. But you wouldn't know anything about that, would you?

What's going on? said Ela. Do you all even work here?
A man was at her feet, digging his nails into her toes, drawing blood. My wife would give her eye teeth to be able to have children, he said. Her blooming eye teeth! What do you have to say to that, eh?

Another man at her elbow, twisting the skin, leaving red welts. Do you know what my family could've done with your money?

One more man climbed on to the hospital bed and squished his foot into her belly. You shouldn't be allowed to run your own business. You should be at home, looking after your husband, raising a family.

Stop it! I screamed. I tried to force my way into the room to save her but there were too many neighbours in the way, blocking the door, pinching her, cutting her.

Stay out of this! they said. This isn't about you!

A man elbowed me in the tummy, his wife threw me to the wall and punched me in the side of my head.

Ela! I shouted. Remember the woman whose bungee cord broke!

Joe, she shouted back, her voice carrying into the corridor. I don't know what that means!

VIOLATIONS

Shasta Grant

———

Naomi brews coffee during naptime while showing me the latest inspection report: *monitor the nap mats and repair or replace as needed when the foam material is exposed, as it could become a choking hazard.* She complains about the cost of new mats while I drink the coffee. I imagine one of the children in her care choking on the foam. I think about the consequence for my sister if they did and feel a momentary surge of happiness. I take the carafe and refill her cup, then mine.

Her house is overrun with children: Jeremy, his finger digging inside his nose, Smelly Melly, Trevor with the knotted shoelaces, and the after-school kids. Naomi collects the meager checks from each exhausted mother on Friday afternoons: fifteen dollars for after school care, fifty dollars for full day. She ticks the names off the list in her register book, tucks the checks in an envelope. I'm embarrassed for her, cobbling together a life like this.

Naomi's known for the best in-home daycare in town. Everyone calls her Aunt Bubbles, a nickname from when she nearly drowned at the lake. She was ten and I was eleven that summer. We were swimming to the raft when her head slipped under, her arms flailing, bubbles forming on the water. The lifeguard had jumped from his tower as Naomi's head surfaced again, gasping for air. Safely on the sand, everyone gathered around and murmured how lucky she was to be alive. My mother stroked her wet hair, my father bought lemonade from the concession stand and held the straw to her mouth.

She's still reading sections of the inspection report out loud. I know what kind of caretaker she is. I've seen her yank the children's arms. She doesn't help Trevor tie his shoes until it's time for his mother to arrive (*I can't be tying his shoes all damn day*, she says). But these aren't the kind of violations the state inspector cares about. He cares about fire drill records and mulch beneath the swings.

I wish I could write my own report: *Aunt takes daughter into own home when it's not her place to do so; environment not suitable for a teenager due to inadequate supervision.* I have not forgotten what happened all those years ago. Naomi thought of Emily as belonging to both of us and I wanted to tell her to get her own damn daughter—even though Emily wasn't a good one, she belonged to me. Strung out on drugs and arrested for shoplifting nail polish and hair scrunchies from Ben Franklin when we had plenty of money to pay for those things.

When I wouldn't go down to the police station to get her, she called Aunt Bubbles. Naomi let my daughter move into the spare bedroom upstairs with the double bed we had shared as girls and skip school whenever she wanted. Some days Emily helped watch the kids, a different set back then, but always at least one child who smelled like pee. Other days, Naomi let Emily run around with friends, cooking up god-knows-what kind of drugs in basements and trailers. One day Emily called me crying, words slurred, begging to come home. I offered to take her to a treatment center and she hung up on me.

Naomi lets these children in her care now run around the backyard without ensuring their safety. She doesn't rake and replace the mulch beneath the swings. Just like she let my daughter run around town on the back of Justin's motorcycle with no helmet, even though she wasn't eighteen yet.

Last spring, when Naomi was in the bathroom, I removed the outlet covers in the living room, stuffing them in my purse, just to see if she'd notice. She didn't. The next report documented the violation: *outlet covers missing from living area that is accessible to children in the program.* She swore Trevor did it and I nodded in agreement: he did seem like a naughty boy.

For months I waited for the middle-of-the-night call. For Justin's motorcycle to crash, for my daughter to overdose on cooked-up drugs, choke on her own vomit, or someone's trailer to catch fire and incinerate everyone inside. It doesn't matter that the call never came, it could have. Maybe part of me wanted it to: an end to the teenage drama, a reason to pretend I didn't have a sister.

We don't speak of that time now and maybe Naomi thinks it doesn't matter. We are all we have left so I keep coming here every Friday. *Family is everything*, we say, kissing on the cheeks. I like the noise, the chaos, of Naomi's house. My daughter lives with some friends now. She cuts and perms hair, waxes eyebrows and upper lips at

Elite Hair Salon on Main Street. Maybe she could have been more if she hadn't been allowed to run wild that last year of high school.

Our coffee cooling, Naomi continues to read the report: *a bottle of Clorox wipes was found under the bathroom sink in an unsecured cabinet.* She's indignant about these small violations. I want to tell her that these inspections reveal what I've known all along.

At three o'clock, the after-school kids come pounding through the door, backpacks dropping on the floor. Jeremy, Melly, and Trevor emerge from the dining room, where they had been napping on the mats with exposed foam. Melly has had an accident. Naomi swats her hand and instructs her to get the Clorox wipes from the bathroom and clean the mess.

I get up to leave and Naomi asks me to stay, to walk to the bank with her. She wants me to watch the mothers file through with their checks, telling her what a godsend she is, how they couldn't do it without her. My sister is no saint though. I've known that since that hot August day when she pretended to drown in the lake.

AN OLD WAR HOG

Desmond White

—

The substitute teacher was an old war hog bristling with spears struck by fingers now bone and buried. On the board was writ Mr. Chaika in a quick cursive and the room was a foliage of desks and chairs chopped by tusks. This was unmistakable pig sign. The hog growled as students entered (cautious and sniffing rudely at the stench), and then attacked, churning chairs into charwood, perforating a student's backpack, lifting the boy into the air until, with a shake of its head, it threw the boy into a desk (now driftwood). The others circled the snorting substitute, dividing its attention with fidget spinners. They were at a disadvantage stepping over bodies from the previous class. Several times, the hog pawed lined paper and ritz crumbs, eyes stained red-root, hairline sharp as broken glass, a tusk chipped (its point in an assistant principal's ass now covered by a silver scar). Once the hog had choked on a filing cabinet, giving its throat a gurgle and a red saliva. Once a spear pierced its lungs—the pink gum long-healed over the ancient wood. The class clown sharpened a yardstick. The valedictorian pointed a remote at the ceiling. The ceiling projector spat light into its eyes. The class clown, proving his head in times of trouble, brought the yardstick on its rump with a smack—sending the substitute charging from the room. All was quiet except the clack of hooves on tile.

COMMON NORTH AMERICAN LIFESTYLE PREDATORS AND HOW TO EVADE THEM

Jane Ridgeway

———

The creatures smelled failure quickly.

Monday, Joel was laid off from the advertising job he had always regarded with slight contempt, a stop-gap meant to get him through the post-college years, one which had never blossomed into worthier opportunities.

Tuesday, he kissed Carla good morning, her lovely cheek pillow-creased, leaving her with a tender lie of omission and spending the day at Starbucks, pretending to be at work.

Wednesday, the firm sent home a slender envelope of COBRA information, which Carla opened. She greeted him at the door (as he returned from a more expensive coffee shop this time, one that made him feel as if that next, better job would materialize soon) with the envelope beginning to crinkle from the tension in her hands.

"I've got this under control," Joel said. "It's just a blip."

She left to spend the night at her sister's downtown loft anyway. "It isn't safe," she said with sad eyes, holding the door frame. A small shrug, as if to say, *you know how it is.* He did. They all knew. They'd all seen what happened.

Thursday in the subway station, Joel saw long, spindly fingers out of the corner of his eye. The fingers emerged from the dark well alongside the tracks, waving gently, scenting the air, twiddling in his direction. Joel began to sweat into his sharp business casual, donned that morning in his lonely apartment in anticipation of miraculous phone calls, unexpected interviews. The elderly woman waiting beside him stared at the searching hand emerging from the darkness at the edge of the platform, then glanced to Joel, the darkness, Joel, the fingers. She gathered her shopping bags and hurried away down the platform.

Joel abandoned the subway and Ubered across town to a co-working space, where he painstakingly copied and pasted lines of his resume into the application for a rival firm.

My passion for advertising is unequaled, he typed, swallowing back the cold brew and bile that rose in his throat.

When he tried to hail a ride home, Joel discovered that his data plan was gone, his phone a glossy brick. Hunched over his laptop in the lobby of the coworking space, a frantic chat session with a representative revealed that without the corporate discount from the firm, his monthly payment had not gone through.

On the train home, other passengers edged away, not making eye contact with Joel, as the long dark fingers pried their way between the car doors, not yet forceful enough to pry it open.

"What?" Joel's heart was racing, but he flung his arms wide in a show of bravado. "Do I have something on my face?"

Debarking, Joel averted his gaze from the dark mass limpeted to the side of the car. It wouldn't come for him yet. He still had time. An apartment, a girlfriend, a credit card. A family who loved him.

Joel broke the news on a video call home. His mother looked near tears.

"You can stay here as long as you need," she said, voice quavering. "I saw a hiring sign at Ace Hardware. I'll make up your bed for you."

His father looked just the way he had the night Joel, nervously taking a date to the movies, crashed the family Volvo into a bollard right there in the theatre parking lot. "Just do what needs to be done, son," he said. "Whatever it takes."

Joel didn't go to the coffee shop the next morning, didn't change out of his pajamas, stayed in bed sending LinkedIn messages to acquaintances: a college roommate, an old professor who'd gone into private industry, a woman he'd kissed once in a shameful, drunken hallway moment at an advertising conference. He watched the read receipts appear on these messages, but no responses were forthcoming.

The phone company still wouldn't reinstate his account, and now something was wrong with his joint checking account with Carla. He sent her a

Facebook message.

Hey can we talk? Isn't this a little dramatic?

The read receipt popped up moments later and hung there, damning as any quiet phone line.

Joel shuffled downstairs in slippers and robe to check the mail, where he found a thick packet from the firm with informational pamphlets: *Filing for Unemployment* and *Protecting Yourself From Common Lifestyle Predators*. Joel flipped through the Table of Contents, then to the "Early Days" section:

Because Lifestyle Predators can smell failure, it's important to rebound promptly from any incidents of unemployment, romantic relationship breakdown, medical crisis, or academic failure. Remember: they can smell you! They know what you did!

The manager met Joel on the way back to the elevator, stopped him with a gentle hand on his shoulder.

"Lease is up at the end of the month," he said with regret in his voice.

"We'd like to renew," Joel said, clutching his pamphlets.

The manager shrugged: you know how it is.

The creatures were at the lobby doors now. Their fingernails tapped and scraped at the glass.

"I can't have this in my building," the manager said. "Scares people. Ain't safe."

The drumming at the glass intensified.

"Please," Joel said. "Please, I'm begging you."

The manager backed away, into the doorframe of his own apartment. Joel could hear the TV blaring in the background, the toddler shrieking, a vacuum running. A world of the manager's own, needing protection.

Joel's sad cat lady neighbor was waiting for the elevator ahead of him but skittered away when she saw him coming.

"I'll get the next one," she said.

"Real nice," Joel said, hitting the *doors close* button. That bitch was safe, but not him?

He thought of Carla, of her pillow creases and mussed hair in the morning, of the apologetic reply that could await him upstairs even now. A win. A point in his ledger. Please.

A clang from above; a great weight dropping to the elevator roof. Fingernails beginning to skritch at the access hatch.

Please, he thought. Please. A win.

CAMP POTOMAC

Brendan Stephens

—

W e were at Boy Scout camp, and it'd been six days since either you or I showered. No one had noticed that I had gone so long because I sometimes swam in the pond's dark water. But everyone knew about you. Soot blackened your fingernails, bug juice stained your smile, and grease clumped your hair. Even the mosquitos stopped targeting you.

Neither you nor I had even got our Tenderfoot rank yet. We weren't even in high school. We were sort of friends—moderately pleased if a teacher put us in a group together, but we rarely talked outside of scout meetings. We were bunkmates though neither was our first choice.

For the past few days, I'd heard murmurs of dragging you out of our bunk and forcing you into the shower's cold water—a joke with the older kids that spread through the troop, growing in plausibility until it felt like only a matter of when. I didn't tell you. Half of me assumed you already knew, and the other half was sick of boys holding their noses when they walked past our tent. It was mostly an exaggerated joke, but, between the two of us, there was a damp, sour smell that took a few minutes to adjust to. If I had any other bunkmate, no one would have noticed. I barely talked to you anymore. We spent too much time together, and I blamed you for the jokes.

It was the last day of camp. Everyone's parents would be picking us up in the morning. One of the older boys invited me into the forest along with him and a few others to smoke hand rolled spliffs, the tobacco and marijuana acquired through an older brother. I wasn't the type of kid to get asked to break rules. I was a pastor's kid—the type of kid who guarded the answers to my test with a wall of folders. I knew this was about forcing you into the showers.

"At this point, he's breaking the Scout Law," the Scout Master's son said. "A scout is fucking clean."

A seventeen-year-old Life Scout with a wispy mustache said, "He looks like a damn animal. He doesn't even seem human."

I didn't say much, didn't even smoke, but I promised I'd force a tube sock in your mouth before they rushed the tent that night. Trying to stop them would only draw attention to me. Part of me wanted to see you humiliated.

That night, after the bonfire, I waited in the dark for your breathing to slow to a quiet snore. I crawled out of my sleeping bag already wearing a black shirt and my darkest blue jeans and sat waiting for the signal. Before I heard a bird call that wouldn't have convinced anyone, I heard their footsteps—a crunching of leaves and snapping of twigs. I stood over you, and for a moment considered shaking you awake and telling you to make a break for it. But they would have known it was me, and I knew how boys like us acted. By the time we made up our minds that there'd be violence, it was already too far.

When the call came, I pulled down your jaw and shoved a clean sock in as far back as I could.

The older boys threw open the tent flap and pinned you to the bed. You writhed and wiggled, but there were five of us. I pinned you down by the shoulders, leaned in close to your ear, and I told you to quit fighting it or we'd kick the fucking shit out of you.

We carried you down the gravel path lit only by moonlight. When the wooden building that housed the showers could be seen in the blue glow, you stopped struggling. You must have given up, felt resigned. Your weight still felt heavy.

Inside, we didn't set you down. We dropped you onto the smooth concrete. One of the boys had a pin flashlight. You pulled the sock out of your mouth and said you'd shower—it wasn't a big deal. But by now it wasn't about being clean at all. It was about violence and being noticed and lacking luck. It was about something that you can't quite put into words. Something about controlling another.

You stripped off your clothes. You piled the clothes in the corner and turned on the shower, not even wincing at the cold water. You lathered and washed like you weren't being forced. I'd never seen a naked body in person before, not even a family member by accident. In the shadows you looked like a corpse. The older boys were right: you looked less than human.

But they wanted the struggle, to force your screaming head into the stream as you pissed yourself. Even I felt it, until I couldn't bear it anymore. Your back was too us. I balled my bony hand into a tight fist. Without form, I hit you in the back of the skull as hard as I could. You collided with the wooden tile wall with a thud. My knuckles felt broken, but it didn't matter. We turned off the water, pummeled you, snorted like hogs at you, spit on you, turned the water back on, and hid your clothes in a rhododendron bush outside. Grime and soot and worm guts and sweat and urine and blood swirled down the drain. Given the chance, you would have done the same to me.

COLD AS CHARITY

Rob Metcalf

———

He hated it when they asked for money. She stood in the yellow light of the late-night street and looked at him in desperation. Her eyes glistened.

"They kicked me out without even asking how I'd get home."

He looked past her, at the cracked paving stones that led to his apartment building. The heating would be on by now.

"Where have you come from?" he asked.

"The Royal London. I was in there overnight but they've put me out on the street."

He nodded, then reached up and scratched his chin. The shadow of his nose fell across it like a sundial: time to go home?

"They kicked me out with no money. Can you help me? I only want to get home."

There were tears now, shining softly on either side of her nose. A pale face with freckles and a mouth turned down at the corners.

He paused, and a voice said, they're good at it you know, don't fall for it. He saw his father sitting at the end of the family table, dispensing the wisdom of kings from a suburban dining room.

The girl wore a hospital smock and undershirt, her bare legs incongruous in the cold, a contrast to the skinny jeans and suit trousers of the sporadic commuters leaving the station. A woman looked over her shoulder and quickened her pace. He thought of following her example, but something—some charitable instinct perhaps? —something held him there.

"Where do you need to get to?" he asked at last.

"I need to get to get the train."

"I might be able to help you," he said, and reached into his pocket. He had some change and it was really no trouble to give her a couple of pounds to keep her moving. If standing around in a hospital gown on Whitechapel Road in winter was a ruse to get a couple of quid, then it was a lousy way to make money.

He placed the coins in her hand and they shone in the streetlights. She looked down in disappointment.

"I need to get to Tunbridge Wells," she said.

She ran her hand through her wiry brown hair. Her eyes met his and then looked away. The hospital tag around her wrist was dirty and frayed.

"I've only got a couple of pounds," he said, "but it'll get you to Charing Cross."

He couldn't be expected to pay a fare out of London for a complete stranger. Someone at the station would be able to help her if she was genuine.

She regarded him silently.

"Perhaps you could call someone at home - get them to pay your fare from Charing Cross?"

"I live alone," she said. She continued to hold his gaze. Was that defiance? Or something else. It hardly seemed right to make his generosity a source of grievance. Anyway, he had an excuse.

"Look, I've really only got the coins in my wallet. I wish I could help you get all the way home, but I'm sure someone will..."

"There's a cash machine," she said, and pointed to the corner. They have elaborate schemes, these people, he heard his father's voice again. But she was leading the way out of the bright lights of the tube station towards the darker corner of the street where a cash machine glowed dully from a hole in the wall. Her hospital gown billowed like a foreign flag as he began to follow her along the pavement.

"You live round here, then?" she asked.

"Yes," he replied, "up the way," and he indicated the general direction of his apartment building, down the street towards the hospital from which she had supposedly come. He thought of the lounge in his apartment and wondered why he wasn't sitting comfortably on the couch with a glass of wine. He sighed and his breath formed a ghostly cloud in the cold air.

"Busy round here. And no-one stops to talk to you," she said.

"It's an interesting place to live, and close to the City, which is..."

She'd stopped in front of the machine and was pointing helpfully at the card slot.

"Could you get me twenty quid, please?"

Just this once, he thought. No fun being stuck out here in a hospital gown, beggar or not.

He raised his card to the slot but then noticed a flashing message on the screen: Sorry, this machine is out of order.

"It's not working," he said.

She scanned the street.

"There's another one over there," she said, pointing vaguely further down the road.

Don't get taken for a ride, boy, said the voice in his head. But he disregarded it. He was a kinder man than his father, and hated the thought of transferring that man's cold and miserly attitude to someone in need.

She led him down a side street popular with Jack the Ripper tours during the day but largely deserted at night. And there, in the pooling yellow glow of the streetlights, she began to mug him.

"Alright, mister. I want your wallet and your phone. Now."

"But the cash machine is just there," he said, not yet fully understanding how their roles had shifted. The jaundiced gleam of a knife made the change explicit.

He felt a rising pressure in his throat, as though he were about to be sick, but he fought it and tried to remain calm.

"Okay," he said, "you know I don't have any money on me. So if you'll just let me get to the machine I can get your money for the train."

"The train?" she said.

"To Tunbridge Wells," he reminded her.

"I'm planning a longer trip now mate. So you'd best give me your wallet and your pin number."

She was no longer the pitiable waif abandoned by the public health system, and the hospital smock now resembled a butcher's apron.

"Please," he said, "I only want to get home."

THE DANDELIONS

Lilian Vercauteren

—

When the lawnmower broke, we did nothing. We never talked about it, we just watched the grass grow long around it. After each storm, a wall of weeds slowly surged towards us. Where there was once soft lawn, thick, thorny branches clawed up from the earth and covered the white picket fence. The mailbox seemed to grow a wig, then disappeared in a clump of ivy altogether. We left the last letters addressed to us in there, unread, in their green tomb that would turn their skin and our names in ink to ashes, a monument to us. It was an unspoken truth between us that when vines crept up the porch, through the swing and underneath the doors, we knew not to bother. Before long, we didn't need to close the curtains, because greens draped from the gutters.

Our leafy shrubs hid us from the world. There was an ease to this world that lost all its sharpness, its edges round, its noises muffled. People came by to see us, to ask questions, tempt us to change. Some only drove by and looked, shaking their heads without words. Others tried to convince us to cut our lawn and repair the fence while we still could. "Those weeds don't belong in your lawn," they said. They wanted us to use chemicals that could fight for us and make the grass green and make the yellow flowers bend their necks and lose their color. They wanted our lawns to not be spotted with these nuisances. They didn't want to stand by and watch those flecks turn into soft white globes that when left alone would let go when the wind comes to take them, slowly, in their own time.

We only listened to the branches of the oaks sigh heavily over the hedge that was now our roof. Birds roosted up there. There were other beasts. We smelled them, heard them, caught glimpses of beady eyes in the dark. We were scared, sometimes, of this new, green world that was so full of purpose that it made us feel we weren't even there.

Eventually the doors covered in moss wouldn't open anymore. The power went out, though the house buzzed and trilled, as if it was trying to shake itself free of its skin. The moldy walls around us flowered thicker. Roots pushed up through the drains, lifting the house from its foundation until its bones creaked. They came reaching down the chimney and spilled from the kitchen sink, like they were hands searching for us. Our bodies were heavy and sank deep into our soft carpet of leaves. We were alone and the world was wild and we let it. We watched the wilderness grow up around us, until on a quiet winter's night, the wind came for us and we were ready.

Artist: Katiana Robles

THE WHITE WITCH OF GHETTO LANE

Tamra Artelia Martin

—

"Our new neighbor is a demon." Beebee spoke as if she were spitting out revelations to hungry ears, her words attempting a normal occurrence rather than confirming our newest local import was a spawn of hell.

We both knew she meant the young white guy who moved into Old Widow Maldonado's spare room two weeks prior. In a neighborhood of black and brown, he stood out like a grain of rice in darkened sand.

No one ever came in or out of Ghetto Lane. Everyone just existed, living there all their lives until they died without recognition or accomplishment.
We weren't in the hardcore ghetto, but the renovated shotgun houses and uneven dirt road screamed poverty, giving a nickname for generations.

"Why would you say something like that, Beebee?" I asked.
She rested her legs up on the banister as she sipped on the diabetic-sweet tea Gran made for us to cool ourselves. Stifling heat created sweat that beaded down her brown skin as her toes brushed up against the same-colored wood of the porch. "It's true, Nellie. Mama said so."

I rolled my eyes and continued dreaming of the fantastical. I wondered what battled neighborhood demons. "Let me guess. Your mama saw his pointed tail and horns, so God told her he was a demon."

"No." Beebee sighed. "She saw him bury bloody rags in the backyard. After she prayed on it, God revealed to her that he was a demon."

"Because God has nothing better to do than to make her think all white people are demons."

Beebee's mother was a certified Bible thumper who believed half the neighbors were spawns of Satan and other abominations, especially those of us who never went to church.

It took years for her to accept Beebee's friendship with me because my Gran and I never attended any religious services. Gran always said if she wanted to get closer to God, all she had to do was go outside and look up.

Belief was my myth, an emotion made up of fear and loneliness. Where was my belief in something?

Beebee shrugged. "I'm just telling you what she saw."

"You don't even live next door to him. How did she see him bury anything?"

"I don't know, but he's shady, Nellie. I know it."

I thought of his naturally tan complexion and hair the color of toasted cinnamon, which made me wonder how white he truly was, but in this neighborhood, he was as white as you could get.

"He's probably a regular human trying to get by like the rest of us," I said. I glanced over at Old Widow Maldonado's blue and tan house, hoping to catch a glimpse of him.

"Something's wrong with him." Her words slipped away as a breeze finally consumed us.

***

I left my sensibilities and logic on Gran's front porch as I walked to his backyard. Moving through the night never felt more freeing. A satisfying sensation melted through my skin and embraced my bones until I stood over the freshly packed earth where the *bloody* cloths rested.

Arms encircled me from behind.

"They think you're a demon," I whispered into the night.

He nuzzled my ear. "I'm a witch. Not a demon."

"I thought only women were witches."

"Men can be witches too."

His chest rose against my back as his breathing tickled my neck, giving a movable melody to midnight.

"Is your offering soaked in blood?"

"Syrah. A wine offering to Earth Mother."

"Earth isn't my mother."

"She's mother to all, even the unwilling and stubborn."

His nonsense made more sense than any religion.

I turned in his arms. "Are you calling me stubborn?"

"I call you a challenge."

"So you don't worship Satan?"

His laugh filled the night and flowed back into me.

"No, but isn't all worship just another form of magic?" His smile reminded me my insides were real. Pangs and clenches in abundance.

This was our back-and-forth ritual, my probing questions followed by his gentle compliance.

His lips tasted of sunlight and moonlight entwined like a Celtic knot, a revelation of power and wonder. In one kiss, he showered me with praise and baptized me in sensation.

The tan of his skin contrasted with my darker shades of fresh earth like the mound covering the offering to his goddess. Scents of mandarin and bergamot lingered on his cheeks from aftershave, two of many smells he taught me to touch without fingers.

Was it a sin to trace his star tattoo from point to point with my tongue when it reminded me of living?

We slept under the glow that filled our slice of Ghetto Lane, and I breathed in the first tasty breath I took since my birth. My pores sucked them in until they were sated.

Maybe it wasn't so bad to be the neighborhood demon.

DRINK

William R. Soldan

—

1. Dominic is digging his holes again, searching. His fortune, he says, he buried it out here in this sun-beaten sea of sand and sage. It was at the foot of the cottonwood along the wash, where the rain ran thin like veins—and then the flood. Or it was under the skull-shaped rock on the western edge of this land, this once-ranch where I was raised, or beneath the heap of rusty chains that rests among the tinder like a heavy coil of snakes? He can't remember, he says. It was right here. Or maybe there. His body sags, shoulders slanted like the undone fences, face poorly hung, a portrait on a crooked nail. He plans to take his fortune and buy a drink, he says. One for every ghost that roams these high desert hills. "There are many ghosts," he tells me, "and I'll soon be one of them." He knows this, he says, and he knows he will be thirsty. "But I don't expect a fancy-pants city boy like you to understand."

2.

The fortune was not a fortune, after all, but a stash of musty cash, soft as blossoms from hands and time. Hardly enough to cover the gas it took me to get from L.A., much less a round for every soul beyond the veil. He's at the final fence post now, three eastward paces from X-marks-the-spot, spade biting into the still-wet sand. He'd be getting warmer had I not unearthed the cigar box days ago, before the rain and before they let him come home. Seizures. They're getting worse and more frequent. "Really, your father should be admitted permanently," they said. "But he's of sound mind and nothing if not persistent." He was only half lucid when I first arrived. That's when he told me about his fortune, pleaded. "We'll be so thirsty," he said. It took some time, but it was there, three feet beneath the dust. A life's hoard. Little more than a pittance. I should probably say something. Tell him to stop digging. Remember the rain, I should say. The flood. This kind of land can't drain quickly. The sand has turned to muck. Nothing is like it was. Maybe I should give it back, his fortune. But he needs to eat, and I need to feed him. Besides, I have an idea the search is all he has left to live for. I tell myself this, not for the first time, then he thrusts the spade again into the ground and his ageing frame seizes, a stone stanchion for one eternal second before he falls. The life's weight is sudden. My shoes are bricks in the thickness, but still I run.

3.

My Hyundai dies inside the canyon, and I have to climb, cutting my hands on sheer faces. My palms have grown soft from years away from this place, but my bones, they remember. There's a bluff above, where he would tell me stories as a child, his eyes and throat alight with liquor, shrouded in a cloud of hand-rolled smoke. Stories of tricksters and familiars and La Llorona, the weeping woman. Stories about where the stories come from. Stories about where we've been and where we go. "I bought the most expensive brand," I say, sitting on the edge. The cork squeaks free. I drink, and I hold the bottle high, mouth to the moon. My chest is a forge, and in my fist a poison jewel. "Drink," I tell them. "Drink." Even the sky is choked with ghosts.

THE ART ROOM

Susan Lilley

—

"What kind of name is Jerzy with a 'z' anyway?"

"He was named for that writer, from the 60s. His parents were unconventional, I guess." Kel leaned back in the lawn chair and held up her hand against the sun. My two-year-old explored the bug world in the coarse Florida grass. We were doing what we always seemed to do that year in the hours between naptime and dinner—telling true stories and drinking white wine spritzers, her yard or mine. Still in our twenties, we saw youth evaporating like fog on the roads behind us. We luxuriated in this brief sabbatical in lives that filled up fast with work and family and duty, time speeding up ever since.

"But seriously, how did you manage it? I mean, at *school*?" I loved this story—I loved all our stories, but this was my favorite, Kel's tale of forbidden love, only a few years back, but in another lifetime. I already knew the details, but we went over them again for the sheer pleasure of it. Jerzy had been her student assistant, 17 years old. A magical age between boy and man, he told her. He was bold in his ardor, with his dark shining ponytail and Cherokee cheekbones. He did some research and declared her the tallest teacher in the school, even including the men. He said she was a rare willow tree. He was not to be denied.

He spent every spare moment in the art room with Kel, helping with all the physical labor it takes to give teenagers the means to make beauty. Canvases to be prepped, clay to be organized, easels, paint, every kind of paper, big charcoal pencils for sketching. Long tables had to be cleared every afternoon, and Kel's radio played at low volume on her desk, messy with school forms and notes and plans in the days before classroom computers.

It started one Thursday in October right after the witching hour, around 4:30 when the faculty and staff parking lot was almost empty. Jerzy turned the volume up, rocked back and forth to the rhythm of Bob Marley and pulled a joint out of his front jeans pocket. He asked with his eyes, and Kel followed him out the back door to an alley between buildings where nobody ever went. When he gave her a shotgun, she noticed that they were the same height. After that, she knew she had lost control of the situation. They took their time cleaning up that day, and when Bad Company's "Feel Like Makin' Love" came on, she laughed at the sheer insanity of it all and carried an armful of brushes into the storage closet. He followed.

Kel and I had fallen out of frequent touch the last few years, so when she called the other night out of the blue, it was a lovely surprise until I heard the trouble in her voice.

"I need to talk to you. And oh, how are you and the family and everybody."

I could tell this was not a catch-up call. "Fine. But what's up?"

She asked me if I remembered that story about her student all those years ago. I giggled like the 25-year-old I was when I first heard it.

"Course I do, woman. Ancient history! So what's going on?"

"Ancient history, huh. I am terrified. That shit could come back to haunt me any minute. Don't you see what's going on? #MeToo? And all those terrible priests. Even women are being called out now. "

"Hardly any. And only famous ones. Come *on*. That dude is probably grateful to this very day for the adventures you gave him." I realized during her silence that this was exactly what a guy would say. She was in earnest, and frightened. I asked if she had heard from him. She had not.

"How old would he be now, Kel?" For some reason I avoided saying his name. Jerzy. I found the current version of myself mildly horrified by the old tale that once seemed so wickedly cool.

"Oh, Jesus, I don't know. In his fifties."

"Weren't you only five years apart when it happened? Think how little that would mean now. I mean, your James is a couple years younger than you for God's sake."

"And what if *he* found out?" She sounded choked up. When Kel married James, nobody made rob-the-cradle jokes.

"Look, nothing is going to happen to you. Stop watching cable news." I added lamely, "Trust the universe."

"I'm trying not to look him up online. Just to see where he is. His life."

"Just don't," I said.

Her voice was shaky and low. "I dream about him."

I bet she does, I thought after we made promises to get together and said good night. I could recall vivid details myself, and I had never even laid eyes on Jerzy. I suddenly felt like a ghostly third party in an old, dangerous secret between the two of them. I was the only one she ever told about the school year full of weekday sex, of guilt overcome by wanting. How shocking life is—the things we do so impulsively and lightly that tip our lives one way or another.

The affair didn't end dramatically, just fizzled when Jerzy graduated and drifted into his real life. Kel spotted him that summer outside a movie theatre and realized that in all those delirious months, they had never been to a restaurant or a movie or any public place together. Kel replaced him with an age-appropriate boyfriend and life went on. No moral consequences, it seemed. But now she dreams the smell of paint and turpentine, his warm breath close to hers as clothes fell away in the art room closet. Of the times they fucked in his ridiculous car, the back seat held together with gaffer's tape. The pointless vows of forever he pulled from her in that heat. I wonder what he remembers.

BUDDY HOLLY IS DEAD

Sarah Viren

—

T he first time I heard "American Pie," Lucy and I were about to break into the Buddy Holly Museum in Lubbock, Texas. I'm sure I'd heard it before at a Kmart or on someone's radio when I was a kid, but until then I'd never really heard it, not the way Lucy made me listen to it, with the earbuds all jammed in tight, one in her ear and one in mine, and the volume up as high as she could get it while her bare legs bounced beside me, her body brushing mine with each bounce and me still clutching the baseball bat we had grabbed for breaking the glass doors in. "Listen, listen!" she screamed in my other ear as the tempo slowed and it became obvious something bad was about to happen, and so I listened, just like she said. It had been my idea to break into the museum in the first place. We were drinking whiskey and sometimes when I drink I start wanting to do something to make the world move. And then there'd been a Buddy Holly song on at the bar, "That'll be the Day," it was, and it all seemed so perfect. We were two blocks from the museum and I already had the bat. But then Lucy got it in her mind that I had to listen to "American Pie," really listen to it, so that we could sing it out loud together as we broke into the place, and so she had stopped the whole break-in in media res and insisted that we sit down there right under the big Buddy Holly sign and listen to all eight minutes before we arrived at my part of the plan. I had to admit when we got near the end that she was kinda right. It was a pretty fucking sad song, even though you can't quite tell why from the lyrics. I guess it's just knowing that he died and him dying means the music died, only right when I was thinking about all that sadness and what it meant, the music actually did fucking die. I jerked my head up from where I had been looking—at this point on the ground where the butt of the bat met the concrete—and when I looked over at her, Lucy was staring hard at the dark screen of her phone screaming "No," as if the world had just ended, which, I guess, in a way it had. I almost told her then but I chickened out, but what I was thinking was how pretty she looked and also how I'd heard once a story about how Buddy Holly's glasses lay in some field in Iowa for years after the plane crash before someone found them and realized what they were worth, how so much of our life is like that, really, us in a cornfield not realizing what's right next to us, screaming into a dead phone that the music couldn't really fucking die, could it?

MY VISIT TO THE PSYCHIC

Pat Rushin

—

A t first it seemed like a harmless diversion, a bit of fun on a lunch date with the girls, but when my wife started seeing the psychic on a weekly basis, I couldn't help but turn skeptical.

"What do you need a psychic for?" I asked her. "You do understand it's a load of horse shit, don't you?"

But apparently she did not, because soon her visits went from once to twice a week.

"It's a waste of money," I complained.

My wife didn't seem to care. She began to depend on her psychic in what I considered to be an unhealthy way. She couldn't make a decision without psychic consultation, be it where to allocate her 401k contributions, which shade to dye her hair, or what to make me for dinner. On the advice of her psychic, she quit her job, insisting that both the cards and the crystals augured only ill omens from her continued employment. When I countered that our swiftly depleting bank account wasn't exactly a harbinger of good times to come, she simply shrugged.

Soon she was seeing her psychic daily.

"Where's my dinner?" I asked her. "Did you wash my blue dress shirt? What's with all the *dust* around here? When is somebody going to clean the toilet bowl?"

But she just smiled dreamily and turned away, ignoring me as usual.

Then one day she went to an appointment with her psychic and didn't come home. Not that day. Not that night. Another day and a night went by. A week. I ran out of clean underwear. Pizza boxes and Chinese take-out cartons covered the coffee table.

Enough was enough.

One evening after work I drove cross-town to the address I had from the psychic's monthly invoices. It was a dark and dreary neighborhood of trashy-looking rowhouses. I found the place, a wide brown eye painted on the front door, and knocked. I knocked again. I banged my fist repeatedly.

Finally, slowly, the door opened. A buxom young woman in short shorts and a skimpy tank top stood staring at me. She was dark-haired, dark-eyed, with a tiny black mole at the corner of a wide mouth and a row of piercings laddering their way up an arched eyebrow. I could smell my wife's perfume mixed with another strange smoky fragrance, and my heart skipped a beat. I tried peering into the room behind her, but it was dark, too dark to see anything.

I folded my arms and glared at the girl. "This has gone far enough, young lady!" I began, voice stern. "Where the hell is my –"

Her icy little hand gripped my arm, taking my breath away mid-sentence.

"Watch yourself," she said, dark eyes glittering crystal, and now I could see nothing but those shining black eyes burning into me. "I know all about you," she purred.

IN DEFENSE OF KILLING BETSY ROSS

Ryan Little

—

For eleven years before it all went belly up, I worked at the American Patriot World reality park over in Middleton. For the last seven years, I was also the manager of the schoolbook depository at our second-most popular attraction, the Grassy Knoll Gun Range. We rented out rifles for any Freedom Lovers or Militiamen who did not bring their own. Some would complain about the eight Liberty Bucks each .22 caliber bullet cost, but all I had to do was point to the sign above the gun closet that read: FREEDOM ISN'T FREE.

For a guy who started out taking tickets for the Stars and Stripes Forever Boat Tour over at the mini Great Lakes, the fact that, just a few years later, I ambled around the American Heartland with a vintage Colt .45 revolver in a side holster garnered me a certain amount of respect. Single mothers who came to the park would even occasionally ask me to stand in for their fallen men once a month on Family Values Daguerreotype Day.

I couldn't take my lunch break at the Independence Day Buffet without getting mobbed. This is where I could usually find my son, Luke, when he would come to visit, stealing away with boxes of bear claws, cakes, and doughnuts to feed old Betsy Ross. Luke was a chubby, inferior sort of kid who still cried when he talked to his mother on the phone and found it impossible to hold eye contact with an adult.

When I'd catch him with an armful of sweets, he knew he was in for it. I'd slap the box out of his hands, and I'd tell him, "What did they tell you about feeding her this crap?"

He'd offer up some excuse—"But she loves when I give her desserts."

"She won't eat her natural diet no more. And next time you get caught, you're going to get yourself banned from the park."

A father's duty is to make a man of his son. Whenever investors came to take the tour, I was given the power—the honor, really—to offer them special access to some of the attractions. On the 4th of July that year, I made Luke tag along on the grand finale, which was to let the investors shoot at our motorized half-sized replica of Kennedy's motorcade. "The only real question," I'd said to the group, "is whether you gentlemen prefer the sixth floor of the book depository or the fence on the other side of the grassy knoll." I gave the boys a "watch this" wink and handed Luke the rifle.

"Oswald."

With surprise, Luke tried to hand the gun back to me. He sniveled.

"Just take the shot." I looked him dead in the eyes. "Time to show me what you're made of." Then so the others could hear: "Everyone's watching, son."

Luke raised the rifle and trained it unsteadily on the motorcade. *BLAM. BLAM. BLAM.* Missed. It was like he couldn't shoot the floor if the Earth was rotating. I had the boys circle the motorcade around again and stop the procession. Luke blubbered to himself, his eyes filling with tears, the barrel of the gun dancing in front of him... And then a certifiable miracle happened. *BLAM-O.* The Kennedy doll's head exploded clean off. Fake blood spattered everywhere. Pride swelled in me.

The investors cackled at the spectacle. But it wasn't Luke. It was one of the investors who had snuck around to the knoll. He yelled, "I'm C.I.A.!" Luke dropped the rifle and ran off.

When we got down to the Zapruter Photo Shoppe, our Jack Ruby impersonator approached the VIPs and whipped out a donation pledge contract instead of a gun. Did they ever get a kick out of *that*.

Jack leaned in. "Better get up to the entrance, Wyatt."

Luke's favorite attraction in the park was a hippopotamus that lived in a bog just in front of the Constitutional Congress Bar-B-Q Pit. Long before it became a theme park, this place was a private zoo. Zebras, monkeys, panthers, the whole deal. Most of the animals had been sold off. But this decrepit hippo survived in a small pond, mostly because no one could figure out how to get her out without losing an arm. Someone came up with the bright idea of stapling a revolutionary flag over the zoo's old signage and putting up a new sign proclaiming the old girl "Betsy Ross, Defender of American Values."

When I got up to Betsy's pen, I found a crowd of people videotaping, snapping photos, and waving tiny American flags. As the crowd jostled, I could just catch glimpses of a boy inside the fence of Betsy's enclosure, tossing something from a big bag into the water. The giant hippo bubbled up with a great snort, her gigantic pink mouth agape, her jagged ochre tusks snapping shut with each catch.

"He's feeding the hippo cupcakes with the stars and stripes icing!" a woman yelled.

"This is the most patriotic thing I've ever seen," a man said.

Pushing through the crowd, I could just make out Luke pitching cupcake after cupcake. Dozens of them. Betsy lumbered out of the muddy water and hulked toward him. Her engorged belly sagged so low it just about scraped the ground.

Luke held out the last cupcake and drew her out further. He backed as far as he could go against the fence.

"Luke," I cried out.

With her inches away, Luke held his hand steady and dropped the cupcake into her gullet. The beast swallowed. Luke reached out and rested his palm on her snout. She huffed and then seemed to calm. In the triumph of that moment, my boy had tamed the beast.

The crowd cheered. Cameras flashed.

With a start, Old Betsy reared back several feet, moved with a great whine toward my boy, and cracked open her immense mouth—the inside streaked red, white, and blue.

N n' N

Rosa Boshier

—

Neil was a strong man. His arms barreled out with knotted muscle. He wore his onesies proudly. For lounging around the house, he sported any solid color. They were good for naps and for yoga. For special occasions, he wore sequins.

It was on one such occasion that he spotted Neyla.

Neyla had changed her name from Marjorie some time ago because she felt it did not fit into the fanny pack of her soul. Her rural Ohio beginnings were not who she was either, so she escaped for the mecca of this twinkle-lit city, always covered in fog. A series of odd jobs and meditation retreats had led her here, to this dance floor, where she felt her most luminous self. She rubbed the bangles on her arms, then threw her arms up in gratitude for She above.

Neil caught the arc of her out of the corner of his eye. The sea of half-naked bodies parted.

Neyla glinted like the Playa at Burning Man under the now-you-see-me-now-you-don't sparkle of a disco ball. She grooved like a well-trained snake, then locked eyes with Neil across the dance floor. Neil shimmied over to her, making sure the light hit the most flattering spots of his onesie. She swung her head around and her hips followed in a semi-circle so Neil could see the plump outline of her bottom pressing against her floor-length skirt. She made unmistakable eye contact over her shoulder.

Neil held cactus arms up in the air and rocked his hips back and forth, careful to keep at least a three-foot distance from her. Again, she held his gaze, then pounded her feet in a faux flamenco step within the vicinity of his arms. She turned around to excavate his spirit with her eyes. He hoped she would find what she was looking for.

She must have, because soon she was moving her arms in an ocean-like motion and sashaying towards him. He paid homage to her decision to dance by mimicking her move. They rocked back and forth like the very tide itself, under the full moon of the disco ball. Neil felt the strength of their psychic connection pulling them towards each other, over and over. The song ended, and Neil gently pointed to the tea station so that they could talk. With a flicker of a smile she consented, and stepped with bare feet off the dance floor.

With a loving look, he handed her a thimble of green tea. The sun of her face rose to meet his. "Is that lavender I smell?" Neil asked.

Neyla batted her eyelashes. "Why, yes. It's an essential oil I made myself."

Neil smiled, making sure to deeply explore the browns of her eyes. He knew the gathering did not allow scents, but he would let it slide.

"What is your inner Goddess telling you right now?" Neil asked.

"That I am the most radiant beam of light," she said, opening her arms out and expanding her chest as if to give him proof.

His face grew very serious. "I honor that," he said.

Thus was the beginning of N&N, a match made in the heaven of mutual loving. After a few months of gentle courtship, they moved into a battered Victorian together.

For a while, life was a steady stream of farmers markets and pickling parties. Then, she saw him sitting at the kitchen table with The Carton in his hand.

She threw a handful of homemade granola in his face. "Soy milk?! Really Neil?! You KNOW the mass destruction of the soy industry!"

Yes, he knew.

Looking back, he thought perhaps he had deliberately sabotaged things. Somewhere in his subconscious he must have known the match wasn't right. She was sauerkraut and he sweet potato fries: the two just didn't mix. Slowly, he watched Neyla's root chakra turn from red to pale pink, until finally, all of her was gone. The only evidence of their love was a forgotten bottle of Doctor Bronner's in the shower. The lavender scent.

For a little while, he was glum. Wore a deep blue onesie to match the shade of his soul. Then one day, the sequins in his closet called to him. He found himself spinning in front of his mirror, prisms of blue, yellow, and pink light illuminating his room like Christmas ornaments.

He hopped on his steel steed and made the pilgrimage to the dance floor. As he slithered between bodies he saw her, Myra, formerly named Janet, glistening like a mermaid under the lights' rhythmic pulse.

COLLATERAL DAMAGE

Nancy Hightower

—

B eatrix Kiddo, aka Black Mamba, attempts to break though the coffin where she's been left to die. Her captor left her a flashlight before nailing shut the lid, though a flashlight does little good so far underground. But now Beatrix can see the narrow walls, the low roof. She remembers Pai Mei's warning that one must be able to hit an enemy only three inches away. Her knuckles are already torn and bloody after three tries.

You're diagnosed with bipolar 2 disorder and put on medication to reroute your brain from the killing machine that it is. You go to therapy, give up alcohol, and exercise daily. Still, your plants wither and die. The turtle you're petsitting has disappeared. Friends slowly stop calling and you wonder if your brain has killed them too. You use whatever's on hand: fork, keys, knife—doesn't matter how dull so long as it reflects a little light. You draw enough blood to prove at least you're alive.

Pai Mei would knock Beatrix on the head with his staff when she missed a beat while punching a block of wood, made her use chopsticks to eat even though her hands shook uncontrollably. He knew the value of pretending to be human when your body betrayed you. The enemy is constant, unmoving. Even in the dead of sleep, she would strike the wall. The wall always won.

This morning you wake up strangled by the bedspread. The voice inside your head whispers you're a prophet of God. It speaks in tongues as you burrow into the covers. You eat breakfast and try to find the turtle even though you know it's been abducted by aliens. You're afraid to take a shower because the bathtub is coffin shaped, only smaller. Once you step under the hot jet stream, the voice inside your head whispers that you've been baptized and never have to leave. You buy hundreds of Christmas lights and string them all around your house. *What prompted this episode?* a friend texts. You rummage through a litany of answers: *menstrual cramps, job pressure, demon possession, because it's Wednesday.* There's never enough story.

Meanwhile, Beatrix escapes. Another assassin takes revenge on her would-be killer using a black mamba snake. Assassins love metaphors. This is how Beatrix kills Bill: pointed fingers darting into his chest, a dance around his heart until it explodes. You wonder if this is how your best friend felt in the last moments of her life, her depression dissipating into a chorus of balloons. You still haven't washed your hair, and the stack of work on your desk has grown into a small hill. The turtle might be buried underneath it. You try to ascertain how much air you have left with every strike of your fist. There are nights you hallucinate seeing the stars, and days when sunlight is merely a diffused beam from the flashlight, your knuckles scraped so raw from the wood, you can only call it love.

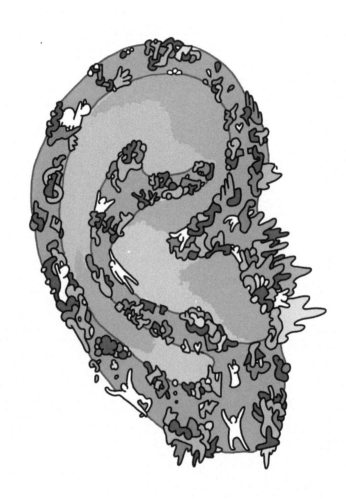

Artist: Paulaidan Minerva

STARRY NIGHT

David Morgan O'Connor

—

L ove, Art, Money, and Merch; in Five Acts

I.   Not my fault the guy cut his ear off.

II.   Started with the shower curtain back when my job was memorizing lines: Shakespeare, O'Neill, Tennessee Williams, Brecht. Back when I used to write trigger words in soap on the transparent glass or plastic whenever scrubbing. Back when I believed art could be transient and move hearts to action. On the line, *O for a muse of fire that would ascend the brightest heavens of invention*, I started swirling the O. The gesture started all slow-mo Tai-chi, morphed into a Karate-Kid-wax-on-wax-off, then got melodramatic Hollywood like some two-bit soap-opera serial killer trying to scour crime blood off my hands. And zip zap zop, *this wooden O, the very casques that did affright the air in Agincourt*, the image struck like a round-house to the jawbone and life changed.

I jammed a transparent plastic sheet into my 3D color printer, downloaded the image, jiggy-jigged the alignments, and tapped print. I thought the ink would run, especially when wet, but it didn't. The image held and I stopped learning lines in the shower. I took walks, used recordings, back-pocket slips of paper between grocery lists. I enjoyed my shower and the image for what they were, almost a single task.

Today I memorized: *How rich art is, if one can only remember what one has seen, one is never empty of thoughts or truly lonely, never alone.*

Are you? Can you?

III.　　　Two months later, I fell in love with an impulse woman. After our fifth shower together, she said, "You know, you're the first white guy I haven't hate fucked. Can I have this shower curtain?" "Sure," I said, "You know, you're the most honest woman I've ever met." She took the curtain home. I printed another. Three weeks later, after another shower together, she said, "My sister fell in love with that curtain. Can you print another?" "Sure," I said, "You know, I think I love your mind more than your body."

And printed another curtain.

That Christmas was our first. I bought a swanky printer and kegs of ink. We printed beach balls, umbrellas, socks, posters, backpacks. She hand-painted teapots. We gave Starry Nights to everyone we knew and loved. Her family was huge, mine tiny, and everyone was merry with what they received. So were we with our work and giving.

That New Year's Eve after sharing our resolutions and bodies, she said, "That painting's public, right? No copyright. Older than what? 90 years? We can sell that shit."

And we did.

Yesterday I memorized: *That is how I look at it; to continue, to continue, that is what is necessary.*

Can you? Is it?

IV.　　　Our first trip to China to find a manufacturer was a mind-fuck. We were already making more than we could manage. Had a live-in-work-loft in Green Point. We always smelt of tint. Often got busy while the printer chugged. Talked about the color of our hypothetical babies. But curiosity jigsawed us in Beijing. I got sick on dodgy Peking duck. She started doing business on the sly with an Italian fashion-mogul.

Lockets. iPhone cases. Hammocks. Lingerie. Yoga tights. Pillows. Nail polish. Guitars. Head phones. Our wallets sold like hot cakes. We couldn't maintain. Fuck, we even laser-sprayed a Volkswagen van. We printed to order and automated everything except our joint signatures, even our love. Stinking rich, we drifted apart. Never had our rainbow babies.

Tomorrow we should memorize: *When I compare myself to others, there is something stiff and awkward about me; I look as if I had been in prison for ten years.*
Would you like to?

V.   I guess Van Gogh's *Letter's to Theo* and unfettered ear really has nothing to do with all this making bank off *Starry Nights*.

HUMAN INTEREST

Ron Burch

—

Someone got us a subscription to *Human Interest* magazine, one of those rags that dishes on celebrities and has overwrought emotional stories. We don't know who did it. We don't know why. Was it a joke? We've asked our friends if they were responsible; no one has admitted to it. The magazine follows us from house to house, mysteriously appearing at each new address, with the correct current address, even though we didn't forward it. We stopped forwarding all our mail in our attempts to escape it. We used to receive one per month. Then it became one per week. One per day. Five per day. Ten per day. Even more sometimes.

I ask the mailperson if she would stop delivering it.

"Sorry, honey," she replies, a slight drawl to her voice, "it's my job."

"What can we do?"

She throws a plastic-strapped bundle of the latest issue out of her white truck and onto the lawn in front of me.

"Better talk to my supervisor," she says, jamming her truck into gear and gently rolling on to the next mailbox, which only receives a garish circular and what appears to be a gas bill.

Inside the house my husband Tim tells me about the faded actor who at the age of 50 is fathering a child. About a rock star's new boyfriend that she's kept concealed for months from the press. How a famous actor has been having an affair with his nanny. Tim reads the stories aloud as I try to cross the wooden floor, *Human Interest* magazines scattered across it like landmines. I attempt to cross without slipping and falling. I catch an open one with my right heel and slip but catch myself in time. Tim relates the story of how a daytime talk show host is beating her battle with alcohol. Tim was never like this. He watches sports. He likes action movies. He doesn't even like to read. We used to talk more, in the first couple years of our marriage, but that all ended before *Human Interest* even began arriving.

I call the magazine. Their automated system informs me that the order was placed by a third-party company, and I would have to talk to them. It doesn't give me the number so I spend the afternoon tracking it down. Finally, I call it but get a recorded message saying that they are closed and to call back. I look them up on the Internet but there's no address for them. They don't have a Contact page and I cannot find an email address.

Tim tells me about the former baseball player who found God and is now a snake-handling preacher in southern Ohio. My husband's stopped eating and enclosed himself in our bathroom. I ram the door, getting it to open, pushing aside a pile of *Human Interest* magazines up to my knees and find him fully clothed in the bathtub, the magazines heaped on top of his red flannel shirt and faded jeans. He tells me about a new allergy drug: its side-effects are stroke, cancer, and heart palpitations. I hand him half of a Gala apple and watch him take a bite before he forgets about it, the fruit falling out of his hand, lost to the narcoleptic effects of the magazine.

"Tim," I plead, "we can't keep going on like this."

"Andi, honey" he smiles, "there's a new drug for impotence."

"You're not impotent."

"According to this ad, I will be someday."

"Tim, there's so much going on in the world. The news, for example, look what's happening to our world."

I hold up my laptop to show him the articles online. He pats my knee absentmindedly and puts down the magazine. He digs his hand into the pile on him and surfaces with another one. "Ooh, the summer special issue."

He hasn't gone to the office for a week. He's allowed his cellphone to discharge, and it sits there like a dark husk. He barely talks to me anymore. I'm afraid I'm losing him.

I walk to our post office, a faded brick building on Magnolia. Part of it is boarded up, including the two turrets that sit on each side of the front. The line flows out of the door and I wait my turn. When I get to the head of the line, I plop down a tattered copy of the magazine and say, "Stop the delivery." The bearded employee shakes his head and hands me a printed card of the Postal Employee's

Responsibilities, pointing a trembling finger at *#4) Deliver all mail to the recipient.* I ask to speak to the Branch Supervisor, but I'm informed he's away at a conference.

At home, the accumulating bundles of the magazine in the front yard are gone. Perhaps someone took them until I realize that the front door sits wide open. Tim perches on the floor in the living room. He sorts through the bundles. I sit next to him. He doesn't even acknowledge my presence. It's like I'm invisible, fake.

"Look," I say, "these two models have adopted a new baby."

Tim, surprised, suddenly looks up at me and smiles. I gently take his hand and together we flip to the next page, the soft swish of the turning paper like a whispering lover.

IN THE HEADLIGHTS

Brittany Terwilliger

—

I want to be home, where no one can enter my skin. I step on the asphalt to warm my soles, but now I am exposed. Turn to look for headlights, imagine car tires crunching over my toes and feel the cracks and breaks through my whole body. Back to the grass, which itches with midnight dew. I look back again. He probably hasn't noticed yet, but any minute now. I should really stick to the ditch, but it's muddy down there and probably full of snakes. The porch light, my destination, buzzes in the distance. I wonder if they're home. I wonder if they're lunatics. I wonder if this is going to turn into a *Texas Chainsaw Massacre*-type situation. I wonder if they're kindly old people. I wonder if they're asleep. I wonder what I must look like. Summer dress. Feet covered with mud and wet grass. Streams of black sadness down my face like the cover of a Courtney Love album. I'm not some sad, fragile little thing. I'm not your victim. I can take care of myself, if I can just get away unseen.

I look back and see the headlights creeping now, far behind me. That's got to be him. There's nobody else out here for miles. That was what we'd liked about it. Hidden away. A break from ourselves. A break from the demons that pursue us slowly and unrelentingly as horror movie monsters. I slide down into the ditch and lie flat on my belly. The grass feels like a thousand bugs entering my skin. I laugh at how stupid this is. How did I even get here, face-down in a fucking ditch, in the middle of nowhere? I want to be home, quiet and safe. Home, taking a bath and emerging all clean and whole and demon-free. Above, the car creeps slowly by. The cold, sticky wet is seeping into my dress. Mosquitoes whine in my ears, their needles pricking my neck. I see the beam of a flashlight shine up and down. I hold my breath and close my eyes. I want to evaporate into the air like mist. I want no one to mourn or remember me, just let me disappear.

The car keeps going and I stand upright. I step faster through the shadows. The ground is uneven down here, all mud and soft-topped mole tunnels, and I imagine my ankles twisting and snapping. How long would I lie here like a fox in a trap until someone pounced? How long would it take me to crawl on hands and knees to the house with the porch light? I stop for a moment to breathe in the lush darkness. When it is this dark, there are so many stars.

The porch light gets closer, and hot blood floods me. Out in the open, clear as day, the porch light is both salvation and threat. Kamikaze moths tick-tick against the bulb. The porch is screened-in, and I can almost taste the crackly peels of paint hanging from its ramshackle walls. I sprint across the yard and open the creaky screen door. I throw myself inside and collapse on the astro-turf next to a dusty wicker chair. I lie there for a few seconds, breathing slow breaths. The plasticky green bristle sticks in my knees and hands. The house's interior door opens. There is a kind-faced old woman in a long, white nightgown thick as sponge cake. Hallelujah.

"What are you doing?" she says, looking me up and down. She looks unsure about me, and then I see the butcher knife at her side.

I open my mouth to explain, and the screen door creaks behind me. The stony eyes of my boyfriend emerge. My insides collapse.

"What in the hell is going on here?" the woman says.

No one speaks.

The woman looks at my boyfriend, then at me, and decides that he looks like the one she should be talking to. "Is this girl with you?" she says.

I know I can't say it out loud now, but I stare at her face, pleading. Don't make me go with him. Let me use your phone. I'll call someone to pick me up. Look, I'll wait by the porch light. You can watch me the whole time.

"Yes," my boyfriend says, performing a sigh. "She's with me. I'm so sorry we bothered you, ma'am."

The woman gives him an incredulous glare. "Well," she says, "tell your girlfriend she can't just go trespassing on other people's porches."

"I will tell her that," he says. His fingers grip my arm, yanking me toward the headlights.

HUMMINGBIRDS AND THINGS LIKE THAT

Epiphany Ferrell

—

It began in Tina Ludden's garden. You wouldn't just guess that because Tina Ludden was widely known to favor all things organic. She had a butterfly garden and she had a vegetable garden and she'd never use Miracle Grow, only compost, and her gardens, both of them, were known to be among the best on the block. She held the record for the most Bright Spot awards.

And then that new guy moved in. Henry Tuttle. Of course he'd have a name like that. Three-bedroom house and just him in it. He planted a butterfly garden too, and it was nice, but it wasn't like Tina's. In the beginning, she even gave him some pointers. We all lived to regret that.

Well, not that specifically. It was the damn bird feeders. Not the feeders for finches and cardinals. The hummingbird feeders.

Mr. Tuttle had a knack. His butterfly garden might not have been as nice as Tina's but oh, did the hummingbirds throng to his yard. He had eleven feeders at the beginning, when he and Tina were still friendly. Eleven! And he had to fill them daily. Sometimes twice daily. In fact, as he carried the filled feeders to their perches in the butterfly garden, he was often swarmed by hummingbirds. The Weekly Star did a story on it. Front page.

Tina put out some hummingbird feeders too. She had three. And she only needed to refill hers once, maybe twice a week. It was weird, we all agreed, that here Mr. Tuttle had all those hummingbirds and Tina had so few. It didn't seem fair. Tina hated to ask so she hinted and was coy and complimented Mr. Tuttle's feeders until he, remembering (because she reminded him) that she had helped with his butterfly garden, gave her his secret. He mixed his own hummingbird food, not relying on that commercial stuff. And, Mr. Tuttle confessed, he increased the sugar content. He doubled it in fact, to a ratio of 1-2 rather than 1-4 as recommended. The hummingbirds loved it.

Well if that's all there is to it, Tina thought. And she made a hummingbird food that was 3-4 ratio and she colored it and flavored it with grenadine. There was nothing to suggest too much sugar was bad for hummingbirds. She knew that from an online search. Maybe they'd fly a little faster, she thought.

But that was only part of what happened, as we all know now. The increased sugar, or maybe it was the grenadine, made them fly faster, sure. And they grew bigger. And more aggressive. Mr. Tuttle had a video of himself swarmed by so many hummers he appeared to have sprouted wings himself, and it went viral. And then Tina had one that put his to shame. The neighbors got in on it too, especially Sally Musgrove, but her videos never took off like the Tuttle and Luddon videos.

The hummingbirds were big as blue jays by July. By August, they were the size of hawks. National Geographic came and the Discovery channel.

It's hard to say who first got the idea of putting blood in the feeders. Or if anyone did. Maybe the hummers got a taste for it all on their own. You couldn't put your cat or dog outside. And you didn't dare not feed them, those bloodthirsty hummingbirds the size of eagles now, or they'd attack you as you got into your car in the morning.

All those thrumming wings kept up a near steady breeze in the neighborhood and the noise was constant, even at night. Some of the hummingbirds had become nocturnal.

Scientists came, conducted interviews, captured samples, most of which they released with tags on their legs. A few of the scientists thought it was the next step in evolution; some said it was tampering with a protected species and any of us with a feeder should be prosecuted.

It's rumored the military was interested in our big hummers, too.

And just when it was becoming unbearable, the hummingbirds were gone. Migrated, we assumed.

The last one seen in the area was a young one, only big as an owl, caught on heavy twine hooked onto its leg tag. It was nearly worn out, but still thrumming the air with its iridescent wings. Sally Musgrove's teenage girl was on the other end of the string, lying on the stone wall in the park, the twine wound around her wrist, her arm moving up and down as the bird tried to escape. Her lips were red from lipstick and the rest of her, at least what was visible, was white as snow. Bloodless.

Someone shot the hummer and its taxidermied body is in the library. It's on some list of curious oddities and people from other states stop by to see it.

It's getting to be spring again now and if our hummingbirds are returning, they are late.

Mr. Tuttle has moved away. Tina Ludden knits caps for newborns now and her garden is gone.

No one knows to this day what Sally Musgrove's daughter was doing with that hummingbird the size of an owl on a leash. I'll never forget how she looked, lying there so still with her hair moving in the draft of beating wings.

The kids say they see her sometimes, standing by the wall, silent and white, her hair moving in a breeze that isn't there. Some say ghost, some say vampire. Kids. They'll come up with any kind of story. There's no such thing as ghosts and vampires. And if there were, things like that don't happen in this town.

TONY AND THE BREEDERS

Sean Patrick Mulroy

—

"**D**o I miss my family? Sure. I mean, I guess so. My brother, Frank. We used to have fun when we were kids, and he was easy to talk to, at least, for a straight guy, right? It's been a little hard, since...you know. But would I take it back? Hell no. And I don't think anyone out there is being honest with themselves if they're saying they want to go back to the way things were."

Tony leaned back in his chair, and took a long sip from the highball glass on the table to his left. He tried to remember everything that he'd been told before the interview—don't stare at the camera, don't look at the boom, don't squirm, don't touch where they pinned the body mic. He felt uncomfortable in his suit, uncomfortable underneath the bright lights, uncomfortable being asked personal questions on live television. But wasn't this the life he wanted since he was a kid? Hadn't he gotten exactly what he wished for?

Of course he had. Hence the camera crews, the fancy gifts, the sudden rush of followers on social media. What Tony had done was the biggest news since last year, when all the fundamentalist Christian people were on TV talking about the Rapture. It wasn't such a crazy thought—millions of men had gone missing overnight, and then there'd been the toads everywhere. It was a weird time for everyone.

"People have been saying what you did was unforgivable," the interviewer raised an eyebrow. "Others are calling you the gay messiah."

"The gay messiah! That's a new one." It was not, in fact, a new one, but Tony figured it would flatter him to seem surprised. Perhaps it was surprising in a way, to hear it said out loud by someone as famous as the woman sitting across from him, but what in this bizarre new world was shocking? What could possibly top the last two months?

A year ago, while everyone else was going on about the Rapture, Tony and his brother Frank were packing up their car and hitting the road. The disappearing men, the waves of brown toads spilling out of every house, Tony and Frank had seen enough movies and read enough salvaged Sumerian texts to know the work of a wishing amulet when they saw it. It took months of research, tracking the path of the toads and reading the bones before finally they pulled up to a humble ranch house in a run-down suburb of Missouri, and knocked on the door. An old woman answered, and after they explained to her why they had come, she'd let them in. Tony and Frank sat down in the kitchen while the woman rummaged through the kitchen drawers, looking for the amulet.

"Now I know it's around here somewhere, boys, give me a moment."

"Take your time, Mrs. Everest," Frank said. "We're in no hurry. We just want to get everything back to normal."

"You don't have to tell me twice, young man. I just want my husband back." She reached towards the back of a drawer, and with a sharp tug and a clang of cutlery, produced a beautiful necklace with a dull green jewel at its center. "Ah here it is. Don't know if it'll do you any good, my daughter and I gave it a pretty good try." Mrs. Everest dropped the amulet into Frank's outstretched hand. "There's a homemade shepherd's pie in it for you two, if you can make the darn thing work again."

Tony reached into his equipment bag and pulled out a glowing loupe, which he pressed to his eye.

"Hmmm. I think maybe—oh here's the problem. Look, Frank." Tony passed the amulet to his brother, who turned it over in his hands.

"Makes sense." Frank pulled a bag of sand out of his pocket, and emptied it directly on the amulet's green jewel. "It's a Volun, Ma'am."

"It is not, is it?" Mrs. Everest sighed in consternation. "I could have sworn that it was Middle Eastern. Look at that detail!"

Frank shook his head. "Nope, Roman. Trust me, if Tony and I know anything, it's Roman artifacts." Frank slid the amulet across the table to his brother.

"Just the one wish for each family, then?"

"Yup. Wonder how it got all the way out here?" Frank blew gently on the green jewel, and it flickered like a dying campfire. Tony joined him on the second breath, and the light inside the jewel finally began to beam again. The three of them stood there, looking at the wishing amulet as it pulsed with energy. "Alright T, you ready to end this nightmare?"

The plan had been to get the amulet, and one way or another use it to fix things back the way they were. It should have worked. It would have worked, in fact, if Tony hadn't been possessed by the strangest impulse. Quickly picking up the amulet, he looked at Frank, and then at Mrs. Everest.

"Wait, Tony, don—"

***

Tony took another swig of his drink. The interviewer stared at him.

"And that was that. I mean, a flash of lightning or whatever, some wind, standard Strega stuff, and then—"

"And then there were no more straight people."

"Right. Look, I know people are angry. If it helps, what I said exactly was, 'I wish everyone on Earth was gay.' I didn't think it was going to make everyone disappear like this. I just thought, y'know, more culture, less overpopulation."

"Well, the Earth is certainly less populated, that's for sure. Do you have anything to say for all the people out there who are missing their loved ones, or for any of your fans?"

"I mean, I'm sorry, and you're welcome, I guess." Tony laughed, and the amulet around his neck shifted slightly, brushing up against his body mic. For a second, the touch of metal on metal sounded almost like a little chuckle of its own.

CLASS REUNION *OR* I'LL USE YOUR ENTRAILS TO BIND OUR LEGS FOR THE SACK RACE

Michael Grant Smith

—

I glance across the table and you squint back at me. Our eyes lock above your corn-on-the-cob captured between wee fork-handles. I've never known anyone who used them, and yet here we are at this picnic and you brought your own. In a velour-lined leather-bound case. Were we high school enemies so many years ago? Friends? What is clear now is that we are both survivors and today you are my antagonist. I smile in reply to your attempt at intimidation; my goatee glistens with barbecue sauce.

Does your wife cut your hair? You don't have to answer, because I can see she buys your clothes. I push more food into my mouth, without regard for enjoyment of what I put in there. I eat for strength and the stamina to outlast my foes. You seem to sense this as you open a wet-nap packet (you brought that as well), dab at your buttery visage, and then impale another ear of corn. It becomes clear to me I must focus. Protein is for winners. I stab at some ribs—the ones on my plate. Your time will come soon enough, my unworthy adversary.

When you arrived this afternoon—your wife all a-bristle like a battleship, progeny like salamanders scampering around your feet—my hopes for a day of food and fun were scraped into the trashcan downwind of our table. Everyone else brought a covered dish to share, but you threw down an open, half-eaten bag of potato chips. Your youngest brat grinned greasily. You packed your tanned cheeks with my homemade rumaki and stuffed more of it into your pockets "for later." I wanted to smash you with a croquet mallet and induce your face to resemble a shattered bowl of salsa.

Condensation from the iced tea pitcher drips into my sandal and saturates my sock, hustling me back to the present. Inexplicably our wives sit together, their hair interlocked in a cat's cradle of collusion. They whisper and giggle, pausing only to cast disapproving glares at the two of us. Abandoned plumbing repairs, broken tools, overdone steaks, poorly cut-in trim painting, stained briefs—what good to me are your secret failures if my own are revealed? I am betrayed. Likewise, I will not permit myself to be cast as the villain in my life's own play. This ends now.

I rip asunder three of those little single-servings of black pepper and sprinkle the contents onto your corn. One, two, three. The once-golden ear now looks as if you rolled it in cigar ashes. You stand up, unbutton your Tommy Hilfiger blue chambray, and fold it over a chair. I can see you've been working out. The woman I married wolf-whistles. I peel off my Hanes Beefy-T Crewneck and toss it to the ground. Sunlight reflected from my pale jiggly flesh forces witnesses to blink. Your eager smirk sags into a kernel-studded snarl, which devolves into a mask of stark fear and doubt.

Yes, you've gazed deeper into my eyes, in which your demise plays out as surely as one of those drunk-driving videos we watched in health class our senior year. I smack taut pigskin. Lava-hot needles sting my hand but I barely wince.

Flag football: family-friendly fun, or blood sport of modern gladiators? For the first time in your life, you're about to understand something.

Moreover, I can win this.

OUT OF SEASON

Michele Finn Johnson

—

T wice a year, the 4H people bus us out of our rundown suburb to show us another way of life full of pollinators and cow manure. That's where I meet you. Our eighth-grade field trip to the apple orchard and you carry bushel baskets up empty and back full, your jeans worn, seams faded to the color of ocean foam licking down your legs. You get the seal of approval from Vanessa. *Just the farm boy, but so hot.* Vanessa knows boys and knows hot, and so I know too, by proxy. Maybe your name is Samuel. *I bet he's sixteen, she says,* and we robot-nod, filling our baskets fast for the chance to brush against you. In my frenzy, I pick up fruit from the ground. You take a bushel from me; you frown at the wormholes pimpled across my apples.

The wind picks up and Vanessa's hair whips into all of our faces. Her girl scent smells expensive, learned. You lean in to grab another bushel; Vanessa's hair spider-traps across your face. *This crazy wind. I just can't control myself!* Vanessa retracts her wayward strands, and you say *No problem* as if hair swallowing excites you, and then the two of you are off in the orchard. Your slurps and wet, wet, wet sounds broadcast beyond full bundles of ripe McIntosh. I bite into a sour Fuji and listen as the 4H lady drones on and on about the dangers of a late spring frost. How can 4H lady not hear you? Vanessa's shirt buttons misalign for the entire bus ride home to our dilapidated civilization.

At home, I pull out a smooth, pink-veined rock from the pocket of my apple-picking jeans. I'd found it nestled in the root of a Gala tree. It seemed logical at the time, pocketing that rock, imagining handing it to you—*Something to remember me by, Samuel*—right before I'd lean in, letting you know it was okay to kiss me, to sniff my ordinary girl smell. I'll rub that rock and dream of you, tonight, every night, Samuel. My decades-old, hand-me-down bed creaks for you.

Back in our pot-holed neighborhood, we ride our bikes until either nightfall or a cowbell or some mother's screech skittles us back inside. Vanessa toots her clown-y bike horn the whole way home as if her whereabouts need any more press coverage. It's obvious to everyone that she's not long for this neighborhood, that someday soon, she'll look at the skinny streetlights that protect our street and see them for the rusty, dim beacons that they truly are. Watch her as she drives her chrome-wheeled SUV away, Samuel. Your open palms extend to her in a half-wave, half-picture frame, your farm-boy face so special and then—there it is, faded. Out of season. But I'm still here, Samuel. Open your eyes.

PIECES

Chuck Augello

———

"I'm falling apart," Lizzie says.

It's true. Last night I found her ring finger on the floor by the bathroom sink, the gold band catching my eye as I brushed my teeth. Otherwise, I might have missed it—her skin tone blends so well with the tile pattern.

I picked up the finger and rinsed it, then slid off the ring and dropped it in her jewe-lry box. This morning, after making the bed, I saw a lump beneath the covers; I pulled back the sheets and there it was, her left foot, still warm in a pink cotton sock.

I try to be encouraging.

"You can still do a lot with one foot," I tell her.

There is a lot of crying in our house these days.

***

During lunch Lizzie's nose falls into the soup. I rescue it with the salad tongs and wash it in cold water. I have a red Igloo cooler in which I keep all of her parts. I save everything. I believe in reconstruction.

I always thought she was so strong. She acted like she didn't need anyone, ever, certainly not me. Sometimes she'd walk ahead of me on the street as if we were strangers, yet I still fell in love with her. After three months we ran away and pretended to be newlyweds. On the streets of Vancouver, she slept in the sun on an old park bench, her head nestled in my lap. I stroked her hair and woke her with a kiss, our lips magnetic and bright.

In bed she pulls away from me now. We haven't made love in months, maybe years, but I've never lost my desire for her. When she undresses I sneak glances. I have a keen imagination.

It started with her fingernails. She lost three in one day and the rest in a week. At first, we suspected a vitamin deficiency but after three weeks of supplements the nails failed to regenerate and her big toe fell off next.

I constructed numerous theories blaming her parents or her job or a cabal of Wall Street bankers, but she dismissed them all until a single suspect remained.

"It's your fault," Lizzie says. "You ignored things and now look what's happened."

"I love you," I say—my mantra.

***

I come home late and Lizzie greets me by the door, her eyes dewy and raw. She hugs me, and then hands me her ears.

"I'm sorry," I say, but I don't think she hears me.

Every relationship has its blunders and grievances. So much relies on interpretation. I write out a sticky note and tape it to the fridge: *Dear Lizzie, the human mind has a great capacity for forgiveness.*

I go upstairs and kiss her goodnight. Her lower lip waits for me on the nightstand beside her contact lenses and a half-empty bottle of Lexapro.

***

There are days when Lizzie doesn't lose anything, and I think perhaps we will make it. We've tried dozens of remedies. For a week she drank nothing but green tea and dandelion extract. I've massaged her skin with a paste of red wine and St. John's Wort. Her MD had success mending her with lasers and stitches, and for a while she seemed whole again. We held our breath, hoping it was over, but five days later I found a finger on the coffee table and a toe in the shower.

This I have noticed: pieces never fall off when others are around. With her friends she is happy and light; her giggles fill the air like butterflies in a Disney cartoon. With me she is angry and morose, but I keep hoping for the best. To show her my love I rent the honeymoon suite at a posh hotel, buy her pretty lingerie and decorate the room with roses and scented candles, scour the love poems of Pablo Neruda to find the perfect bon mot to pry open her heart.

But the honeymoon suite stays empty.

"This is awful, it has to end," Lizzie says.

"But I love you."

"Can't you see what's happening?" She shakes her head, her eyelashes falling like dark snow. "We always knew this was a mistake."

I list the many kind and loving things I have done for her but by now they are meaningless. If this were a television show on TV Land a wise father played by Tom Bosley or Robert Reed would set his arm around my shoulder and identify the lesson: loving someone is never enough.

***

Her friends arrange a trip to Florida for the healing powers of the sun. I go online and find a Facebook group of men in similar situations. Apparently, Lizzie and I are not unique. Sometimes the men meet at Starbucks and share photographs and spouse parts. There's a blogger in Istanbul who recommends a home cloning kit available through E-bay for under a thousand bucks.

If you have enough cells, you can bring back almost anyone.

***

I stand in the hallway watching as her friends pack her suitcase and carry Lizzie toward the door. "I love you," I shout, but the only response is the front door slamming shut. Flakes of skin dust the hardwood floor like confetti from a long, gruesome parade.

As I walk upstairs and crawl into our bed, I understand why Lizzie never said goodbye. Lying on the comforter is her tongue, pink and moist.

I hold the tongue in my hand as I drift into sleep—imagine it growing in the warm Petri dish of my palm, the cells multiplying and dividing until piece by piece, Lizzie comes home.

Artist: Katiana Robles

LET'S GET LOUD

V.G. Anderson

—

You strip out of your blue leggings, gently stretch your flesh-tone nylons into place, and tuck your short wide penis into as comfortable a position as possible. Your nether regions are humid and sticky. Baby-powder is a foregone conclusion. You were out till dawn dancing with friends and arrived late to practice this afternoon. You've been a Jennifer Lopez impersonator in Las Vegas for two years, and you've been choreographing new moves whilst lip-syncing "Let's Get Loud" for the past few hours. You planned it carefully. Every detail. Down to the white and silver shimmery halter dress and knee-high white-leather boots Lopez wore during her 1999 FIFA Women's World Cup performance. It was electric. You're excited to bring that energy to your stage. You've been in love with J.Lo since you won a look-alike contest at a local mall in ninth grade. You gifted the nail-polish-set bounty to your mom because you had a hard-enough time at school for being a short effeminate Latino boy, but you kept the gift certificate for free drinks at Orange Julius that summer.

Your friend Alejandro recently returned from his mother's funeral in Texas, so you'll no longer be pulling "overtime" doing his Christina Aguilera show two nights a week. That's a relief. You haven't felt like a genie in a bottle since you were beaten unconscious at your high school in the Wholesale District of Los Angeles then stuffed into a locker. You spent the night there. The morning security guard set you free. No one at home noticed you'd been gone. Your mom's drug dealer is gay, and you'd been fucking him since your sophomore year, but he never checked up on you. You found them both unconscious on the sofa and put yourself to bed. The calculus-test you missed and subsequent GPA-drop cost you a scholarship, but you hadn't planned on going to college. You were always Vegas-bound. Your first love was burlesque dancing, but you weren't born with the optimal body shape for those costumes—too square.

You've been saving for gender-reassignment surgery for years. Hormone treatments have been consistent, and your breasts are coming in nicely. Your implants will be minimal to achieve J.Lo status. Also, classier than some of the oversized melons your female friends forked out way too much of their sugar-daddy's cash to balloon their already ample chests Playboy-bunny style. Tacky. Though you still get drunk and motorboat your friend Scarlett's tits on weekends.

You slip the mini dress up over your ample thighs and narrow hips shimmying it into position. You're feeling spicier by the second. You own your stage and take your audience on an audacious adventure of Latin hip hop dance appreciation. At least that's what you write on the back of your headshot when canvassing the strip to book new gigs.

Every so often a Christian "do-gooder" hands you a pamphlet selling salvation for a "small" percentage of your income equivalent to a full month's rent. "Good thing God's accounting for inflation," you said once, then asked for another pamphlet and wadded them up on the spot, using them to "freshen up" your bra stuffing.

It's impossible for people like that to bring you down. You've come too far from being chased by gang members down alleys; half hoping they'd catch you because you longed for physical affection. Mom had been warning her friends to keep their children away from you for years. "They might get infected," she'd caution. Most nodded in agreement before you were sent to your room. But you had YouTube and movies and video games, and you preferred to avoid having to show everyone your penis to "prove it existed," which had somehow become standard procedure over the years.

The drums cue your hips to sway. You might as well be a million miles from southern California. Throwing your head back to the horns, you position your long, caramel wig with blonde highlights over your fishnet cap and tug it into place, reposition a bit, then dip into your bobby-pin tray.

"Fierce," Alejandro says, smacking your ass as he prances by.

"Sorry about your platinum Afro wig!" you say. "I underestimated the drop of the ceiling fan."

Alejandro throws up stop-sign palms. "No troubles, papi! If I do "Fighter" one more time my regulars are gonna revolt."

Remembering you haven't given Alejandro his cut for booking the Aguilera shows you performed, you hand him a roll of twenties.

He squeals and gives you a quick peck on the cheek. Then he's off to do shots and buy blow before tonight's performance.

You prefer to avoid drugs. The rush of the show is enough for you and, with the hormone treatments, drugs tend to throw you too far out of whack. They also make it difficult to drag yourself out of bed in the morning and to the gym. You take pride in your hard ass and toned thighs that make your J.Lo impersonation more authentic than most. You're sure.

Your cell phone buzzes and "Mom" appears on the screen. You haven't sent money for a while. You select "reject" and take a mental note to PayPal her some cash later tonight. She kept you out of foster care after Dad was deported then disappeared. Money is the least you can do.

Tony, your stage manager, walks up. His cotton V-neck is a size too small and accentuates his tan biceps. He cases you up and down looking ravenous and out for destruction.

"You comin' over after tonight's show?" he asks.

You consider playing coy, but you know your cheeks are flushed brighter than your peach blush. You nod and give him a growl. *Mom will just have to wait.*

He kicks up the volume on the sound system. You throw some exaggerated hip sways his direction as the horn section amps the crescendo. It's gonna be a great show.

BETWEEN THE LIKING AND THE PRETENDING

Cathy Ulrich

———

If I were a rental wife in Japan, my husband would be a salaryman with pants that needed hemming. They would droop around his heels. When we met for dinner, he would smile when he saw me, always smile, pull out the chair for me to sit.

I know you like gentlemen.

He'd say this in English. The wife I was replacing would have been American, like me. She would have been the kind of American Japanese people expect when they think of Americans, not someone like me, dark-haired, quiet, tattooed. I would have to wear a blonde wig, long sleeves. I would have to smile more than I usually do.

If I were a rental wife in Japan, my husband would smile at me and I would smile at him. We would smile at each other.

I would ask him wifely things — *are you eating well, are you getting enough rest, you're not drinking too much, are you?* — things a long-absent wife might ask. That would be our story; I would be his long-absent wife, returned from America to visit. He wouldn't know my real name, wouldn't know I had a Japanese boyfriend, panic attacks, a drinking problem. He would call me *o-mae*.

It's been so long, he would always say. *Hisashiburi*, like a teenage girl.

Hisashiburi, I would say, reach out and touch his hand.

If I were a rental wife in Japan, I would make sure not to linger too long, touching my husband's hand. I would surreptitiously check the time — ten thousand yen per hour — I would smile, I would smile, I would smile.

The waiter would bring a bottle of French wine to our table. The wife I was replacing would have liked things like that: bottles of French wine, rare wagyu steak, salads with vinaigrette. When I was being her, I would like those things too. Or I would pretend to. There wouldn't be so much difference, I would think, between the liking and the pretending.

My husband would take my hand.

Hisashiburi.

If I were a rental wife in Japan, I would let my husband hold my hand like that, fingers entwined, on the table. His hands wouldn't feel so different from the hands of my Japanese boyfriend. He would hold my hand and talk about the weather, about his commute, about his coworkers. I would remember he hated one.

Oh, Tanigawa, my husband would say. *He's still the same. Always the same.*

And we would shake our heads together, *oh, Tanigawa.*

If I were a rental wife in Japan, I would make my excuses when our time was up. I would let him pull my chair from the table, let him kiss the side of my face.

Only hands can touch, I would remind him, *remember, only hands.*

I know, he'd say. *I know, I forgot.*

You're just so like her, he'd say.

He would smile again, and I would smile again. There would be something so peaceful in all the smiling.

I don't mind, I'd decide, and let him kiss the side of my face again, somewhere between liking and pretending; my Japanese boyfriend would say, when I returned, *do you love him?,* standing at the kitchen sink in our twelve-tatami apartment, *do you love him,* back to me, shoulders taut.

I could never lie to my Japanese boyfriend.

Sometimes.

When I'm her, sometimes I do.

Ah, my Japanese boyfriend would say. His hands would be wet with dishwater when he finally turned round, wiping them dry on a dish towel, standing barefoot across from me and me barefoot across from him, feet aching from the heels the American wife liked to wear.

I would reach out, touch the side of his face, think of the difference between liking and pretending. I wouldn't smile, run my thumb along his cheekbone.

Hisashiburi, I would say.

12 AND COUNTING

Scott Paul Hallam

—

My wife Michelle and I had a sinking feeling when Joey was born. Nine months to the day after our first child, Jennifer.

We didn't have sex for weeks after Jennifer's birth; the gynecologist said it wasn't safe. And Joey wasn't premature. Fully formed and raring to go. The doctors baffled. A biological oddity.

It took ages to conceive our first. Clinical conversations held in sterile, white offices. Pills and shots. Wives tale solutions like rosemary vagina steams. Prayers to St. Anne.

Even though devout Christians, we kept a statue of the Egyptian fertility goddess Bestat in our bedroom, which we kissed before having perfunctory ovulation sex.

Something must have worked. Too well.

Baby three, blonde-headed Jackie. Ten fingers, ten toes. Arrived in seven months.

After baby four showed up in six months, spunky Jasmine, the media caught wind of our circumstance. Reporters, armed with microphones and videocameras, mobbed our now cramped ranch home.

We signed onto our own reality show. Michelle, Michael, and More.

For a while, we almost enjoyed ourselves. Sprawling McMansion. Free diapers and baby food from show sponsors. Cash from strangers. Nannies around the clock. Even talks of a book deal.

But the babies kept coming. Jessica, baby five, in sixteen weeks. Jason in nine. Lucky number seven, chubby Jeffrey, in a breakneck five.

The fickle public soon lost interest. Our show canceled. The free gifts and cash slowed to a trickle, then stopped.

It's not like we didn't try to stem the baby tidal wave. We tried abstinence. No dice. Baby eight, James, tumbled out in one month flat.

Next, the doctors performed a hysterectomy. Three weeks later, baby number nine, Jade, appeared. Michelle's uterus grew back.

Our babies' cries bounced off the walls, reverberating like electric drills in our ears. But one look at their cherub faces and guilt washed over us. We slugged down more black coffee and continued the round-the-clock childrearing.

My wife's body was now a battlefield, shelled over and over. Ginger hair streaked gray. Loose skin and C-section scars. Her eyes liquid, beyond exhaustion.

Our bank account lost the war too. My mother-in-law hospitalized from a stress-induced stroke. My two brothers stopped speaking to me.

I even lost my job at the firm from falling asleep in court.

The eleventh, Jeremiah, arrived within five days of the tenth, perfect baby Jeraldine. The doctors don't even congratulate us anymore. We don't smile or laugh. Our few remaining friends and relatives have kept us upright.

By the time we arrived home from the hospital with our new bundle of joy, Michelle's stomach looked distended. Did we have days or hours?

This is why I'm telling our story on your program. A plea. Babies to good homes. Not sure how long Michelle can hold out; the doctors think sixteen, seventeen tops.

So, show up at our door, bring the proper papers, and little Jasper is all yours. I heard him pop out of the oven just now.

NEW PRICE

Scott Garson

—

My ex wants to lower the price on our house, I guess so it will sell.
I am amenable.

I use that word, anyway.

She takes it, I know, as me being funny, me doing something to cast our dealings in vaguely ridiculous light. Which is probably accurate. I mean in terms of my goal.

I'd probably rather give commentary on this moment than have to live through it.

"Five," she says. This in response to me asking how much she would like to come down.

I muse on the question of why she won't say it in full. Because 'five' by itself can get me to 'thousand'? 'Five' is enough? Because each word she has to give me here takes something out of her? Or because 'thousand' is hard, being closer to 'dollars,' being closer to time and cash we've invested in getting the house and property ready for what our shining realtor from hell has called a "potentially fast-warming" market?

"Five's okay."

She gives me a nod, says she'll talk to the shining realtor.

I'm aware of how differently she and I are handling the end of our marriage. I've ditched caution. I'm liable to speak any words that feel like they want to be spoken. As I do now.

"My shrink, coincidentally," I start, "my shrink says I should consider lowering my price on lots of things. My time. My attention."

"You don't have a shrink."

"Are you sure?"

"If you did, you wouldn't call them your shrink." She looks at her watch. "I have to go."

Her way of handling the end our marriage: to change. Become suddenly purposeful. A person so far from the woman I've known that I can nearly imagine someone pointing us out to one another, doing the introductions.

I give a wave.

Her car passes in silence.

What next? I loiter in dirt by the curb. By my monthly apartment. Because I'm worn out, because four cups of coffee won't do much against black-hour sleeplessness, or because I'm soft-headed in general, which is to say sort of useless and dumb, I let myself think of a different street, a quieter street at this hour. With peeping birds. And a sign out front, and a decent price, with new floors, new hickory cabinets, handsome pressed-tin backsplash. Everything new. Everything ready, I think, for some couple to make a new start.

BROKEN KEYS

Jennifer Fliss

———

It wasn't long into their relationship that her "I" key stopped working. She started typing things like: "want to have sex" and "like beer & cheese." He took from these what he could and thought how lucky am I? I found someone who gives and gives and gives. Selfishness is not a trait he likes.

They wrote about their frustrations with jobs, friends, parents. He asked about her hair. Had she ever cut it? She asked about his roommate. Favorite meals. Her: takeout Thai. Him: homemade gnocchi. *It's so easy, anyone can do it.* She mentioned she had a window herb garden but didn't like to cook. He scoffed, but he didn't tell her he thought this was ridiculous. He talked about his recent case; he was an attorney. He began to type "tho" instead of "though" and "U" instead of "you," as if the effort for him to acknowledge who he was addressing was too much.

Like a piano with dead keys, it was beautiful until it wasn't. She saw the problem, of course, acknowledged it within herself, but didn't want to say anything. She couldn't afford a new computer and didn't see how she could replace the keyboard alone. All her letters, her words, slowly lost their meaning. M and E were the next to go. And soon he read her missives as that of a passive woman. In theory he didn't like this, but in reality, as he stared into his screen, his own face vaguely reflected back at him, he thought that this was, in fact, the way it should be.

She typed and typed, late at night, at work, on the train to and from, and she wasn't being any more understood no matter how much effort she put into explanations. Her friends said *ditch him* and *swipe left babe*, though that wasn't the kind of app she'd found him on. He responded between the hours of nine and eleven at night.

Eventually he wrote "we are going to meet IRL."

She typed, *ok!* Deleted it.

He saw three bubbles.

She typed *"what do you want to do?"* Delete.

The bubbles disappeared.

She listened to the hissing of the heater in her little apartment, something she associated both with warmth and danger. She had learned how to avoid the radiator during the winter, one burn too many had left a scar on her forearm that still throbbed.

He typed: *"Girl please."*

Girl? she thought.

"What was all this for then?"

She typed an angry mash of letters. *"Tnwfuwifnwijjufhrvrf."* Delete.

The bubbles reappeared. Disappeared again.

He typed *did I do something to offend you?* and *don't say you're that kind of woman.*

That knd? She cursed her lack of an "I." She dragged her cursor to the *Log Out* icon. Hovered there. Clicked *My Account* instead, clicked and clicked and clicked until she finally found, hidden amidst a throng of text, *Cancel My Account.*

A pop-up box: *Are you sure?*

OAKS FALL

Christopher Ramsey

—

Jack buried both cats under the laurel oak in the back yard of his yellow ranch house in DeLand. He bought their tiny caskets from a company called Pet Eternal that he found online. He never told anyone how much he paid for the kitty coffins, but it was more than he could afford — especially after his divorce. Two years ago, when he buried the Siamese ladies, he made sure that they would be far enough away from where Chad's blow up pool would be set up — come the first of July. It seemed disrespectful for a kid to be splashing about directly over the Pet Eternal Premium Wood Cat Caskets handcrafted in Bangor, Maine. The laurel oak was the only shade on the entire property, and it had to serve a co-parented six-year-old boy's summertime fun and two dead cats.

"For two-hundred dollars, I can trim those branches back," Carl said, lighting his Pall Mall. "But if that thing ever comes down it will take the house, Jack."

"If," Jack said, pondering.

"I know one thing for sure. Oaks fall. Top heavy and rooted in sand."

"That tree is the best thing about the back yard. It's the best thing about the house. It's majestic."

"Laurel oaks are only good for about forty years. Like people. After forty, they get the heart rot," Carl said, taking a long drag off his cigarette. "If you want longevity, you plant a live oak. Those fuckers are strong."

"Trim the top," Jack said, walking away.

"Cash?" Carl said.

"Do you take cards?"

"Nope."

"Do you take checks?"

"Nope."

"Then why are you asking?"

Carl dropped his cigarette onto the grass and crushed it with his steel toe.

"Pick that up. My kid plays back here," Jack said, heading toward the side door of the laundry room.

In the laundry room, Jack pulled a dirty towel from an overflowing basket of dirty clothes and wiped his forehead. It was hot. It was June-in-Florida-hot. He stood in front of the washing machine for about twenty seconds before he picked up the basket and dumped its contents into the old Whirlpool's tub.

In the kitchen, Jack removed a can of Diet Coke from the refrigerator. The sink overflowed with dishes, the trash can under the sink brimmed with take-out containers, and the oversized microwave above the stove served as a protector of bread, cereal boxes, and cookies against the wolf spiders, water bugs, and anoles that Jack had long since made peace with as the co-inhabitants of his yellow ranch house. "It's Florida," he said, explaining his stance against pest control to any new visitor.

The same cohabitating philosophy extended to the outside porch area where a dozen paper wasps nests decorated the entranceway to Jack's front door. "It's my security system and my protection against Jehovah's Witnesses," he said to his ex-wife when she had voiced concern about the safety of their son. "I don't fuck with them. They don't fuck with me. We have an agreement," he said. "The wasps understand what the Witnesses do not."

After peeling back the stay-tab on the Diet Coke can, Jack dumped an ounce of the brown liquid over the dirty dishes stacked in the sink. Placing the can on the edge of the counter, he opened the cabinet above the empty drying rack and removed a liter bottle of Jack Daniel's Old Number 7. He uncapped the bottle with one hand and tilted it until the lighter brown liquid oozed from the can's opening. This ritual helped take the edge off of the morning.

Most mornings.

The falling oak didn't sound like an explosion or even what one might expect a heavy crash to sound like. Instead, it was a silent wave of energy that lifted the kitchen floor up several inches in a delayed suspended millisecond. In that frozen millisecond, Jack didn't hear the Diet Coke can as it landed and bounced on the linoleum. The only sound was the Husqvarna chainsaw's motor as it choked its way to a stop.

The impact of the laurel oak on the laundry room's roof was as swift as it was devastating. The laundry room was an addition to the house that the last owner had built by himself. The concrete slabs under the laundry room were not up to code, but neither was anything else about the addition. "The guy was an idiot," the inspector told Jack when he was buying the house.

A branch about the width of Jack's waist sliced through the middle of the laundry room's roof and pancaked the Whirlpool. The oak's trunk hovered over the large gash in the ceiling, threatening to finish off the last owner's shitty construction work.

"There was some Spanish moss roped around two branches. When I cut one, it pulled the other. That's what looks like happened," said Carl. "Weight and momentum."

"Are you fucking kidding me?"

"I'm sorry."

"Fuck you."

"You're mad. You probably have a right to be mad, but we need to take care of something that is creeping me out right now, Jack."

"What the hell are you talking about?"

"Those tiny coffins." Carl pointed at the two Pet Eternal Premium Wood Cat Caskets that the base of the oak exposed as its roots ripped open the earth. The wooden boxes were as pristine as the day they had been put into the ground. The extra expense, that at the time Jack couldn't afford, now seemed worth it. These were the quality caskets that the Siamese ladies deserved.

"I'm going to call the police," Carl said.

JADED

Wilson Koewing

—

Jade dug around in and tossed aside items from the pile of stuff she kept on the vanity we'd purchased for the bedroom when she moved in.

"What if I'd known you first?" I asked.

"I don't know, Josh."

She found her passport and tossed a bag over her shoulder, returned to the vanity and retrieved her magic wand vibrator from a drawer.

"Vibrator and a passport, huh?"

"All I need."

I followed her to the front door and watched the words etched on her shoulder bounce away through the tight binds of the screen door– *life is meant for living.*

His name was Raif and he lived in the Czech Republic. I'd been aware of him. Known the name Josh didn't compare to Raif. Nothing exotic about Josh. Nothing life changing about a future with Josh. Raif sails you to Grecian islands. Raif waves his hand and gets you across the Croatian border. Raif declares Medellin a "hidden gem."

I wandered onto the porch as she climbed in an Uber. The grey sedan bounced away on the cracked New Orleans street, turned right at the corner and vanished. There was no breeze. The sky was peppered by tufts of thin clouds that resembled couch pillow innards torn out.

***

I remember one conversation vividly. Jade and I at the Carousel Bar in The Hotel Monteleone, revolving slowly.

"Some people have that one person, who... no matter what, they would leave any relationship to be with them," I said.

Jade swirled a neat whiskey.

"They're always out there... and no matter how hard the other person tries... it's just spinning the wheel."

Jade lifted the glass to her lips.

"Do you have someone like that?"

Jade got the bartender's attention. A hunk in a shirt two sizes too small.

"Is there alcohol in this?"

"It's neat," he replied.

Jade held his gaze and he reciprocated. It was oddly flirtatious until he lumbered away.

"It's boring when you act so insecure."

She went outside. The bar slowly rotated until I saw her through the window, smoking beside a potted evergreen. An empty pedicab zipped by. Gaslights burnt above doorways. French Quarter characters passed and crossed streets. A city romanticized through a window. And there she was on her phone.

* * *

I met Jade one night when I couldn't get in a Bywater club because my ID had been washed so many times my face looked scratched out. The door people around town were dicks who cared about their jobs.

That night it had been a young woman with short black hair, tattoos crawling down her arms, and a great smile, who seemed delighted to send me away. I gave her some choice words and went outside.

Jade stood by the door with one leg up against the wall. Her pale white skin bordered on translucent under the dull glow of the club's sign. She wore a red dress and had red hair. Her fingernails appeared painted with white-out. In retrospect, she spent more time than anyone I've known acting like she was posing for an imaginary photo.

I wandered over.

"They wouldn't let me inside. How was it?"

"Why wouldn't they let you in?"

"Must have thought I was dangerous... maybe even a menace."

"You don't look like you could be a menace at all..."

We stood awkward in heavy silence. I gazed at St. Claude bathed kindly in streetlights; hipsters relocated from Brooklyn stumbled and swaggered across the neutral ground.

"Want to come to my house for a drink?" I asked.

She watched a tattooed guy with a red mohawk stomp confidently toward the club's entrance. He gave her the eye. She stared passed him off in the distance.

"Okay."

***

More than once I woke up to Jade sitting on the porch at dawn laughing at the sunrise.

"Jesus, the things people get excited about."

Occasionally the laughter bled into crying then she'd want to have sex.

At night we'd lie in darkness and listen to records. Alt-J and Neutral Milk Hotel, mostly. To this day I can't stomach Jeff Mangum's voice. There exists nothing more self-indulgent and meaningless in this world than *In the Aeroplane Over the Sea*. No one has been more responsible for young women leaving on a whim for Europe in the last two decades to find their Raifs than Jeff Mangum.

I didn't have to investigate far into Jade's Instagram history to find the Raif weeks. Early 2018. Her European backpacking adventure; her lone trip outside the states; which she infuriatingly brought up any chance she could; the trip she didn't want to return from, crying on the phone with her parents, them coaxing her home. The first twenty something in history to do that.

***

With Jade galivanting around Europe, I had time on my hands. I drank heavily and kept unusual hours. I didn't think about her for two weeks. Half past noon on a Tuesday, three beers and two shots in, I decided to unblock her Instagram.

There it was, the last two weeks meticulously documented. A photo outside the Prague airport, Jade's arms around Raif's waist, white 3-D letters spelling Praha in the background. A sunset on the Charles Bridge; The Prague Castle silhouetted behind them. Raif always in sweat-suits owning the look of preposterous Euro-trash. Blurry photos through the windows of moving trains filtered with X-Pro II. A Gondola ride in Venice. The cathedral. The birds. Smoking a joint on a bike in Amsterdam. Posing in front of Matterhorn. Sunbathing in San Sebastian. A dozen Pintxos photos; not even good ones, the garbage that warms on the bar. A selfie on an overnight train to Lisbon. Flashing a peace sign at JFK? #welearnfrommistakes. Back at Louis Armstrong. #happytobehome. Time-stamped one hour ago.

I knew before I saw her rising into view through the tight binds of the screen door, trailing puffs of smoke, that I would open it and let her right back in.

THE ART OF CUTTING

Joshua Begley

—

(There's an art to cutting oneself. Most don't appreciate that. Real cutters—not teenage girls scratching themselves with their fingernails, looking for attention—hide it. Placement is important. Displayed scars kill the art, but more importantly, the body is a highway of veins, nerves, and arteries. Go too deep and you may end up hurting yourself worse than you intended. The final part comes down to preparation. One must have alcohol, a clean knife, and bandages on hand. Infections come easy, and telltale blood drops give it all away.)

John thought this as he sat in Starbucks, scratching his arm under the sleeve, high up near the shoulder. His nails rode crisscrossing bumps. Ants ran under his skin.

"Don't do this." Gmail's welcome screen sat on his laptop.

"Don't do this." He typed in Bethany_Cabe@gmail.com then entered the password.

John bit his lip and leaned forward, expecting to see a name. Instead he saw spam, newsletters, coupons, and emails from her sisters.

John leaned back and closed the window. The desktop picture stared at him. Beth smiled, holding the skirt of her evening dress wide. John smiled and draped a shoulder over hers. Behind them loomed the cruise ship's ballroom.

He slapped the lid shut and rubbed his eyes. When he opened them he saw streaks of blood on the lid. It stained his fingers and trickled down his arm.

"Shit." He knocked over his chair as he walked to the cream and sugar bar to grab a fistful of napkins.

"This doesn't count," he said. He turned to walk back to his table and saw the little man. His bald pate reflected the fluorescent lights, and his eyes were coffee-dark. He smiled at John and saluted with his cup. John grabbed his laptop and left, leaving his coffee on the table.

#

Coffee-dark eyes haunted him. John sat on the couch, not watching the news. He kept blinking, like his eyes couldn't focus.

"What's wrong with you?" Beth said. She sat cross-legged on the recliner, head tilted forward, practically touching the screen.

(There is an art to hiding. A tilted computer screen, a hasty mouse click, a deflected question. Silence becomes a language unto itself.)

"Don't do that," he said.

"Don't do what?"

"Don't ask me like that. It makes it sound like I'm doing something wrong."

"Don't be so sensitive."

"Don't be so insensitive." John winced. *Too deep*, he thought. The ants returned and he scratched the scabs on his arm. *Stupid. Always think before you speak.*

Beth drew in on herself like an armadillo, her face hidden by the laptop and her hair.

#

He waited at the counter at Starbucks. The door opened behind him and the cold wind made him huddle in his coat. He wrapped his hands around his tea while he waited for Beth's pumpkin spice latte. A bouquet of roses stuck out of his coat pocket.

"Don't you just love the bite in the air this time of year?" someone said behind him.

A small, bald man with dark brown eyes smiled at John. He smiled with his lips closed.

The ants returned in force, but John couldn't scratch through his coat. "I guess. Really it just reminds me that winter's coming."

"Don't you like winter?"

"Not a fan."

"I'm not one either. I prefer these between times like now. Not quite alive, not quite dead." He smiled and showed his teeth this time—small, sharp, like polished stones in pink sand. "It's a time ripe with possibilities."

(There is an art to conversation. An art John never quite mastered. The words never quite appeared, and he felt like Frankenstein's monster, grunting and gesturing, making more trouble than headway.)

"I guess," he said and turned back to see if the latte was ready, hoping the conversation wouldn't go any deeper.

"Don't do anything I wouldn't do," the small man said and flicked the bouquet.

#

"Don't do this," he said.

Beth threw clothes into a suitcase. "I'll be back next week for the rest of my stuff. Please don't be here."

"Please, we can work this out. We can get couple's therapy."

She shook her head. "I can't do that." She finally looked at him. "It's over, John."

"No."

"You're a good man and a good husband, but I'm not happy, and I don't love you."

He stepped forward. "Make love to me," he said. "Please, just make love to me."

"Jesus Christ, it's never enough for you, is it? How deep do I have to drill into that thick skull of yours? We. Are. Over."

"Somebody told me this is a time rife with possibilities. It doesn't have to be over."

Beth pushed past him, slamming the door as she left.

(There is an art to leaving and to letting go. Recognizing that it's over is the trick, and acting upon that recognition is the miracle).

John tore open his scabs. His fingers sank into his flesh as he tried to root out the ants.

#

"Don't."

He stood in the bedroom bathroom, stripped to his underwear. Blood ran down both arms. It caked under his nails. He rocked on his heels. He held a steak knife in his right hand.

"Don't."

Rubbing alcohol, cotton balls, and bandages lined up on the sink like good soldiers, waiting for orders, prepared for the worst.

"There is an art to cutting, you know. Anything done with passion and precision can be an art." The little, bald man stood in the bathroom doorway, his dark in his eyes overwhelmed the whites, looking like two pools of coffee.

John nodded at his wisdom and raised the knife to his arm.

"Ah, ah, ah, ah," the little man said. He traced a line on his cheek from just under his eye to his jaw.

John nodded again. He placed the knife against his face and pulled down.

Artist: Katiana Robles

TWO MOONS AND A HUMMINGBIRD

Jo Varnish

——

I once saw two moons in the same sky. I don't talk about it because it felt like something I should hold close, something special. The next day I met Tess.

Not long after she'd moved in, we saw a mouse-hole in the drywall at the back of the bedroom closet, and later, the mouse himself. I called him Morris. Tess called him Timmy.

"I heard Morris last night," I would say.

"Funny. I heard Timmy."

One mouse was manageable. For months, we rarely saw him, and when we did it was late at night. Silhouetted in the darkened room against the baseboard, he would survey the scene before ducking under the door and venturing into the hallway.

"Have fun, Timmy."

"Enjoy yourself, Morris."

Tess and I were a hummingbird, at times darting into life with agency, at others beating our wings furiously with no progress made. She was determined and cultured, much more so than me, and being less so made me a bore. Or maybe the insecurity made me a bore. Confidence is king after all.

"God, you can be such a bore," she said.

I left the basement window cracked open to run a cord for outside lights. Morris invited a date inside. Within a month or two we had little toddler and bigger toddler mice exploring, skipping across the living room floor while I watched television, Tess in the armchair on her phone.

"They're so bold," I said, imagining Morris telling them they need not fear us.

"They have to go," said Tess. "But together, they need to stay together."

We set up tunnel plastic traps that we bought online. The mice would be tempted by peanut butter, walk into the tunnel and their weight would release and close the spring door behind them. The first couple of evenings, we barely sat down in between the clacks of the little trapdoor closing. We emptied them into a large tub, and before we went to bed we drove to the woods to set our catch free. Seeing Tess there wishing good luck to the mouse family, her skin lit by the moon—the one moon—was too much to bear.

"Anna! Where are you going?" she called after me.

"To wait in the car."

Not long after, a deep froideur set in. An evening of red wine, pad Thai and blistering insults, their intent to harm increasing with unsettling rapidity. And, like a disturbance early in a night's sleep, after which there is no return to the comfortable slumber that preceded it, the words thrown that evening were our crash landing. There was no pretense it was anything but an ending and she moved out just a couple of mornings later. I was insulted that she'd leave in the morning hours. Neatly packed bags in the hallway, 'goodnight', and an alarm set. I deserved screaming, throwing clothes in the car, driving off into the darkness without a plan.

She texted me at nearly midnight.

- *Did you check the traps? We didn't look for a couple days*

I went downstairs. One was empty, and the other had a little mouse, one of the smaller toddlers. He was lethargic, not even attempting to dodge my hand. I had left him too long without anything but a smear of peanut butter.

- *There's one there*

- *A baby? You can't release him alone*

I put him in a box and mixed honey and water to make a nectar. I dipped a chunk of bread in it and put it where he lay. His whiskers trembled and he began to eat. I closed the box. After work the next day, I bought him a tank with a mesh lid and named him Timmy. I kept him as a pet, safe. Not alone.

I make a point to look outside each evening, so I don't miss the second moon when it comes. I don't research it, I don't want to know how long I'll have to wait. I want to walk outside and know I am seeing something special, just like last time.

DISTANCE

Justin Brozanski

—

M om meets the half-elf ranger, Stillgar, inside *Everquest*, the online roleplaying game. A makeshift bed of goose down comforters and three cream-colored pillows lay tidy on the computer room floor, because that's where she sleeps now. Blue computer light bathes her body. She wears her favorite nightgown, a white smear of Nair burns her upper lip, and a towel wraps her long, wet, black and silver-streaked hair, high and tight, like the royal cap-crown of the Egyptian Queen, Nefertiti. Her fingers shudder each time Stillgar private messages:

GG on that Crushbone Orc

Yes, Copenhagen's very beautiful this morning.

It's not as beautiful as you, though.

Her husband sleeps, alone, in the master bedroom. The orcish death-rattles pumping through the speakers could wake him. And, so what if they did? If he were to walk in now, would he even understand her needs? Her desires to feel appreciated? Much less what is happening in front of him? That this is more than just some game for her?

The real-time clock reads 1:03 AM and he works in six hours. The same distance between where Mom sits in Florida and where he, Frederick, the man behind Stillgar, must sit in Denmark. If she typed goodbye and slept now, would she have the energy to meet and hunt with him, again? *What are you having for breakfast?* Mom types, and she laughs when he writes *a danish* because, of course he is.

#

Her son logs in as his human monk. At the other computer, Mom sits, still, playing her high-elf mage. She hasn't changed out of her nightgown and, in the monitor's reflection, her queenly demeanor feels less refined, instead pinker and puffier. There's a smell on her, something like garlic, onions, or cheese left alone too long.

Her son punches goblins in the face, for an hour, and, in that time, she thinks how Stillgar—who she knows is Frederick, but still, why not keep calling him Stillgar?—proposed to her. How he offered her a Ruby Dragon's Heart Wedding Ring which promised a +7 save to her fire, disease, cold, magic and poison resistances as long as she wore it. How she accepted his proposal. Her own wedding rings, the real ones, made of white gold and diamond, clack against the keyboard. What had they ever protected her from? The real-time clock reads 5:30 PM. Her husband would arrive home, soon.

Her teeth clench. Any more pressure and they might fracture. Her fingers command the keys to cast an attack spell and the goblin her son punches explodes in a storm of colorful fireworks.

"Hey, that was my kill," he says.

Mom instructs her high-elf mage to meditate. When she stands her body feels like a tree in Florida during a torrential rain, ready to bend. If she tells her son about her weird video game lover, what then? Would he 'get it'? He is a teenager, after all, and don't teenagers feel the need to be loved, to feel angst, and loneliness? Isn't that their thing?

But.

What if he didn't? Would his rejection bow her so far, she breaks? Would he try to kill her lover in player versus player? Would he tell his dad her secret? Would he quit the game? Would they take the game away from her?

"You know he has other women when he leaves on his business trips," she says. *Finally.*

Her son looks down, first at his keyboard, then the ground, then her. His face is riddled with pimples, his hair as greasy as hers, and she can't help but think they must smell very much alike. *But things don't have to be like this, do they?*

"I know," he says. "I just didn't know if you knew, too, but I guess I should've known better with you sleeping in here." His hands tap at his knees like he's typing a message for help or to find some way to logout of this *situation.*

And, it was a situation, wasn't it? She had come this far.

"I've met someone," she says. "In the game. He's asked me to marry him, and I'm not entirely sure what that means, but this is something for me. I thought you should be a part of it. Or, at the very least, know."

Her son stands. Will he leave and shut himself up in his room? Will he spit in my face and call me a whore? Will he end my world?

Instead, he wraps his gangly arms around her body. She feels him squeeze her, tight, and she can't help but let her face drift into his razor-burned neck, where she cries, and says, "thank you, thank you, thank you."

The garage door whirrs.

The car door slams.

Keys rattle.

And, she waits, in her son's arms, in the warm glow of computer light, to the sounds of vengeful goblins tearing their unmanned characters to pieces, for her husband, for the questions he will ask about his crying wife, and whether she will, finally, now, tell him about the other man who saved her soul from the ghastly specters in the City of Mists; who camped for weeks to pluck a flower, just for her, from the coral gardens of the jealous undersea God; who lives six hours in the future; forty-eight hundred miles away, and yet, is with her always and forever; or, not.

FOREST OF FRIENDS

Claire Polders

—

V ic had his eye on a promise, a potentially fixable cool box buried underneath the junk. He was digging it up when the rain, only nagging before, began to bucket down. He rushed to the edge of the dump and found shelter in the shed where the boys often got together, especially when it poured and trash-diving became more dangerous than rewarding—nobody wanted to fall through the soaked mush and be trapped forever. Like Dennis.

The boys shared one cigarette between the six of them, outsmoking the chemical tang of the closed air. They whined about how much life sucked, until Ras, the self-proclaimed poet, gave birth to a plan that sounded flowery and heroic. He used words like "inspiration" and "alliance," and sketched how the boys would be adored if the plan flourished. Enthusiasm rose immediately, yet also fear. It surprised Vic that only one kid protested openly. When had they all grown so bold? The youngest boy was nine, the oldest twice that age. After the lonely coward had left, the others eyed one another warily. Would the coward talk? Should they go ahead regardless? Then came the secret knock, and Vic opened the door. The boy had returned, no longer a coward. He stood there, drenched and dripping, saying, Please count me in. They all shook hands, fraternity soaring. Together they would reach the sky.

Each boy pitched in to collect the cloth—stealing, begging, hunting—and soon they had a bunch. Trickier was getting the scraps connected. They had rescued a Singer from the dump and had sufficiently repaired the thing to do the job, but sowing had seemed easier when their mothers and sisters had worked the machine. Vic was proud to know more than the others and taught his friends how to seduce the thread through the needle's eye, how to zigzag. In the shed, revolutionized into workshop, the boys swore and sucked their thumbs, secretly happy. Sacrificing their blood confirmed their bravery: one plan, one heart.

On the big day, Vic woke up early, before the sun, before his mom. He moved stealthily. She'd never allow her kids to put themselves at risk. *You protest what you don't understand*, she would say. *Because there's never a good explanation*, he would reply. From under his bed, Vic removed the suitcase he'd taken from the shed, and he carried their clothed plan to the other boys, who were waiting at the back of the girls' school. Only a year ago, they had marched against the school's opening, against the law prohibiting girls and boys to be taught together, in one classroom. Vic could still point at the spots on his body were the batons had left him bruised. Now, Ras hushed last-minute doubts. To resist means to be wounded at least once.

The boys joked as they got dressed, the sun rising. Despite their anxiety, there was something wonderful about their clothes, self-made, unauthorized. They would own themselves again by looking like others. They took their position at the school's entrance and remained unobserved for a while. In their long skirts, their faces still beardless, they simply resembled girls waiting for classes to begin. Since the Regime had banned women from wearing pants, Vic had hardly seen a girl outside her required costume. Whenever a woman disobeyed the rule, she was fined, intimidated, or worse: arrested. The official punishment for Contempt of State was unpaid menial labor, but anything could happen, and no one would know. Some girls came back pregnant.

A teacher arrived at the school, did a double take, and smiled broadly. A mother dropping off her daughter looked as though the devil had come for her soul. Some girls cried when they noticed the boys standing tall like trees, and they joined the gang to form a forest of friends. What courage they had together, what union! Vic held Daisy's hand—warm and soft skin—and felt like they should make a tour through town or something. Adrenaline pumped a triumph he would later call love.

Before the sirens broke the calm, before the batons, a lone reporter showed his face. He snapped shots and fired questions. What are you trying to accomplish? Vic didn't answer, nor did any of the other boys. A goal beyond the day was never part of the plan.

FAIRYTALES

Kieron Walquist

—

I

    Selling heirlooms online, pocketing pennies from tip jars, shaking vending machines and performing surgery on our piggy banks, my father is King Midas—money is his life source, the blood that flows through his veins. We're the rosewater that washes his treasures and makes them cheap.

II

    In the frozen section at Walmart, in the park past the seesaw, along theater 5 amongst strangers at the movies, my mother is the mother from Hansel & Gretel—abandoning us to fend for ourselves, to find our way back using invisible bread crumbs. Her presence during her absence would've been far more satisfying than any candy-house.

III

    Following behind her car, searching for her in the mall, peeping through her bedroom window and interrogating his friends about her, my brother is Peter Pan—never growing up, usually high as a kite on pixie dust, certain some Wendy girl will happily follow him to his Neverland. Be he's just a lost boy.

IV

    Once in my arms, now out of reach, out of the neighborhood, out of state, my one and only boyfriend turned out to be the Gingerbread Man—run, run, as fast as you can. He did. And never came back. Perhaps I wasn't sweet enough or in the perfect cookie-cutter shape.

V

Emaciated to portly, colossal to miniature, received to disowned, my sister is Alice—taking pills and tea from mad acquaintances, eating cakes and tarts when famished, then retching to downsize. She's petrified over how the world will see her. We tell her she can't go on like this—she'll end up disappearing like Cheshire. But to her, everyone is Tweedledee and Tweedledum when it comes to her pain.

VI

First Doc, then Happy, next was Sleepy, perhaps even Bashful at one point, my aunt is Snow White—seven, eight, maybe nine little suitors competing for her love, for she's the fairest of them all. At least that's what she believes the mirrors she admires so much are telling her.

VII

No one's The Piper or Rumpelstiltskin. No one wants a child to look after.

VIII

Wigs, lipstick, dresses and polished nails, my uncle is the wolf from Little Red Riding Hood—attending dinner parties, getting fixed at the beauty salon and gyrating amongst drunken company at the disco-bars as "grandma" rather than "grandpa." We've chastised his lifestyle; ostracize him from family outings and reunions, stating that his behavior isn't normal. He says we need to accept him— the real him. But, really, he's just a wolf in sheep's clothing.

IX

A laptop that sat alone at a Starbucks, a TV that blared snow through a bay window, a motorcycle left running on a curb, my best friend is Goldilocks—taking candy from actual babies if they're munching on her favorite flavor, stealing clothes off store mannequins, exposing artificial parts. She's dealt with many angry bears due to her sticky hands. One day, she'll rob the prisons blind.

X

Castles in the skies, bystanders with animal faces, oceans existing under puddles in sidewalks and shadows that predict the future, my grandmother is Sleeping Beauty—dreaming of fantasies amplified by her Alzheimer's; stuck living in the wrong world. Prince Charming died long ago, so she might never recover.

XI

I use boards for structure, feathers for lift and wax to hold it all together. I'm Icarus—searching for a brighter life. The sky's the limit. However, as I chase my dreams, my little heart giving everything, I lose sight of the ground and run into reality that is as sweltering as the sun: dreams only come true in fairytales.

NURTURE

J. Bradley

—

The blood peels itself from napkins in the trashcan next to the bed, the duvet in the hamper, Lana's underwear crumpled on the bedroom floor. It converges together in front of the bedroom door. It bends and twists a plea one letter at a time: H-E-L-P-P-U-T-M-E-T-O-G-E-T-H-E-R. "How," I ask. The blood forms a tiny head, neck, and shoulders just to answer with a shrug.

Lana didn't understand why her body rejected the thing that might have become Paul or Pauline. A few days after it happened, I caught Lana in the bathroom looking at her stomach in the mirror, her fingers studying it like a black box. I wonder whether the boy who would probably break his collarbone on a moped or the girl whose teeth would be as briar patch gnarled as mine made it and Lana's body decided to spare them the cruelty of living. I only inspect at my testicles when I'm alone in the shower so Lana can't see how I'm trying to figure out what went wrong on my end.

I offer to help Lana shave her legs. I put the flecks of toilet paper with her blood on it in my cargo short pocket when she isn't looking. I rescue used tampons while they're still wet, squeeze them into the blood after it forms a baby bird's beak and makes chirping motions. I move furniture around the house to help Lana open her shin, a toe or two. I promise the blood not to say anything to Lana until it has enough to form a larynx to greet her, arms that will never let her go.

IT'S A LONG WAY FROM HERE TO THERE AND BACK AGAIN

Rachel Smith

——

You brought the bats home the week before I left. Three furred faces wrapped in newspaper shrouds. You boiled them with garlic and ginger, and ate them with buttered white bread.

I'd never seen them for real before, only in those nature docos I made you watch on Sunday nights. Their screech and squabble always reminded me of our kids that time we went on a family road trip – piled three small bodies and all our things into the back seat of the car and hoped we would make it up and over mountain passes.

Turned out the middle child got car sick and the other two discovered a talent for torment. The roads were long but there was no turning back once we got started. You know how I get; when the proportion of commitment invested is nearly equal to the total attainable sum of the whole bloody exercise, I have to push on.

Some things seemed clearer though, compressed down into that small space between sun visor and foot well. As you drove us through one-shop towns I pried back the past 17 years, layer by layer. Under it all there I was – my face looking out as if the whole world was a breath away.

Now I tell the kids the truth, or my version of it anyway. That bats had been your favorite food when you were little like them. That beauty can be found in the darkly veined leather of a wing, in a tributary of capillaries raised to the surface of the skin.

THE SWAN MAIDEN'S CHILDREN

Bethany DuVall

—

O ne day, her little daughter was playing hide-and-seek with her brother, and she went behind the wainscoting... and found there a robe all made of feathers, and took it to her mother. As soon as [her mother] saw it, she put it on... and flew away.

When the hunter came home next morning, his little daughter told him what had happened... So he set out to find his wife in the Land East o' the Sun and West o' the Moon.

-Joseph Jacobs, Europa's *Fairy Book*

The Hunter's Daughter

The man stands tall with a dark brow. Carnivals are beneath him. But he'd heard of Leda – everyone had – and so he slips beneath the frowsy tent.

After the performance, he pays the ringmaster for a private audience with the maiden. He waits in the master's own train car, eyeing the grimy, unmade bed and the red corset lampshade.

The door opens, and a tiny bundle of pale skin and feathers stumbles through as if pushed from behind.

She catches her balance.

The man removes his top hat – the felt one, not the silk today – and begins to circle her, examining every inch of the curious fusion of feathers and flesh. They say the girl is a half-breed, abandoned with her half-breed brother in a cabin of furs and guns and taxidermied geese, no parents for miles. Indeed, it is a flawless costume. He pulls at one white pinion protruding from the girl's sharp shoulder, but it does not come loose.

"Ow."

"That hurt?"

The girl does not look up.

The man finishes his orbit and stands in front of her, surveying her nakedness. She is flat and small.

"Take off your feathers."

For an instant, the girl meets his gaze – even her eyes are white. Delicious. She twists to reach her own back, arm crooked across her neck. He watches. Her slight hip bone juts out.

She yanks. "I can't," she says, fixing her gaze again on the rickety floor.

The man settles himself on the master's messed bed.

"Try," he says. "I believe in you."

She clamps her jaw in concentration, pulls at the plumage on her wrist. A bruise rises under the shaft, but the feather remains intact.

"Leda," he says, "come here."

She takes a diffident step. "My name is not –"

The man shoves two fingers into her mouth, pressing down on her tongue. She gags, and he presses in further, down her throat, holding the back of her neck with his other hand. When she stops resisting, he takes her by the shoulders and tears feathers from her skin, one by one.

The Hunter's Son

Dark curls frame the woman's face. She stands stiff as a rod. Carnivals are beneath her. But she'd heard of Zeus – everyone had – and so she slips beneath the chintz tent against her better judgment.

The performance does not disappoint. Young Zeus is every bit the god: white as snow, a ruffle of feathers, taking tiny, delicious Leda under the ringmaster's narrow gaze. He hesitates only once. The ringmaster raises the whip, but does not need to use it. The show goes on.

After the performance, she pays for a private audience with the god. She waits in the master's own train car, a mess of scarlet and beads. She straightens the amethyst sheets.

The door opens. A scrawny bundle of skin and feathers lurches through, as if pushed from behind.

He catches his balance, and she circles him, hawklike, examining every inch of the feathered boy. She pulls gently at one bright pinion protruding from his spine, but it does not come loose.

"Ow."

"That hurt?"

The boy glares at her. Even his eyes are white. Remarkable.

"A god cannot be hurt by a mortal woman."

The boy says nothing.

The woman finishes her orbit and stops in front of him, surveying his nakedness, his smallness. "Take off your feathers."

"I can't."

The woman settles herself on the master's messed bed, poofing out her dark skirts with delicacy. "They didn't want you, did they, half-breed?"

He takes a step backward.

"Zeus," she says, stretching long fingers out to him, curling them around his bony wrist, "you don't need to disguise yourself with me."

"My name is not –"

The woman closes her mouth over his. She grasps at the feathers on his back, tugging at them, calculating how much force each quill can withstand, gobbling his screams as she pulls.

Twins

They squat together on the steel tracks between the contortionists' wagon and the aviary car. Wherever they are, the train tracks are always the same. The peacocks squawk from within their cages.

Phoebe stares into the dead night. Her brother dabs her gapes and gorges with ointment.

"How will I fly away if they keep taking my feathers?"

"They'll grow back." Sampson scrubs dried blood from the down on his sister's neck.

Phoebe flinches.

"Sorry."

Phoebe turns to him. She contemplates the purpling bruises scattered across his shoulders and chest, each punctuated by a ruffled, but intact, feather. They never pull his out.

"I understand why Mother left."

He meets her colorless eyes, the only eyes in the world that match his own. They do not belong here. They do not belong anywhere. "I'll carry you. When my remiges fledge in. I'll carry you."

"I'll be too heavy."

They both know she's right.

Sampson studies Pheobe's mottled bald patches. The real Zeus had been a monster, but even he didn't mutilate Leda.

A cluster of new pinions grows from her left side, just below the rib cage. He leans in to be sure. "Tomorrow night, keep your arms down if you can."

"Why?"

Sampson points at the fresh growth: long, structured quills.

Phoebe twists to see. "Wing feathers." Her voice is a hushed prayer.

Sampson scoops a blob of ointment and pastes the elegant remiges to his sister's skin so they hide in the slight contour of her waist.

Phoebe stares at the winking stars.

SURRENDER

Kevin Hogg

—

A crid smoke filled his eyes, calling him to give in to temptation. Breath came in increasingly painful gasps, and going on was not worth the effort. Even the dancing flames invited: "Quit fighting. Become one with us. Fall to the floor and be free."

A barely audible whisper tickled his brain. A call from the next room? He paused and heard it again. "The oath." There was no second-guessing. The voice came from within him. His chief had made him recite the oath when he took the job—concern, courage, strength, wisdom. Defeat played no part in these values. Rejuvenated, he pushed on to the only door remaining in the hallway. Locked.

He lifted his arms, only to find how close he had truly come to giving up. His axe lay abandoned where he had paused, too distant to be of any use.

Legs almost anchored to the floor by fatigue and protective gear, he summoned all of his strength and delivered a sharp kick to the door. Nothing. He kicked again. The door held. A vision of his wife flashed through his mind. He must keep trying; he would hope for the same if his family was in peril.

One more kick sent the door flying open into the room.

There on the floor lay his worst nightmare—a man and a young girl lay unconscious on the floor.

A man. In all likelihood, a provider, maybe the provider, for this family. Probably married to the hysterical woman he had seen outside. And a girl. Life barely begun, she couldn't be more than seven. Clad in pajamas, with long blond hair covering the back of her head.

Amid the inferno and its choking fumes, time remained to save only one of the victims. There could be no second trip, and the remaining firefighters were off trying to save the neighboring houses. Nothing in his training could prepare him for this decision. Either choice condemned the other, and himself, to a life of guilt.

Still unsure of his next action, he strode quickly toward the bodies. He grabbed an arm from each and pulled. They slid an inch or two. There was no way he could bring them both through the flames. At this point, it would be a miracle if he could save either one.

He caught himself gazing into the spreading flames, reviving their siren song. Only one path remained.

Removing his mask, he whispered, "I'm sorry." Then he lay down between the bodies, grasped their hands, and waited.

Artist: Kaylan Stedman

THE DISTRACTIONS

Liza Monroy

—

Y ou drive up on their lawn, throw the Buddha through the window, and pass out in your own vomit. It isn't your proudest moment. But what was? You haven't taken a risk in your glossy little life, much less on something that could end so spectacularly disastrous. So here we have it: the most admirable thing you've done. Your car, driver's side door flung open, headlights beaming into their living room, sits with its engine still running. Their formerly elegant windowpane reduced to shards of shattered glass glinting across moonlit grass as if they were ice flakes. Not that ice flakes would occur in LA, but it's the first thing that comes to mind. What does happen here: a stone Buddha with a broken nose. You, in a similar state, supine on the lawn. If only you could see your hair. You spend six hundred dollars at Jean-Claude for that look, only this version is much better than anything he does, all matted and mussed like that, natural. Your mascara-streaked cheeks and smeared lipstick. Your pretty trench coat, white button-down blouse, and pink jeans covered in grass stains, mud, and vomit—the contents of every single craft cocktail from the fancy little speakeasy around the corner on Santa Monica. But don't worry. You still look pretty.

   I would know. I've been watching you for years. First on Friendster then MySpace then Facebook, Twitter, Instagram, Pinterest, and of course the reliably consistent Google. You have been an independent filmmaker, a magazine writer, a curator of miniature works of art. Mostly you have been a mother. I'm sorry about your kid, the diagnosis. It must have been so hard for you. I can't imagine since of course I am not a mother, if I was I wouldn't have had time for such close observation of minutia, the trivial details that obsess me, the true reveals of other lives. Lives like yours. Unexceptional and wholly absorbing. It's why I do what I do.

By that I don't mean the stalking. I mean my job. Or rather, I made the stalking my job, though I preferred to call it curiosity. I became so good at my job that within a decade they called me the female Mark Zuckerberg in the press.

Female, always predicated by female, as per usual, "the female version of this interesting guy, the female version of that accomplished dude."

Fuck them.

They're just the male versions of me.

Get off the Internet, Mimi, I told myself so many times. There is nothing for you there. At least, nothing good. But I lost hours, I lost days to my distractions. There was no getting off. It was with me everywhere, wherever I went. I needed it for work. I needed it for everything. Mostly, I needed it for connection, even if the people I was connecting with had no idea that's what we were doing.

But there's you. Drunk and passed out on their lawn. They don't know how much time you spent with them. With their second selves. Or at least she doesn't. Don't worry, he won't reveal your connection and I won't come out from behind these hedges. I am so fucking happy to be here. Your celebrity-worthy semi-public meltdown is the ultimate reinforcement. I've been hoping for a long time that this would happen.

You looked too perfect to be a real person.

But I should have known. It's always the perfect ones who have the darkest sides.

You wake to them standing over you. The fractured early sunlight splits your eyes.

"Definitely never seen her before," the man says.

Liar.

"Well she can't be a stranger," the woman says in a French-accented lilt. She sounds like a cartoon and looks like she stepped out of a 1940s movie. "She's done this on purpose. There must be a reason."

"Maybe it's you," says the man. Trying to turn it around, flip the situation onto her. Classic.

You try to roll over to sit up but your head is now as heavy as their precious stone deity lawn ornament—missing, now returned.

Are you sad now? Satisfied? The answer is at the touch of an icon.

Emotional Read-Only Mode

I'm so glad I created it.

THE GIRL IN JAKE'S RED HOODIE

Maura Yzmore

—

I was going to hang out with Jake today, but Mom insisted that I haul this lame basket of groceries to Grandma's instead. Supposedly, some fresh air would do me good. Whatever.

Jake said he could pick me up at Grandma's afterward, so it wasn't a total loss. I put on the red hoodie he had left at my place last week and set off into the woods.

When I was little, I would see squirrels and rabbits along the path to Grandma's house. These days, the woods were littered with needles and used condoms.

As I approached Grandma's house, I heard howling inside. Hairs stood up on the back of my neck.

I knocked on the door; there was no answer. I knocked again and heard a commotion.

I pressed the handle; the door was unlocked.

"Grandma?"

I put the basket on the floor by the front door. The house was dark. I could hear labored breathing from the bedroom. I went inside.

"Grandma?"

"Hi, honey. I was napping."

Still in bed, she turned on the lamp on her nightstand. I winced at the sight.

"Grandma, why are your eyes so big?"

"Presbyopia. My eyes look gigantic with these glasses on."

"Grandma, why are you so hairy?"

"Menopause. It's mostly on the chin, though. I know, I look like the goddamn Bearded Lady."

"Grandma, why do you have such big teeth?"

"New dental implants. Do you like them? I hope they're worth it. I've spent every last penny on them; if I hadn't, I could still afford laser eye surgery and facial hair removal."

I heard a noise in the closet.

"Grandma, what's going on? Is someone else here?"

"No, honey, don't go in there!"

I opened the closet and saw a burly man in a wolf costume, looking sheepish.

"Grandma, what the hell? Who's this?"

She sighed and threw off her covers, revealing a matching wolf costume.

"Honey, this is Wolfgang; we met online. We like to...dress up. Honestly, I wasn't expecting you to stop by today."

My mind was blank.

"Hi everyone! The door was open..."

I'd never been so happy to hear Jake's voice.

"Bye, Grandma! The groceries are by the door! Nice to meet you, Wolfgang!" I didn't wait for an answer as I ran outside, dragging Jake by the hand.

"You look great in that red hoodie," said Jake on the ride home. "So, what exactly happened in there?"

"Wolves," I shuddered. "Fuckin' wolves."

BRIDGETOWN

James R. Gapinski

—

I.

Portland's nickname is Bridgetown. There are a lot of bridges. There are the old ones that everybody knows: Hawthorne, Steel, Broadway, and the like. Then there are the newer bridges. There's a bridge made of pressure-treated wood that stretches from your middle school locker to your cubicle. There are several glinting metallic bridges that sprout from one high-rise to the next, smashing into crystalline windows, erupting into chaos before becoming a static skybridge between each column. There are a contorted series of rusted footbridges that spiral out of your bedroom window and meander toward your ex's neighborhood. There is a misguided bridge that plunges into the Willamette River, skimming the bottom, emerging miles downstream in the Industrial District, and fish flop upon this bridge for a glimpse of what happens on land. There are bridges that lead to Seattle, arcing over the I-5, casting a shadow over the anti-abortion billboards that dot rural stretches between these two cities. There is a retractable suspension bridge that rises above Downtown, made specifically for easier access to the food carts, allowing you to walk around the corporate complexes and drop near plates of falafel and hummus.

II.

The aforementioned bridges all make sense. They go places. They have a *Point A* and an accessible *Point B*. But there's one bridge that doesn't. It's a complete fuck-up on the city planner's part. This particular bridge sprouts straight up from Gateway Transit Center, offering a vertical impasse which some outdoorsy people dare to freebase. On the other end of the bridge, some say there's another city—a cloud city or a parallel dimension city or a mirrored city. Some say there's just mist and broken cinderblocks. Some say there are colonies of birds nesting at the top, forming their own communities and cultures. Some say its heaven. But mostly—if you ask those who have climbed the bridge—they say this bridge dead-ends into a twisted mess of road, hung mid-atmosphere, sprouting into a dozen new bridges.

THE SPELL

Meg Pokrass

—

B efore you fell in with Serena, the snake charmer, your caravan was a sad and quiet place. Now she slides her lips around yours, spits her wishes straight into your mouth. You draw on those wishes, swish them around and swallow them whole. Her last lover, Tiny Bill, an albino midget with a heart of gold, has been missing for a month.

"Sad about Little Bill?" you say. Serena screws off her bracelets and rattles them like a hymn before setting them on your nightstand. Pauses as if digesting your question, as if it isn't as interesting as your leg. She slips down on you, everywhere on you and moves her mouth over your dead knee.

When you performed in the main ring, before your big fall, you used to think about the dignity of ropes, how many ropes you'd dangled from thinking about the wrong kind of woman, how many times ropes nearly killed you but saved you instead.

"Not really," she says, hovering over your knob. "And Bill never did me the way you do me." It's been every night this week, this sideshow for your heart. You feel dirty and free of your body, on top of the world. She is the most unwholesome beauty you've ever loved and you feel like you've found your real act in this world.

You can taste your own saliva as Serena goes higher and faster. You start to burp, but stay completely still. Your peg leg seems to thrill her the most, but it's pinching you now, setting limits.

"I need to take this off, Babe," you say, and so you do.

She watches you pull it, poised and gleaming. Keeps her face next to it, sniffing the edges of your shiny pink stump smiling from ear to ear every time, as if she's never seen anything so perfect.

"You ain't shown me anything I haven't wanted to see all my life," she whispers, holding your stump like a snake baby in her arms."

"Nobody is sinless," you say, about Bill, but she doesn't even twitch. Her lips make nests in your hairy back while you sleep, and you dream of being a boy again—flying on rope swings over the quarry back home. When you wake up, in the middle of the night, you can hear her gliding right in.

HOLIDAY OF THE FLIES

Erik Deckers

—

D **ay 1.**
It started when someone forgot the cereal.

Someone forgot to refill the cereal supplies at our coworking space. There are dozens of us, tech entrepreneurs who share desks in a large open-concept office where we work on our individual companies and projects. I run my writing business out of there, so I was the natural choice for recording what happened when the office managers left us alone for the holiday week.

The space is called Canvs, and it's pronounced "canvas," but it's missing the second 'a', because we're young and hip and hate unnecessary vowels. One of Canvs' perks is free cereal and milk for members. There's also coffee, snacks like peanuts and granola bars, and even fresh fruit.

The office is closed for the holidays, which means the managers are at home. But Canvs has 24/7 keycard access, so some of us are back at work the Monday after Christmas.

Except someone forgot the cereal.

We think it was one of the managers, but they wouldn't give us their cell numbers.

There's still milk, but only half a gallon of whole milk, and a barely-touched gallon of skim milk. We laugh about it being "the American beer of milk" and dump it down the drain.

We refer to the people on the other side of the office, the ones with permanent desks, as the Settlers. We laugh and make crude jokes about their name and the states of their relationships. In the afternoon, one of the Settlers wanders over to our territory, and we drive her out with shouts of "THIS IS SPARTA!"

Later, we raid the kitchen and eat most of the fruit and all the snacks. Supplies mean survival, we tell ourselves. Without food, we can't work. Without work, we can't provide for ourselves or our families.

Day 2.

We arrive at the office early, before the Settlers arrive, and finish the fruit. We search for more food, but the refrigerators are empty. We curse whoever forgot the cereal.

We combine the remaining creamers into a single glass, which makes six ounces for our coffee. We crouch around the machine as it brews, like cavemen around a cooking fire. The coffee is hot, and we are pleased at our fortunes. We burn the empty containers to cover our tracks.

.

That afternoon, the Settlers twice send thieves to the kitchen, but we turn them back. On a third attempt, they steal half a box of granola bars we had stashed away for an emergency. We send a small raiding party to retaliate and burn down three of their desks. We steal the granola bars back and take a jar of peanut butter as well. One of the Settlers breaks his arm in the melee. Supplies mean survival.

That night, as I go to sleep, I think the skim milk may not have been so terrible.

Day 3.

The Rovers have captured the bathrooms! The Rovers have captured the bathrooms! We now hold most of the western sector, and control access to the kitchen and the only bathrooms. The war council believes we can take the entire office by week's end.

Meanwhile, the Settlers find an emergency exit and use it to go to the bathroom at the Hamburger Mary's on Church Street. The Hamburger Mary's staff doesn't mind, but the Settlers feel awkward, so they buy an order of fries each time they visit, which they throw away, because they're "counting carbs."

We control the bathrooms but need food. A noob cries and wants to quit. We berate him for being weak, and tell him if he wants comfort, he should work from home. He relents and stays with us, but he disappears the following day. We never see him again.

.

Supplies mean survival.

It's become our mantra. We chant it before we raid. We say it before we scoop the coins out of the fountain and spend them at the vending machine. My wife says I've been saying it in my sleep for the last two days.

.

Day 4.

A raid on an art gallery yields mixed results. There's plenty of food, but it's all organic, and most of it is vegan.

Skullhammer the Javascript designer cuts down one of the artists with her USB keyboard — a found object sculptor named Jane. She and Skullhammer were friends, but that was in the Before Time, when Skullhammer was simply Elizabeth, and they were in the same book club.

In the afternoon, we sweep through a nearby comedy club, which is home to an improvisational theatre troupe. They are quick to adapt to our surprise attack. Windrunner, the network security consultant, is stampeded by war cows, and they place his head on a pike outside the ticket window.

The war council says if we don't get food soon, we may have to surrender. I worry my bones are getting brittle from the lack of milk.

Late in the afternoon, we enter a ceasefire with the Settlers, and agree to let them use our bathrooms if they bring us fries from Hamburger Mary's. We barter one order of fries for two bathroom trips; three, if they're loaded fries. We give them access to the women's bathroom and designate the hallway as the Neutral Zone. No weapons, no shields.

Day 5.

It's a holiday miracle! We find six boxes of cereal under the manager's desk. She apparently bought them before she left and forgot to put them in the kitchen. We gather with the Settlers in the conference room, and they share three gallons of 2% milk they'd hidden in one of their dorm fridges.

It's a wary truce. We're happy the war has ended, but our hands never stray too far from our weapons as we eat.

That night, I stop at the grocery store on the way home, where the deli manager finds me weeping in front of the skim milk display. She calls my family, and they take me home.

THROUGH THE REEDS

Maria Pinto

—

You have stayed, stubbornly, a frog. My lips are green from their efforts to cure you—they're pond-logged and wrinkled. You don't seem to remember the procedure. You think I'm an amphibian fetishist, or that I came to look for my own reflection in the water, but found you instead. Either way, you've said, we're compatible. You keep croaking about gourmet flies and crickets and about lily pad real estate and about how beautiful our polliwogs will be. Through the reeds, I hear your friends say that, years ago, before your first marriage, you had a full head of hair, expressive mammalian eyes, a goddamned castle, an affinity for your own species.

RELUCTANT ORPHEUS

Teege Braune

W hat does one think when one sees a dead friend at the supermarket? You feel the now familiar skip of your heart as you catch her in the corner of your eye, your brain swirling with hope and its twin agony—acceptance. This isn't the first time in the last few months you mistook another for her and were forced to apologize awkwardly, your grief renewed in your chest. Surely this too is some doppelgänger with an eerily similar visage who has grown used to strangers in public places asking, Don't I know you? You keep your glance low, not wanting to embarrass yourself again, but she, with a sly grin on her lips, approaches.

There is no mistaking her. You could never fail to recognize the freckled nose, streak of white amongst auburn locks, and caduceus tattoo near her left ankle. The unmistakable features of one who was once so dear.

You might chalk her death up to some kind of error or bad hoax had you not been the one to find her body seated on the sofa. You started to ask her what smelled so bad before you noticed that she didn't lift her head or blink her big eyes, that the stench was coming from her. The funeral with her mother, who had always hated you, sobbing into your lapel, the nights spent alone but for your guilt, your desperate inability to remember her as anything but a corpse. These are not rituals we observe for one still among the living.

Best to continue this ruse of estrangement. Your head down, you dart for the nearest aisle as though you forgot something very important, as though to escape. Examining a box of cereal with grave interest, you hear the tip-tap of delicate steps approaching, coming nearer with purpose. You pretend to read the list of ingredients, your heart thudding in your chest. When the footfalls come to a stop just behind you, you cannot help but turn towards the gaze boring into the back of your skull.

Her bright eyes; her rosy smile. Death has been kind to her. She radiates with health, and finally you have found the young woman she had been before those last months. Her bones do not jut out from beneath baggy clothes; her hair is not limp and thin; and her skin lacks the waxy, gray hue it had when last you saw her alive.

What else to do but greet her with warmth? Pretend she's merely been away. Why won't you tell her how much you miss her, of the tears you cried for her? Plead for the forgiveness you have needed to put your life back together again. Tell her now what you could not when she was with you. Why must you feign joy at the unexpected reunion for which you have so longed? Why are the knuckles of your clenched fists turning white with terror?

Behind the myriad of smells of the supermarket, the bakery's aroma, the sweet hint of ripe peaches and apricots in produce, the pungent waft from the fish counter, and the antiseptic scent of cleaning product, you notice a distinct odor of rot. You cannot help but shiver, shiver and tremble, when she lays an icy kiss upon your cheek and wraps around your neck arms as cold as clay.

PUTTING ONE'S AFFAIRS IN ORDER

John King

—

S am needed to take an emergency-level shit when he went to buy that gun.

He had slept with Dianne, a co-worker, whose husband Jake was now apparently homicidal. Dianne had fled to her parents' house in New Hampshire the day before.

Sam hadn't seen Jake, but then again Sam was avoiding work and home.

He had three .45-caliber bullets jangling in his shirt pocket.

Was Dianne worth it? Sammy thought to himself, but he really couldn't imagine an answer because his intestines were gurgling and roiling with debris that seemed volcanic and uncertain in velocity. His face was slick, sweaty.

Sam stepped into a restaurant. The men's room and the women's room were locked. He waited amidst the potent aromas of sushi. Every customer who entered the place looked like Jake, alert white dudes in preppy clothes.

Sam hobbled outside.

A block from the restaurant, a pawn shop loomed with cheerful neon. He inserted himself inside its fortified door.

"Got a restroom?" Sam asked.

"For customers only," said the clerk, not looking up from his copy of *Variety*.

"I want to buy that," Sam said, pointing at a revolver underneath the glass.

"ID and permit, please," said the clerk.

"Can I use the bathroom first?"

"Nope," said the clerk.

Sam slipped his hand into his pocket. He kept his loins tight as he unfolded his wallet and submitted his driver's license and concealed carry permit over. He concentrated on his steady hand.

The cluttered shop smelled like new plastic. Sam gazed at the front door.

The clerk scanned the electronic stripe of the card. "The background check will take about ten minutes."

"Can I use the bathroom now?"

"Nope," said the clerk.

Sam smiled as he sweated. *Was Jake really bonkers?* thought Sam — trying not to think of his squirming intestines — *or was Jake just mouthing off as if he were crazy?*

Dianne has the sweetest smile in Florida, he thought. He was a grinning statue for the next several minutes.

"Credit card?" asked the clerk.

Sam gave him the plastic and waited for the sale to be completed. He signed the form. Each breath seemed to agitate his quivering guts.

The clerk handed Sam the card, the gun (placed inside a case), and a receipt. "Bathroom?"

The clerk paused, sighed, then pointed to the bathroom behind the showcase.

Sam was crying as he struggled to lock the door with his heavy purchase in his hand. He couldn't get his belt unbuckled without putting the gun down. He could feel things moving inside him.

He dropped the card and the gun on the tile and slid the lock.

He undid his pants and collapsed onto the porcelain.

He was no longer in control of his body as he reached down with his trembling fingers for the case.

Then the door opened, exploding the clasp of the lock.

Sam turned around, spewing, and howling, one finger touching a bullet, one hand digging inside the case.

Artist: Kaylan Stedman

BEEHIVE

Karen Gonzalez-Videla

———

H er body was covered in holes, as if her flesh had been munched on by earthworms. They were spread around her with the symmetry of a machine-made pattern, but sometimes they twisted around the bends of her face and disfigured it. The constant exposure to honey had loosened her skin so much it resembled a damp sponge, and when she flexed her muscles, streams of honey oozed out of her limbs until she retched at the sweetness.

Every few seconds, a bee popped out of one of the holes and circled around her. They popped out unannounced, sometimes emerging from the hole on her upper lip and other times from the hole on her lower arm. Sometimes they sprung from her chest and became entangled with the fabric of her blouse, so they buzzed louder and louder until she freed them.

The woman sat by the edge of a lake, her feet tucked underneath her thighs. It would take only one brush of water against her toes for her body to turn into a tornado of bees, a commotion of buzzing ready to explode. She had hoped for some peace, some time away from the mothers who put a protective arm on their children when she passed by, or from the store owners who refused to allow her tiny little pests inside their stores. The lake was the quietest place she knew.

Yet the bees never stopped working. She could feel the buzzing inside her eyes and inside her breasts, a presto performance on the violin that had decided to live within her in an infinite replay.

She sighed.

Ten or so bees flew out of her and dispersed across the landscape. They were the laborers, searching for nectar to bring inside her body. They worked and worked until the woman's nostrils dripped with honey, until the sweetness accumulating in her mouth forced out a series of repeated gags. She begged them to take a rest, to let her throat regurgitate the honey until there was nothing left inside her but a sour taste.

But the bees didn't listen, for they had a duty, and where the woman sat down in despair, a circle of pollinated flowers yielded new seeds.

INPATIENT

Philip Elliott

—

At the clinic they fed us pills like they were biscuits. Those pills made the tongue loose in my head, my left arm numb from the elbow down. Sometimes the world would smolder at the edges. Patients came and went, people from every kind of background but all with one thing in common: no longer capable of contributing to civil society, they needed to be kept out of sight—losers, loners, dreamers, freaks; God forbid they ever make it onto a TV screen.

Anna-Lucia was one such patient. A bi-polar twenty-year-old of Italian descent, she bristled with fierce energy. A permanent darkness hung beneath her eyelids, as if she had never learned how to sleep, but her body moved with the ferocious, unpredictable rhythm of an ocean harnessing a storm.

"Sometimes I have this dream," she told me once as we both sat on our beds in nightgowns. My bed was opposite hers, rain slashing at the window. "Always the same. I'm at a funeral, the coffin right in front of me. There's no one else there, just me and whoever's in the coffin. At first, I'm confused. Why is there no one else here? Does no one love this person? So I step over to the coffin to see who I'm grieving." She swept dark bangs out of her face, exposing badly-healed gashes on her wrist. "And it's me. It's me in the coffin." She chewed on a nail. Some moments later, she angled her head like a chirpy little bird, and said, "Ever fuck a girl?"

Another time we were watching TV in the break room. A giant cartoon duck scuttled about the screen, declaring its insanity to us all.

"What the fuck are we doing in here?" she said.

"Learning to live again, or something," I said.

She shrieked a laugh at the ceiling. "All I've learned in here is that there is a serious amount of fucked-up people in the world."

"Everybody's fucked up."

"Not like we are."

The cartoon duck had somehow acquired a bow and arrow, looking to commit murder.

She said, "I think I'm going crazy in here, man. I'm going fucking crazy."

"You were already crazy. That's why you're in here."

She stuck out her tongue and grabbed my face with both hands. Then she kissed me. It seemed to shock even her. 'Hey, wanna see something?" she said. "Follow me."

She bounced up from her seat and ran out of the room. We weren't allowed to run in the clinic but the staff had long since quit telling Anna-Lucia this. She did anything she wanted.

When I reached her bed, a notepad lay opened on her lap. 'I drew it for you,' she said. On the page two female figures soared out of an open window, gigantic smiles carved into their faces.

"Is that me and you?" I said.

"Excellent deductive skills."

"I wish my boobs were that big."

She laughed, eyes shining like diamonds in her skull. "Artistic license."

"I guess that's why we can fly."

"Oh we're not flying. We're falling. Together."

Anna-Lucia and I showered at the same time every day, chattering to each other from adjoining cubicles. She'd step out of hers completely naked when finished, blissfully secure in her beauty. Sometimes she'd talk so much that I'd be dressed and ready to leave and she'd still be standing there in the nude, dripping.

But one time we went to the showers together and everything was different. She looked at me strangely as she opened the curtain. "I'm really, really glad I met you," she said.

"I'm glad I met you too."

She smiled and stepped inside.

I was surprised when a few minutes passed and she still hadn't spoken, but I hadn't slept well the night before and was glad of the silence.

Until I saw the blood.

The doctors fought hard to save her, I was told, but she'd severed an artery and the blood loss had simply been too severe. She'd sliced near an old wound. Could be that she didn't want to die, just wanted someone to bandage her up, take care of her.

Anna-Lucia, I never told you this, but you had my heart.

EVERY REACHABLE FEATHER

Gary Fincke

—

There's some, her father said, who are shameful with their pets, and she nodded, thinking of a friend who'd allowed an aquarium of fish to die, something worse than her twice forgetting to feed the dog, then forgetting a third time a few hours ago.

Careless, she said. Selfish. She clutched two brightly-colored paper bags. She said sorry.

Her father looked as if he thought she was giving him a reason to be even angrier. Like she thought the misfortunes of pets could be bound up in a book aimed at middle-schoolers like her who forgot to walk and feed their dogs before they went to the mall with their friends to buy makeup and a dress for the school dance.

There's worse than careless and selfish, he said.

Cruel, she said, mentioning an uncle, her mother's brother, who she'd seen kick his dog more than once, trying it out like a plea-bargain.

Try this on for size, he said. There's a man I know whose wife bought herself a parrot. Maybe you know who that fellow is? No? Well, that fellow you don't know hates his wife's parrot for its squawking.

Like an echo, she said, and he gave her that look again.

Like squawking, her father said, but that fellow owns a snake, a big one he's always talking about. I love that snake, he says. Never makes a noise. Hardly ever any sort of mess. And after a while, he set that boa loose to coil around the parrot's cage, which, it turned out, quieted that pretty thing down.

She wanted to say she thought that parrot would scream, but instead she said, I guess so, and her father nodded.

You'd be right about that, he said, because the parrot went mute like all it could do was listen for what that snake might say or wait for what that snake might do.

She waited while her father took a couple of deep breaths like he was about to go underwater. She wished she could put her new-bought things away.

That fellow's wife, her father said, she claimed the snake had driven the parrot crazy, that parrots who shut up are depressed, but you want to know how you would realize it's crazy? Every reachable feather on that parrot's body is gone. Now it looks like food. If it had hands, it would pluck its head.

Oh, she said, and her father said, oh is right.

There's more, her father said. That fellow, now, can wrap his fat arms around the cage and press his face to the bars as if he doesn't fear for his eyes. There isn't any need for his snake. He does the coiling now, surrounding that bird, then walking away, then coming back to surround it again. That parrot must think it's about to suffocate. And then it doesn't.

This time, when he paused, she said nothing.

Her father stared at her. Which would you rather be, he said, the parrot or the snake?

The snake, she said.

But you aren't, her father said. So, what would be worse, the snake or the arms?

THE ART OF BEING INDUSTRIOUS

Len Kuntz

—

She is busy tracing knife wounds, busy eating her own hair, busy manufacturing crude fetishes. She is busy shredding skin, busy dismantling science, busy fishing the hangdog moon. She is the busiest person you know, this person in the red room thinking red is black, that black is the sound of a blade hissing on the throat on a night in a park by a tree that will never split open as this person will be split open, her blood and archeology dripping on the scarred bark, soaked up by the bulging tree roots, her underwear torn and hanging from a limb, his semen swimming in the wrong direction, in a stream without mercy, on a current without pardon, where the only thing to do is stay busy, to scream and scream, to keep screaming.

THE DEATH TRIP

Rachel Kolman

—

T he prisons went to the moon first.

The idea made sense – at least, it made sense to the lawmakers. What place is more secure for the Earth's worst criminals, they argued, than a place *not on Earth?* Sure, it was mostly paid for by tax dollars, but at least we're still ahead of the Russians, people said. And that's always the place you want to be. The greatest country on Earth, and now, the greatest country on the moon.

Plus, it let us close Guantanamo for good, which made the liberals pretty happy. I mean, I'm pretty sure a lunar-based prison is a worse alternative, but at least no one was being tortured up there. From the stories we heard, it didn't sound half bad. These criminals, the worst of our humanity, were now working for science, collecting rock samples and charting stars and orbital cycles. It turns out, without any other people to rob or rape or terrorize, you could get a lot of work done.

After the prisons were set up, retirement homes went next. It made for some great marketing campaigns. TV commercials, full of slogans like, "live your golden years watching the stars rise with the sun" or "liftoff to life's final adventure." Never mind the cost of the trip was an entire life's savings, but I mean, why did life savings matter to someone moving permanently to the moon?

The overall problem was that there was no return trip. Not yet. Hence the life-sentence prisons and retirement homes. No need for the return trip. In this early phase of the program, there wasn't yet a large enough moon base that could allow vessels to travel freely. Only small cargo ships could afford the back and forth. It *wasn't* a vacation destination. It was a place to send the unwanted, the forgotten.

Anyway, after the prisons and the retirement homes, the next group to go up were the terminally ill, those no longer responding to treatments. I think it was around that time the moon trip finally got the nickname "The Death Trip." I mean, that's what it was. You were meant to live and die completely off the planet. It was assisted suicide.

But *his* supporters, they liked that the terminally ill were into the moon idea. Getting them off the planet meant avoiding a tricky "pulling the plug" scenario. Instead, you went out naturally. "How God intended you to die," they argued. Some advertisers played up that religious aspect, calling it "one step closer to heaven" or "a pit stop before your final destination."

Anything to make it sound more appealing that we're slowly turning the moon into one big gravesite. So far, there have only been a few moon deaths, but eventually, it'll be more dead bodies up there than live ones. Where will all of the moon bodies go? Left out on the surface to freeze? Float off into space? Our bodies returning to stardust?

And now, after the prisons and the retirement homes and the center for the terminally ill, the Death Trip is finally open to volunteers. Well, to anyone who can pay the millions for a permanent relocation to the moon.

When this new phase of the program was first announced, the Kickstarter campaigns were outrageous. Everyone seemed romanced by the idea of getting the hell off this planet.

Remember when all we wanted was to go to Canada?

As for me, I'm glad the program is now open to volunteers. It means being able to dedicate your life to science, and research, and the dream of terraforming the rock that surrounds our blue planet. I mean, from that vantage point, the world must look so peaceful. All blue swaths of oceans and swirling cloud patterns. From there, you can't see the drone strikes or the suicide bombers or hear the news outlets screaming at each other. From there, we must look like one big happy family.

I also hear in the media of the euphoria of living on the moon. People go into these meditative states while gazing down at the planet, watching the sun's shadow dictate time zones and sleeping patterns. To be separate from that, it almost makes it seem as if you are separate from time itself.

Anyway, that's why I signed up. I'm still raising funds, but it looks like I have a good chance of going. It's not that I have a death wish, it's more like a "the grass is greener on the other side" complex. I'm a hopeless optimist. And here, hope is no longer a campaign slogan; it's a foreign language.

Anyway, if I do make the cut, and raise the money, I'll be part of a group that's meant to establish more of a moon community. Aside from the scientists who work the landing dock and receive cargo shipments, this new program would send the first healthy, young, and humane group going to the moon to simply *exist*, with no promise of seeing Earth again.

I get asked a lot by my friends about why I want to go. My default answer is "I'm just looking forward to a good night's sleep." Always the funny guy.

But aren't you nervous to leave Earth forever? they ask. Not nervous, I say, just *curious*. Sure, the unknown seems scary, but instead, think of what I'm gaining. The ability to start over. How many people every day wish they could start over in a new place and be someone else? Maybe it will be lonely, or maybe it'll be peaceful. Maybe I'll find nirvana. Maybe to actually find nirvana you have to leave this planet. Maybe now I'll live out the rest of my life loving the Earth that gave me life, instead of hating the land that's raised me and the people on it.

How can anything so beautiful be considered a death trip?

STRESS CARDIOMYOPATHY

Sheldon Lee Compton

—

T wenty Years and Again

A roach across the floor with light after its body, illuminating cornea-thin wings. There were roaches all those years before, but I was younger then, and my mother not nearly so sick.

The Guestroom

This is your bedroom, baby. I love it, I love it, she said. She ran to the porcelain cat curled on the nightstand. Pink! I love it. I just love it. I had told her I hoped she'd liked it. She liked it, I was sure, for me. A soul so old for a girl missing only three teeth from new gums.

A Picture for Marking His Place

Great Biographies. Stacks of these, a series, in the back bedroom where the old man lived half a lifetime. The books I shuffle like old cards. Thumb-hammering through one, there's my picture marking page sixteen, wincing into the sunlight, standing, as always, in exactly the wrong spot.

Absent

I put the necklace on the sink and rubbed the tips of my fingers across my throat and upper chest. Forever was forever, but the silver coating was fading and the copper was showing. My children reduced to shards of pennies, and I'd not showered in weeks.

The Mercy Prayer

Somewhere there's a road that curves in England. I'm not sure how that helps, but to think of it. A curvy road, flatly paved, that rolls between green grass and ends somewhere where answers spring up like well water. Think of that, and not of this.

THE SIREN

Alyssa Pearl Fusek

———

I caught you with God again, and the lilies I bought you wilted at the dawning, breaking. Noon, I think, with fresh-cut basil in the sink. Green food, green house, green bruises, green napkins—his obsession with green smarts me, mama, don't you know? I don't like catching you and him like that. That kiss was hurtful to watch, violent teeth against plump lips, taking again. I went to the pond to forget, but it's not easy.

If he weren't so mean he'd be handsome, but your God's true breed shows every day, mad and savage as Achilles. We're reading *The Iliad* in English class, mama, you should read it too. So many nights he rages against you, his Hector, his Patroclus, a throw and a crumple against the bedroom wall. I hear and say nothing. *Never trust a man mistrusted by animals,* you once said, you said so, mama, and I still believe that even when you don't. We're animals, too.

God always says bad poetry to mask his control. Today, you put the red pagoda plant you got at the farmers' market in the kitchen window, and God said, *No more succulents on the windowsill, sweetheart. Flutter your lashes at winter & me instead, 'cuz solace is in the genteel curves of your ears & I love it when you listen.* I know you didn't know what he meant, but you did as he said, let God tug on your earlobes. The wince, mama, I saw it. I took the red pagoda and hid it under my bed. Green and burnt red, like your heart since your God came. Too much water and it dies. He knows your true heart is prettier than him. He knows I'm prettier than you, and he has the bite marks on his hands and arms to prove it.

Your God tried, mama, but I'm not you, and that saved me. The horror afterward, green and burnt red. Someday, mama, someday.

God don't go by the pond, so that's my place to be now. *To be,* you used to know what that was like, didn't you, mama? Cattails and sunlight cut by the oak tree, green and gold smeared by spring. Cicadas and the croaks of grumpy frogs. I read and draw and avoid and hum. But at school the boys sneer because they smell your God's failed attempt. The girls with half-lidded eyes offer me a smoke, and I take one to spite you all. Your God doesn't like that kind of impurity. Well, bully him. Bully him, mama, please. But you won't. I beg and you still won't. So I will.

I know in *The Odyssey*—we're reading that next, mama—Odysseus plugs his ears so he doesn't hear the sirens singing as his ship sails by. Your God isn't that smart, and I can't sing, but there's the pond. Deep enough to lick my waist, so deep enough, mama.

He forgets the bite marks real quick. Cut-off shorts showing moonshine thighs does wonders, mama, that I *know* you know, I got them from you. I hold the red pagoda behind my back. Heavy, cool ceramic, and wet soil. I hum, and he mistakes the smile in my eyes for something else.

Stupid, your God. So stupid, his saunter into the water, his leech-eating grin. He's right in front of me, reaching for my arms. So stupid.

The sound of his skull breaking is liberty. Again, again, until blood slicks hair and skin. Water splashes, dark earth flies, sticks to my lashes. It's easy to hold him down when he's barely conscious. I'm helping God trade one darkness for another. I don't need to hum anymore. I smell dislodged mud and copper. The cicadas never stop singing.

He stops moving. Cracked ceramic digs into my skin. No more green now, mama, only red and red, Mama, forever.

DIFFERENT

Francine Witte

—

M y father tells me I'm different. He doesn't say how, or if different is bad. Just leaves the word twirling and swirling around like the time he flushed my not-dead goldfish down the toilet. He said he was teaching me a lesson. Wouldn't say what the lesson was or where the goldfish was going.

My father says get used to it. Again, doesn't say what *it* is. He likes being mysterious. Will disappear for days sometimes, or else he pretends he's James Bond. Tells my mother he wants his coffee shaken not stirred. Stuff like that.

My father tells me not to listen to boys. Not one of them can be trusted.

He says that because I'm different, boys will get me to do their homework. He says boys won't treat me well. That girls like me, who are different, will buy boys presents to get their attention. That boys will pretend they like me. Call me a good egg.

I look in the mirror for the egg part. I'm not yolky or runny or anything. When I tell this to my father, he says, well just be careful.

I *am* careful. And the night my father doesn't come home and it turns into forever, my mother is the one who turns egg. Cracked and shattered, sprawled like a pain-omelet on the couch.

That's when I know I'm different. Won't miss this man who tells me what I am but won't tell me. Leaves my mother and me swirling around and twirling around without giving us even a clue about where we are going.

Artist: Paulaidan Minerva

WHEN WE FENG-SHUIED SEBASTIAN

Christopher Allen

—

This is what we did. We stood over Sebastian with our protractors, compasses and Bagua, punched coordinates into calculators, scribbled *not-theres* and *not-there-eithers*. We licked thumbs and held them to the air. We found the safest, calmest space for our son and *placed* him there. For a pair of decades, Sebastian moored in the northeast corner of the living room. Wind and water lilted through the house. Sebastian was a balmy, unproblematic thing.

Bimonthly, we swung our recliners around to make his corner a stage, to let him entertain us. His Dolly Parton impersonation was a YouTube hit, which our feng shui advisor Keith said wouldn't upset our chi as long as we *kept that shit* away from the spirit gate in the northwest corner of the house. We took such care.

When the other YouTube videos started popping up—Sebastian on a Mexican beach in the arms of a Gandolf-bearded guy named Exodus. Sebastian rock climbing with a giant drag queen named Bob. Sebastian hopping up and down with the Maasai so high you'd think he was made of cloud—we sensed somehow that Sebastian had found friends beyond his corner. Sebastian had left. Sebastian was rising.

We had to act fast. We followed him the same day on Facebook, Twitter, Instagram, and LinkedIn because that's how our Bridge partners Doug and Lara liased with their difficult daughter Yvette.

We found him first on Facebook with a loud and lively timeline and 4544 followers. *Air's thin up here, but it's my air*, he'd posted just the day before at the top of his page. *Come home! Basti!* we commented. *We'll place you in our Money Spot. In our Love Spot. In the Safe Spot on the sofa. We'll fall asleep watching* Dancing with the Stars.

He smiley-faced or hearted every single one of post's 248 comments — except ours. Who were these multitudes rooting for our son? Who said they envied his courage and claimed to live vicariously through him? *Basti*, we commented, *we understand: you're rebeling. We get that. If you don't want to be feng-shuied for a while, it's fine. When you're done raining, just come home: 35.5175° N, 86.5804° W.* Still no smiley.

Sebastian did not come home. He placed himself in the middle of everything, which was a million miles away from our coordinates. He blocked wind and water like a glob of grease in a drain. He caused weather.

What could we do but monitor his ascent and hope for a settling? We screenshot posts, tweets and subtweets. Saved his perennial and popular Tornadocorn gifs. We made a virtual scrapbook entitled "The I AM of the Storm"—a subtle jab at Sebastian's self-centered Jehovah-complex squall—and uploaded it to his Facebook timeline with the comment *We hardly know you anymore.* We wanted balmy back. We wanted the pin-drop stillness of Sebastian in his corner.

And that's almost what we got. Sebastian went silent, left social media, though years later we saw him one last time on CNN.com. The first Category 6 hurricane on record. Unprecedented destruction. The meteorologist described him as "Nature's fury unshackled—the result of a century of environmental neglect." The tremble in her voice was the kind of respect you'd save for weather. Neglect was a strong word. Parenting techniques vary. What did she know?

Recently—on the advice of Keith—we scooted a juniper bonsai into Sebastian's corner, which worked wonders for the house's chi. We would miss that little thing we'd made, always wonder what went wrong with our calculations. But if we were honest, we didn't want Sebastian home, at least not the cataclysm he'd become. We'd had a few rough winters; the roof was getting old. Did we really need another storm?

END IN SIGHT

Paul Nevin

———

I try to avoid touching the new manager, but on his first day he hands me a box of crisps that need to go on the shelves. It's enough to link us, and I find myself in his too-warm hospice room, staring over his wife's shoulder as we watch him die. She turns to face me, as if she can sense that I'm there, but the scene cuts, and I'm back in the shop.

He introduces himself as Tom. He's young, thirty years away from the diagnosis of prostate cancer that leads to that hospice bed. He offers his hand and I shake it, because by then it doesn't matter—I'm already infected with knowing. But I get a weak burst of it again, like an afterimage of the sun.

I tell him my name's Susan. He calls me Sue and asks how long I've worked at the supermarket as we restock the shelves.

That night I tell my husband Jim about the new boss.

"That's nice," Jim says, but there's a flat tone to his voice, a timbre that shows that he isn't listening. He leans forward on the sofa and focuses on the remote, clicking through channels, settling on none.

Jim dies just like this, of a cardiac arrest while sat in front of the television, a fact transmitted with perfect clarity through a nervous handshake on our awkward first date. He's alone, I presume because he outlives me, and I ponder again how long he sits there until somebody finds him, how long he stays on that last channel before someone turns the television off.

Jim finds a programme he's happy with, and he eases back into the sofa, the remote control in his lap.

The next day I'm on the till. Many customers are regulars, and inert, but there's a flurry of strangers who share their death with every banknote or receipt that passes between us. Heart disease, cancer, stroke. I pause when it's an accidental overdose. It's a woman of about thirty, with a toddler. Neither are much older at the end.

"Take care of you," I say as she wheels her trolley away, but she doesn't look back.

I turn to see Tom walking the tills. Someone's decided against the beef in their basket, and it needs to go back in the display fridge. Tom puts his hand out and I give him the meat. Nothing else passes between us.

That night Jim watches a show where couples answer questions about each other to win a holiday—bra size, favourite album, toothbrush colour.

"We should go on this," he says, but I tell him that he'd get the questions about me wrong. Jim doesn't answer, and the conversation ends there, without even the chance to peter out.

I stare at Jim, and I think of our first date, and how I'd let the vision of him dying in an armchair wash over me, like all the others. I didn't wonder where I was in his death, because I never saw myself in his life, not then. But now I do wonder, because it's getting better, this nightly dress rehearsal. He's getting older, easing into the role, looking more the part, and not for the first time I have the urge to blurt out what I saw on that first date.

I imagine myself on the show, being asked how Jim dies, and if he's alone, and if he's not found for a while. Getting the questions right to loud applause.

A week later there's a shoplifting. Tom is in the office above the shop, and I rush up to tell him. Just packets of ham, I say, and not the whiskey cleared out again. I stand over his desk, looming over him like I do at the end.

"Well, maybe they needed it, then, Sue," he says, and he smiles. It's kind, almost beatific, and I feel something shifting, inside me and between us, but I don't know if this is a misfire—if the smile is for me or for the shoplifter.

I think again of his last moments. Prostate cancer can be asymptomatic, lurking sly and unseen for years. Tom could have it already. I could warn him, but I say nothing.

He asks me to log the theft with the police. He turns back to the computer, but he doesn't type anything, and I sense him staring at me as I go back down to the shop.

At home I find Jim quizzing along to a television show. I start to tell him about the stolen ham, but he puts a finger up to stop me interrupting, pausing me rather than the programme.

I march into the kitchen and start dinner. I hear clapping over theme music, and the creak of the armchair. I expect Jim to follow me, maybe even to say sorry, but instead there's the clack of his wedding ring against the remote control as he scrolls through channels.

I feel something shifting here too, as if I've arrived at the crest of a hill, and there's a long and difficult descent ahead of me. I think of Jim years from now, an old man with his television, and I wonder if I do die on him, or if I'm somewhere else when he goes, living another life, dead to him another way.

I think of Tom too, and how he dies. I play it over in my mind, this snapshot of him and his wife. How she turns her head, as if she can sense that I'm there in the room. As if she knows that I'm stood right behind her, watching them.

LEAPERS

Joe Baumann

———

T he Leap is quick and easy. Painless. According to Nora, that is, who leads the way as she and Johnn trundle down the sidewalk in front of me, their mittened hands clasped together. Nora has breasts now and she's screaming at me over her shoulder, her breath puffing out like oversized bursts of popcorn that disappear into the cold air. She swivels, her knit hat bobbling atop her head like the leaning tower of Pisa.

You'll be fine, she says. Then she turns from me and kisses Johnn on the cheek, and he stutters away from her, giggling. Winks at me, his chin whiskered.

The birch tree sits in the dilapidated park where the swings screech so hard you're sure they'll collapse if you pump your legs too hard, nestled next to the tunnel slide that spits you out into a sandy trench that leaves rug burn on your thighs if you don't land just right, calves flexed and heels up. Nora points at the long, low branch that runs nearly parallel to the ground like a tightrope. She nods.

That one. Just walk to the end and jump. Arms out, or it won't work.

Are you sure, I say.

Of course. I already did it. The ground grabs you like a cloud.

The grass is still green even though the leaves have morphed into their blood reds, sunset oranges, urine yellows. The air bites at my fingers even beneath my knit mittens, which catch on the birch's pebbly hide as I step onto the branch, which hovers only inches from the ground like a balance beam.

Come on then, Nora says, slapping her thighs with her pink mittens. It'll be great. Don't close your eyes or it won't work.

You'll love it, Johnn says.

Rainbows and unicorns and trolls, Nora giggles. The trolls will comb your hair like your mom used to. Except, I don't know. It's different.

She would sit me down, I remember, in front of a mirror she polished each day with a rag soaked in vinegar. Humming a song, some lullaby with no words, something she would use to rock me to sleep while I was teething.

Nora stands on the sidewalk. She'll be there after I finish the Leap, she says. The world turns upside down like a dream. The grass puckers and bows, a little bit like water curling into a storm drain in a whirlpool. Your body will tuck and stretch, she says, like taffy or bubblegum. Her mouth is wide and cherry when she tells me this. Her teeth are crooked.

We'll have fun, she says.

Go, already, Johnn says, punching his hands into his hips and shaking his head.

The world is close below me. I blink, my eyes wilting with tears.

You'll love it, Nora screams. I got breasts afterward.

I got erections, Johnn yells.

I know what erections are.

They're great! He smiles.

Everything is yellow and custard. Nora's words whip around in the breeze like the leaves that curdle and crimp into the grass.

The birch teeters, its limbs limping and bowing around me. The branch I'm on dips and raises like a sailboat on the ocean tide.

Leap, Brent, Mona says.

Come on, Brent: Johnn, clapping and exhaling, balloons of air crisping from his mouth.

I close my eyes and bend my knees. The birch groans beneath me, lulling like a diving board.

The world pools beneath me, the grass cringing. There's land beyond the soil. I'll find myself there.

Leap, leap, leap, Nora says. She claps, the sound puffy like a piñata bursting.

Go. We love you, Johnn says.

I close my eyes and clear my throat. The world is a plain, a cracked pipe, an announcement.

The bough bends.

I shudder and jump. The grass bends like Nora says, and the world curls over, lets me seep in like I'm landing in tar or pudding or rubber, and it eats me up. I transform, I move, I stutter. The cold eats at my cheeks, and when I bounce back, springing out, the cold yawns for me, the air gnarly with ice, and I see, I swish: I rise and walk. I own.

FIRST DATE

Rose Andersen

—

Francine liked to make bone broth after a particularly good date. She would wake up early the next morning and spend the first hours of the day chopping, browning, and simmering. She would add a few choice aromatics like garlic and onions, followed by carrots for sweetness. Her neighbor once complained it smelled like a glue factory, but Francie simply smiled politely and shut the door in his face. How could she explain the importance of the broth? The very thought of marrow and blood was enough to excite Francie to the point of unrestrained squeals.

More than once, she considered skipping the process and just sinking her teeth into the muscle and bone. But, she decided, such an act would lack decorum. Making the broth took a full day but she didn't mind in the least. The last thing she did before bed was add the date to the jar and place it in the freezer. Only then, knowing she could enjoy him any time she wanted, could she sleep.

YALOBUSHA

Tristan Durst

—

Living in a dry county meant every Sunday afternoon I got a grape Slush Puppie. No alcohol could be sold from Saturday midnight to Monday noon in our town, so my father drove his old Ford pickup, Big Red, across the county line to John's Grocery, a gas station with pumps but no gas. The contents of John's Grocery were little more than cold beer and enough sweets to reward the children of the beer-drinkers for accompanying their parents on the most noble of quests: procuring enough cold Natty Light to last the entire NASCAR race, rain delays, wrecks, and all.

The Sunday after Dale Earnhardt died, John, my father, and Tattoo Mike, whose upper body was a turtleneck of snakes, pierced hearts, and naked breasts, spent longer than usual with their small talk, so much so that I finished my Slush Puppie before we even got back in Big Red.

"I just wished he coulda seen Waltrip and Jr go one-two. He'da been so proud." John quickly pulled from his beer as his voice cracked on the last word.

"He saw it, friend. I gotta believe he saw it," my father replied.

Sensing my growing disinterest in the conversation, taking pity on the empty cup I pitched into the trash, Tattoo Mike placed two wrinkled dollars on the gouged wooden counter and handed me a king-sized Butterfinger with a wink.

The soda fountain and Slush Puppie machine, as well as the four galvanized steel shelves, holding the candy bars and chips, the same shelves that housed my father's tools in our garage, were all accessible to customers. The beer, however, was behind the counter, in a walk-in freezer that John had to unlock every time someone made a purchase.

The county lines don't butt up against each other snuggly, it turns out, but leave about forty feet of leeway, a no man's land where no sheriff held jurisdiction, just enough space for the only cold beer on Sunday for three counties in any direction. People had a nasty habit of spending all their money on the gas for the trip over, nothing left for the beer, but refusing to go home empty handed.

"Someone wants to steal a candy bar, sure that's annoying as shit, but it ain't where I make my money," John explained.

"Is that why there's no gas?" I asked once I finally understood the game.

"Shit, girl, naw. Ain't never had gas. Just the only way I could get the permit."

Sunday afternoons were for Papa and his Perfect Peach. "You and me, kid, we're like characters in a Pete Seeger song, going out to conquer the badlands."

"*Badlands* is Springsteen, Daddy."

"You're goddamn right it is."

We drove with the windows rolled down no matter the weather, making a game of counting the animals, alive or dead, it didn't matter, out of our respective windows. Totals were wiped back to zero when we passed any of the roadside crosses commemorating travelers with fates darker than our own. In the car we both set to drinking our beverage of choice. "We won't tell your momma," he'd say, though my purple tongue and his reddened cheeks inevitably gave us away.

"You're gonna kill yourself one day," she always said, without malice though.

"Yeah, one day. Just not today."

At nineteen I ran like a lemming off the edge of familial dissatisfaction, blindly following roommates and potential lays. No one else spent rainy Sunday afternoons on the phone, parsing the differences between the album and live versions of "Thunder Road." I grew to dislike my father in the way all college freshman claim to dislike their fathers: in the way that feeling any sort of happiness was the same as being ordinary, in the way that anything short of casual contempt was codependence.

At the close of Thanksgiving, I stood in the driveway and hugged my father like a life preserver. The next weekend, slurring and sliding off of a futon, groping for my own share of parental misery, I indicted my father for being too stupid to buy enough beer on Saturday afternoon to last the whole weekend.

"I mean, he's not an alcoholic. He's just kind of dumb."

When my father grew so old that his mind forgot me, these are the memories I wanted to give back: the blacktop steaming from a just-ended summer storm, classic rock radio cutting out when we drove past the tallest of the trees. I wanted him to remember how he shook with laughter when I asked Tattoo Mike why he always wore the same shirt, how he dropped a beer to clutch his sides.

I brought his turntable and boxes of records to the home, and every time I play "Backstreets" it's the first time he's heard it.

"Imagine that," he sighs as the vinyl crinkles to a halt.

PENTAGRAM

Mike Lee

—

T he Model A broke down on Route 66 as we entered Flagstaff, Arizona. Our two boys, Benjamin and Arthur, tied ropes around the fender, and pulled the car while Benjamin's wife Rose followed behind with the baby.

We followed behind Rose. The kids insisted we stay in the car, but we knew the boys would not make it to the migrant camp with us adding on extra weight.

Irene wasn't well. She has a fading heart. I walk with her, as promised when we married.

My hip ain't the same no more, either.

We weren't farmers. I owned a store. We had a nice house in Dalhart. Built it with my brother in 1919. Poured the concrete foundations ourselves. Irene had the garden next to the driveway. I took my favorite picture of her—we were a picture-taking family—of her in a blue silk dress, with the lace collar, holding her Kodak camera.

We were a picture-taking family. I sold the cameras before we left after the black clouds filled the sky. The drought pretty much had already wiped us out, but the clouds sent us away. Sold what we could and followed the children, like we are now, walking, behind my Model A.

I have the photo of her in my inner coat pocket, wrapped in my handkerchief, as Irene and me follow behind the car. I always am taken by her enchanting smile.

Irene put her hand on my shoulder.

"I am not well," Irene says.

I held her tight as she stumbled into my arms. We put her in the back while Sharon watched over her. I carried my grandson Leonard on my shoulder, singing old army songs.

We're marching to Pretoria, Pray tor ee ya hoo rah.

Hiding behind the solitary cloud above the mountain range on the horizon, the moon is a faithless lover. My feet are hurting. My shoulder was sore from carrying Leonard and my feet hurt.

I pass the time thinking. For example, I believe that, like Moses, Irene and I have made it to the mountaintop, but unlike the prophet, I am likely going to reach this Promised Land at the end of this narrow concrete strip. This narrow path leads to Barstow, California, and continues northwest to Bakersfield. Bakersfield is where we are going.

But I already had my Promised Land. I've a picture of her in my pocket and she lays in the back of my broken-down Model A Ford.

I'm afraid to lose her.

It is night. The family huddled under the blankets in the car. I am holding Irene, wrapped in her mother's quilt.

When I slept, I relived that day in April when the dust blizzard came rolling in, turning the Sunday afternoon into night. I couldn't see in front of my hands reaching out, and coughed for days afterward. Irene stayed in, but despite all our efforts, closing the windows, desperately blocking the cracks with laundry and rags, the dust invaded, covering everything. It was the apocalypse. Irene began crying, her face contorted, constantly wiping counters, and the table tops in the gray haze. Finally, Irene collapsed. She bent forward as if she were shot and went to her knees.

I had already lost the store. The boys were already planning to leave to work on the WPA. So in June, we left.

In the morning, we pulled the jalopy to the camp. The boys worked on the car with a mechanic in return for food and a ride to Barstow. Rose stood on the roof of an old barn, watching over the kids jumping off onto a stack of old mattresses.

Irene went out beyond the shacks, with her grandmother's walking stick. Her grandmother was a Scot and her people came from the Highlands, and the stick goes back to the time of The Bruce, or so Irene was told. I never met the woman.

Irene was dragging the stick along the ground, digging it deep into the soil. When I came up to look, I saw she had cut a pentagram into the ground.

Irene put her hand on my shoulder, pulling me close to her mouth.

She whispered, "You are to close the point that is opened."

Irene passed the stick to me. I felt her rapid heartbeat against my left arm as I pressed hard against the earth.

1985

Cheryl Pappas

—

T hat summer day, we laid our bodies on the beach like lambs at the altar, using our crumpled sundresses as pillows. Smoothed our young skin with coconut-scented oil so it could burn better, for the boys. It was deadly serious. Meanwhile, scenes from the bonfire party the night before flickered into our minds.

"I think Steven walked away with Rachel."

"No way. Where did they go?"

"In the tall grass. I'm not even kidding you."

"Gross. I can't even see them together."

"Beer makes you do stuff."

We had some stupid conversation like that. I adjusted my slippery plastic sunglasses, closed my eyes, and saw red. I loved the feeling of my skin tingling, singeing in the white wall of heat. Baseball announcers barked on some distant transistor radio. My heels dipped in the hot sand.

There was a brief silence between us before it happened, before we saw him—or it, whatever you want to call the thing we saw—walking near water's edge, a little down the beach. We heard gasps of others first before Sheila and I sat up.

He was dressed entirely in black. That was the first strange thing. I mean entirely: black oversized hood with a thin mask over his eyes, gloves that looked too tight, and a black silky robe down to his feet, shoed in the same material. He was also improbably tall, maybe 6'8", and walked as if he was counting to himself or reciting something only he knew. Little waves rippled and slipped over his feet as he walked but he didn't seem to care. His head was bent and through the waves of heat rising from the sand. Hhe seemed even stranger—a mirage.

"What the hell?" Sheila said.

"I don't know what that is," I said.

Along the beach, moms held their open-mouthed kids close. Men stood, hands on hips, all eyes but no movement, no words.

I grabbed my crumpled sundress and clutched it. Sheila did the same. Maybe I knew he would turn, which he did, just then, walking up the beach at an angle, a straight beeline. Everyone in his path took a step back. He walked faster now, with total purpose. I screamed in silence, like in my dreams. When he was so close his figure blocked out our sun, we shrivelled like raisins. He stood over us, whispering, chanting, leaning in, and I closed my eyes. His warm hands took mine to make a cup, and he placed something soft, something impossibly light in it. It was only when his robe brushed the sand past me that I opened my eyes and found in my palms a white lily, powdery with yellow pollen, its petals shaking in the hot breeze. My heart turned to moon: white, cool, endless.

SPARTA

Ryler Dustin

———

T he last time any of us saw Frankie Mazzie alive was on the evening news. Well, not on the news, exactly—more like *around* it. He was there every commercial break, on a low-budget camera in front of a blue background like it was picture day.

A couple of teeth missing. Circles under his eyes like the dark grimy halo below a fridge, just peeking out when you open the door.

The last time anyone saw him in real life, he looked a lot better. That was in Homeroom during free time. We were sitting in the back of the class—him and me and Lee Durban—on the three big, gray computers that huff and whir like there are animals caged inside.

"What the fuck are you writing, Dustbin," Lee said with no question mark. Mr. McKay had stepped outside to lecture some girls about using nail polish in class. The room still smelled.

I pretended to be finishing a sentence to give myself time to assess the situation. *Walk softly and carry a big stick*, my dad says. I get nervous when someone like Lee messes with me, because the only advantage I have in a fight is the element of surprise. Though to be honest the only real fight I've been in was when an eighth grader sat on me while I was tying my shoe, and I stood up and he flipped over and everyone acted like I was tough.

Frankie swivelled to face me. He always had this sort of dead expression, but it was happy, too, like he understood what Mr. McKay called *transience*. He didn't even care if people made fun of him, just looked kind of bored and eventually changed the subject.

He slapped my arm with the back of his hand. His knuckles were scrapped up. "Yo, Dustin," he said, "check it out."

On Frankie's screen were the words B U D D H I S M. Each letter was a different font and color.

"Heh, yeah," I said. "It's like, Buddhism: taste the rainbow."

Frankie stared at me for a minute and then started laughing. He reached around me to punch Lee in the arm, almost falling out of his chair.

"He assigned us his favorite," Frankie said. Mr. McKay, who looked like a greaser with a white mustache, had given each group a religion to research. Each group was also named after a Greek city-state, and we were grouped into them based on what he called our aptitudes. I was in Athens. Frankie was in Sparta. Lee was in one of the other ones. Athens had recently fallen in Olympics points because Tommy Lingbloom had kept making marks on my paper and I broke his mechanical pencil and threw it across the classroom. So, Mr. McKay had taken Buddhism away from Athens and given it to Sparta.

"I'm in charge of the title page," Frankie said.

I gave an appraising nod, like I was on a daytime cop drama saying, "Nice set up. There a pension with that?"

The bell rang. I wiped my hands, sweaty because Lee was still breathing down my neck.

I'd written about half a page of the short story Mr. McKay was letting me do to make up for breaking Tommy's pencil. I emailed the story to myself, waiting for the little swooshing sound like Hermes tucking it in his sandal and flying off to Olympus. Then I hurried out of the room into the dusty sunlight. I didn't look back at all.

After that, Frankie wasn't in school. Athens got ahead again. And then Frankie was around the news, talking about meth, some kind of public service announcement.

Mom was sleeping on the couch when I saw him. "That guy goes to our school," I whispered to Allie, who was doing math on the floor next to me. The shades were drawn against the sun and the room was filled with blue TV light. Frankie's voice sounded like static, like branches scraping the tin sides of the trailer.

"Huh, weird," she said.

I offered to help her with math, which annoyed her because she's good at math. Somehow, I always forgot that it did that.

That night was warm, like it was already summer. After mom went to the hospital, I slept out on the deck behind the trailer, my sleeping bag unzipped so that my legs could stick out. Listening to the wind, I dreamed that Mr. McKay was lecturing me again about fighting Tommy, telling me how disappointed he was in Athens.

When I woke, the wind was hot. There were screams coming from the forest. Human screams, rippling through a crowd the way screams do, like a current, when someone gets in a fight or sees something gross, so that, by the end, the people farthest from whatever is causing it are just screaming because of the scream's momentum, because it's taken on a life of its own.

I stood up. I didn't move. And then the screams dried up and blew away.

On the ride to school the next morning, mom said it had been the sound of geese. "It's eerie. I know what you mean."

I liked how she said that. "I know what you mean." People don't say that often enough, including her. I put my head on the window, thinking about my story, and the Greeks dividing themselves into city-states, and Frankie's sign about Buddhism. Then I only watched the cedars. When I unfocused my eyes, they lost all shape, and I could let them rinse past me like green and brown water, soundless.

Artist: Genevieve Anna Tyrrell

THE BIG PLACE

Kimberly Lojewski

—

W ay out here, the ocean swells up big and mean, crashing on the broken teeth of the tidal rocks with enough force to knock resting seabirds from their perches, and sweep them down into the sea. Sometimes the waves spit up their remains. Guy and I collect tail feathers and broken wings and tie them to the twisted branches of the hawthorn trees in place of leaves. They flutter wildly in warning when the storms come in.

We run against the wind. Against the swirling black skies. The hawthorn trees flap their makeshift wings. Guy's legs are longer than mine. Stronger. Sometimes the rain falls before we reach the glass house on the cliffs. When this happens, we use poppies to deflect the drops of water. The poppies here grow tall and wild. Big enough to wear as hats. They are a vibrant red against the green of the hills and the moss-covered stones.

Green is the first color I know. Ocean blue is the second. Poppy red is the third. Gorse yellow is the fourth. The day I know the grackle black of Guy's hair I feel as if I am on the verge of a tremendous breakthrough. When I learn the silver and gold of the sky I want to weep. I don't. Just in case it might erase me. In the beginning, this island was only different shades of grey. Now there are colors. They pulse at me secretly.

Guy pulls a poppy from a stalk the size of my wrist and holds it over me, making an umbrella, just as the first fat drops fall. They splatter against the waxy petals and roll off towards the ground. Guy says the rain is what makes everything so big in this place. The hills. The flowers. The ocean. The trees.

"Run," he says, and I chase him.

Guy and I feel like strangers, but I am sure we know each other somehow. Under a certain light, the grackle black of his hair has a deep blue shine. This is when he looks the most familiar to me. His features are fine and his skin is luminous. No matter how hard I try, I still can't name the color of his eyes. A splatter of rain lands on his cheek, erasing part of his cheekbone, and I see the silver veins beneath his skin.

The house on the cliff is never warm. This ensures that we always keep on moving. We burst through the door and I throw the wet poppy out into the wind, watching it twirl up into the storm, petals flying. Guy lights a fire but no heat comes. Our house is perfect for looking out of and seeing into. When the windows fog with moisture, the glass shows traces of shapes and designs that we have drawn with the tips of our translucent fingers. We seem to write in different languages. I can't read Guy's drawings just like he can't read mine.

Sometimes, Guy shows me my reflection in a seaweed strung mirror that washed to shore after a storm. It's the most terrible thing not to recognize yourself. My hair is yellow like the gorse and my eyes are blue like the ocean. But my face is blank. Whatever used to be in there is gone. I look anyways. I want to know the face that he sees when he looks at me. If I look long enough I think I will remember it. But my features stay slippery. So does the color of his eyes.

Our house is big. There are glass turrets and tunnels, staircases, and chandeliers. It is a cold and lovely prison. Guy and I sit side by side in the dark of the storm, shivering and watching pale flames flicker in the fireplace. He lights the fire out of habit. He says he remembers nothing about the time before but something in him remembers that fires should make you warm.

I believe that remembering who we are is the key to getting out of this place, but he grows surly when I pester him with questions.

"What's the oldest thing you remember?" I ask.

He frowns. "Finding you."

"And before that?"

He shakes his head. "Just this," he says. "Just the storms and the sea."

I am always cold. Sometimes when I look in the mirror my lips are blue with it. I imagine myself dead in the sand with tiny crabs crawling out of my nose and I wonder what Guy will do without me. I imagine the rain erasing me until I am nothing more than a lonely breeze shaking the feathers in the hawthorn trees. But I am alive. I tell myself this as I sift through fish scales looking for new colors. I am alive. I repeat it over and over as I scrape salt and barnacles from my feet.

We are both looking for a way off of this island. I believe the pictures Guy traces in the glass are maps that he's keeping secret. This smarts extra bad when his hair has that blue-black shine that's so familiar. I hate that he keeps things from me, but I don't tell him about the colors either. I stare at my slippery face in the mirror. I sift through piles of scales. I collect tail feathers and broken wings and tie them to the trees so I can hear the storms coming. I fold poppy petals into thirds and wear them around my wrists in secret splashes of red.

Way out here, the sound of the ocean feels like thunder. If you stand out in the rain too long you might disappear completely. The waves spit up dead seabirds like they are burping up their dinners. In this big place, the cold and loneliness eats away at your bones.

DOG SITTING

Kim Magowan

—

I 'm waiting on my front stoop when my ex-wife rolls up in her beat up Buick and unloads her Great Dane from the back seat. She tugs Hamlet's leash like she's reeling in the world's largest fish. I have to smile at the sight of Colleen, barely five foot two, with that horse of a dog. Hamlet the Dane: that's my ex-wife the teacher's idea of a joke.

I pet the dog while Colleen hauls from her trunk a massive bag of dry dogfood. Some special brand that they don't sell at grocery stores, the pricy kind you have to buy at the vet. Hamlet licks my face. I scratch his rough, meaty ear, veined on the inside, and I wish humans were that easy to win over.

"Thanks for doing this, Hank," she says. "I owe you."

Colleen is flying to Amsterdam to be with our daughter Maisie, about to give birth to our grandchild. Every time I think the word "grandchild," I feel my heart crawl up my throat.

"So put in a word for me," I tell her.

Colleen's eyes are the color of steel. She points them at me. "There are these contraptions called computers," she tells me. "There is this phenomenon called email."

The thing is, I have reached out. But I can't stand looking at my Inbox, hoping for a reply. I flick the back of my hand at her, and she sighs.

"You're so damn stubborn," she says. "Both of you. Maisie inherits all her stubbornness from you. Me, I'm pliable." She does a shimmy to illustrate, which makes me laugh. She looks like one of those inflatable, red, bendy tubes with arms that the gardening place down the street mounts in December, when they clear their lot for Christmas trees. They hook it up to some blower, and it bobs and twists.

"Just put in a word. I'm looking after your damn dog," I remind her.

The truth is, I wish I could extract a word or two: pass my palm over Maisie's forehead to erase her memory. Colleen grew up rich. I picture one of those fancy, stupid utensils her parents had—serrated grapefruit spoons, or those doll-size forks for spearing escargots. I picture sticking one of those forks into my daughter's crenellated ear and extracting some epithets I wish I'd never called her mother. Rug muncher, dyke, whore. Colleen's forgiving, but our daughter isn't.

"Why am I taking care of this dinosaur anyway?" I ask her. "Why haven't you prevailed on Peggy?"

Colleen shakes her head. These days Colleen will come over with a six-pack and watch a Warriors game with me. But she still won't say a word about her love life.

I pat the dog to convey I am a trustworthy, considerate person, therefore my ex-wife doesn't need to give me the steel eye. "When are you coming back?" I ask.

"Jeez, Hank, I don't know," she says. "Maybe I'll just stay in Amsterdam and enjoy being a grandmother. Maybe I'll buy some funny wooden shoes, put my feet up. It's not like there's much to come back to, in this land of Trump."

We meet eyes. I sense she's telling me, without saying it out loud, about the state of things with Peggy. When we were married, Colleen was always attempting to transmit silent messages—"Let's blow this popsicle stand," when we were at some party. She'd get pissed when I couldn't translate. It's like she knew Morse code and I didn't.

"You should come with me. Be there when your Dutch grandson emerges into this fucked up world," she says.

I look at her, and it's Morse code again: long dash, long dash, short dash. Me feeling like a doofus, trying to interpret what the hell she is telling me.

"Then who takes care of your dog?" I ask.

Colleen nods. "Good point."

It's as if we've both been floating and land heavily on my stoop.

"Send me pictures of the baby," I say. Our twenty-two-year-old is way too fucking young to be having a baby; we are way too young to be grandparents. But what can you do? "Give Maisie my love, will you?"

Colleen looks like she's about to launch into her contraptions-called-computers speech again. But instead she nods, and pats both of our heads, me and her elephant dog. From the stoop we watch her car disappear.

OUTLINE FOR LYRIC ESSAY ABOUT CAVEMEN

Nicole Oquendo

———

I'm writing this because he stole my voice. No sense of when or why passed through my apartment's locked door as if it was jelly, to the bedroom. I don't know exactly what he did before he entered my bedroom, or even if he is a he, for that matter, but this person was a thief who held hands like bear claws over my eyes before he—I decided just then it was a he because of those hands—reached down my throat and pulled out the elegant box I had professionally appraised the night before, when over the telephone someone told me I was soothing.

I. He didn't go straight into my bedroom.

    A. He came in, starving, and thrust his hairy bear body into my small kitchen to treat himself to a turkey sandwich.

        i. It was fresh, bought yesterday, but I almost forgot to put it in the refrigerator because the phone rang. Regardless, he sat there to munch on my new turkey, now packed loosely between two fresh, lightly-toasted slices of white bread which were, themselves, lathered with mayonnaise.

            a. The rest of the groceries were untouched. I had, in fact, purchased five items total, including fresh turkey, mayonnaise, white bread, lettuce, and a box of sleeping medication that sill needs to be returned.

            b. Without it a good night's sleep I can't organize my thoughts.

        ii. I didn't open anything before I went to bed; placed it straight into the refrigerator for the next day. Therefore, he would have had to resist the temptations of all the other specimens of food and drink. This pained him, and gave him motive. It's not easy to plan an invasion, or to be deterred once it's begun.

    a. Motive established. My voice was stolen.

  B. He tried to watch the nightly news.

    i. He moved on to my bedroom in a fright, after furiously clicking the remote to find that it only worked in conjunction with my unique fingerprints.

      a. I forgot to buy batteries because I was so excited to go to the grocery store.

    ii. He surfed through all four of my channels, multiple times, to find nothing of interest. Their subjects ranged from infomercials for exercise machines to infomercials about exercise machines. The caveman, being fit on his own time, muscles bulging off of themselves, paid little attention.

      a. It was Sunday, 3:00 AM, when little is on but these snippets of advertising.

      b. I forgot to mail the cable bill check. It's been written out for over a week, on my nightstand where all the dust is.

II. In the event he was actually a she.

  A. She doesn't allow herself to eat after 8:00 PM, so though stopping for a turkey sandwich is tempting, she passes it by and heads for the bathroom, examining herself and all of her furry curves for twenty minutes in the full-length mirror.

    i. Many popular diets limit the intake of food after 8:00 PM because of our inability to burn large masses of calories while sleeping. The food needs time to slip through the body, which apparently doesn't like to digest on its side.

      a. I returned from the store at 7:45 PM, but because of the length of my phone conversation, I was not allowed to eat my turkey sandwich.

    ii. Whether or not my assailant was a man or a woman is, again, questionable, the hands themselves are worth noting again. She's self conscious about the coarse hairs on them, so she strokes them down flat in front of the mirror, pawing at herself, jealous of the magazines strewn across the bathroom floor.

      a. So am I.

      b. I'm starving.

  B. She dragged her flat feet into my bedroom, hungry, and smoothed my hair back while I slept.

i. The theft of my voice was compassionate—she placed her mouth over my mouth, her moustache tickling me awake, before pulling away slowly, and slipping the tip of a hairy finger into my mouth, drawing my voice out between my open lips.

    a. When I ran out, I found bare footprints, not the imprint of shoes. There was a place for each toe in the large marks, pressed like they should be filled with water and swam in, or with clay and preserved.

    b. I'm allergic to whatever it is that robbed me of speech—been sneezing all morning.

I know this is abrupt, maybe unwarranted. And that's fine with me—I need to research cavemen. But in case my theory proves false, the real theory in the theory, I need to cover my tracks, or else no language in the world is going to get you to believe that any of this happened to me. There must be a balance in composition, because all in all I'm glad my voice is gone—I hate being told I sound poetic. The phrase itself makes no sense to me, unless I'm speaking in iambic pentameter, which I make it a point to suppress. There—motive established again.

III. If he/she never came in at all.
    A. It's all my fault.
        i. According to my previous written work on the subject, there's a chance that I did it all on purpose—I can't be relied on for objective commentary anyway because of the differences in perception between people.
            a. I don't even like turkey. It doesn't have any flavor, no matter what I do to it.
            b. All the lights in the house were off. I crept into my own room, digging my toes into the shag carpet as I stepped to feel the fur between the crevices, looked around at the empty furniture, and screamed.
                ia. Screamed.
                ib. Screamed.
                ic. Screamed.
I started yelling while on the telephone.
    i. And didn't stop.
        a. Never started, never stopped. Just was.
    ii. He told me that I used to be soothing, and now I'm erratic, voice quivering all the time.
        a. He's a liar.

LOST GOING HOME

Bradley Sides

—

H enry was always lost, which was fine. But there was a problem: he would never ask for directions. "I'm just not that type of man," he'd say whenever someone called him out. The fact that he was dead—gone, departed, passed on, expired— didn't change anything.

Everyone else could figure it out. Surely, it couldn't be that difficult. Follow the light.

When it was his father's time to go, Reynolds sat up in his hospital bed and declared, "It's brighter than I expected. I'm going to go and lick it." The family cringed, but they knew he was headed in the right direction.

When it was his mother's time, she collapsed in the floor and shuddered, "Look at that. Glimmering like the star that topped my mama's Christmas tree. I'm coming, Reynolds."

Following the light was always the answer, and Henry had done that much—sort of.

As he squirmed on the piss-splattered bathroom floor with his wife crouched beside him, he looked around the room, finding nothing of interest. Then, just as he thought he was beginning to regain feeling in his legs, it appeared.

White. Glowing. Light.

He clutched her hand and told her, "I see the light, Barb. I see the light."

"Follow it," she told him. "Follow it as best you can, you dumb man. And don't you lose it."

He listened. He crawled out of his ramshackle, ugly body and flew toward the light.

It didn't take long—or maybe it did—for Henry to reach the sparkling core. As he stood there, unsure of what was happening, the light went out. He was in the dark.

No one had told him where to go next.

He could've asked. He could've shouted.

But Henry was still Henry, so he sighed and sat down in the darkness. Barb couldn't be long.

MRS. BEE

Sara Comito

—

I *want you like the sudden silence of the chute opening, the twin engine fire now a childhood memory, the earth so far below it makes no sense, panic a clay you can mash into fist shapes like a heart dead cold.*

This she writes into a notebook, smoking a Pall Mall under a maple. An electronic beep and intercom static entreaties, "Mrs. Bee. You are needed in the arts quad."

She's never skydived, so much as touched an airplane, not done anything remarkable beyond escaping the reservation. Which is, undeniably, remarkable. She's also, and never has been, a Mrs., and "Bee" stands for "Hokala." Badger never gets his due as a clever child of God.

"Fuck," Maeve says. She knows which child has vomited and whose leavings will need her scented distribution of sawdust. The weeks decide how they will be observed.

Real good reason to get off the heroin. Or maybe not.

The dented mirror almost helps with the acne scars. When the children leave their violins in the basement, she dances with them like partners. Enacts their shapes for "just kidding." The kid that calls her squaw, she can squint and think words they don't yet know. Welcome to Oregon. Watch the Catholic priest kiddie proceedings. Binge. Purge. Repeat.

I want you like I could start again. Be shot out of my mother's womb. Breathe innocence like oxygen.

She never will be seen in profile. Hair: crow's blue black. Right arm: ringed by tribal tattoo. Education: Master's lost in lost languages. Sawdust: at the ready.

THE MOST METAL BAND NAME YOU'VE EVER HEARD

Patrick Cooper

—

"What's it say?" Dan squinted at the piece of notebook paper.

"Sound out the letters," Shelley said. He paced in front of Dan.

"I am. I'm sounding them out in my head, the letters, and I—"

"Say them aloud then. Sound them out."

Dan dragged his eyes slowly across the crudely drawn logo, a mess of thick Sharpie strokes, and mouthed the letters. "It doesn't—"

"You've got to... stop squinting. You've got to relax your eyes. Lookit now."

Dan blinked hard a moment, then let his eyes rest on the center of the drawing. "I don't—"

"You're not—"

"I am."

"Rest your eyes. You've got to."

"My eyes."

"Give it a sec."

"I can't."

"Ben saw it easy."

Dan pulled his eyes away. "He did?"

"Fucking A. Ben saw it in like three seconds."

"And what'd he think?"

"He loves it. Loves the name. Says it makes him want to puke."

"Puke?"

"Real nasty. He said he doesn't even think the tee shirt place will print it. It's that gnarly."

"Will it fit on my bass drum? The name? Or will I have to get—"

Shelley punched Dan on the arm. "C'mon now, dream boy. Just relax your fucking eyes."

"Where is Ben?"

"Beer run."

Dan glanced at the 30 rack of Pabst in the corner of the basement. Shelley had been tossing back cans since Dan arrived.

Dan said, "But where?"

"A beer run."

"Where?"

"Downtown."

"Where though? I thought I saw his car outside."

Shelley sighed. "You're taking too long, dream boy. Do you even want to know what our new band name is?"

"Why don't you just—"

Shelley hushed Dan. He put his thumb on Dan's chin and gently turned his head back to the notebook paper. "Read it. It only makes sense if you read it."

"Makes sense?"

"If you read it."

"I can't."

"Read it, dream boy. Relax your eyes."

"You keep saying that. More I relax my eyes, the less I see. My eyes are starting to hurt."

"Your eyes are—"

"Starting to fucking hurt. Where's Ben?"

"If you don't read it, I'm going to break your hands."

Shelley was twice Dan's size and twice his age and scary when he drank. Dan had seen him get violent before. Put his own head through the van's window. After a show one time, to scare a teenage girl that was hanging around, he slit his wrists. Just enough to scare her. Substituting musical talent for theatrics.

Shelley looked at Dan with two bloodshot eyes. "So read the fucking name."

Dan's mouth was dry. He looked back at the paper. The drawing had changed.

"Shell... what is this?"

"Read it."

"It's different."

"Read."

"The drawing... it's different."

"Read it quick then. Before it changes again."

"Changes? Fucking... what is this? Where's Ben?"

"It's changing?"

"What?"

"Better read it quick."

The thick black lines of the logo swirled in front of Dan's eyes. He dropped the paper and started to fall over. Shelley caught him.

"Did you see it?" Shelley said, easing Dan onto the couch.

Dan pressed his palms into his eyes.

"Dan, did you see it?"

"See it?"

"Yeah, did you see—"

"Yes."

"What'd it say?"

"I can't."

"Tell me."

Dan told Shelley what he'd read. Then Dan leaned over the armrest and vomited on the concrete floor.

Shelley laughed. "When Ben read it, earlier, Ben saw something different."

Dan wiped his face off with his shirt. "I don't understand."

"Did you eat today?"

"What?"

"Food, dream boy, did you have any today?"

"I did, but it's all on your floor now."

"That's good."

"I don't... Shell, what was that?"

"Our new band name."

"But you said, when Ben read it, it was—"

"Different for Ben, yeah. I think, each time..." Shelley trailed off. Started looking behind the drum set.

"Was that Ben's car outside?" Dan said.

"Did you have anything to drink?"

"Where did you, oh Christ, where did you get the drawing? The logo? Where—"

"From a man lives behind the 7-Eleven dumpster. Traded it for some smokes."

"A man?"

"Gave me the logo."

"Why?"

"He said it was the most metal band name of all time. I'm certain it must be. Listen, I need to know, did you have anything to drink?"

"Drink?"

"Before you came here?"

"I have a Dew in the car."

Shelley sneered. "Fucking... where is, here?" He lifted a water bottle from behind the drums and handed it to Dan. "Drink this."

"What is it?"

"Water. You just puked. It'll take the taste out of your mouth."

"Why does it... it looks cloudy?"

"Fuck's sake." Shelley grabbed the bottle and tore the cap off. He grabbed Dan by the hair and yanked his head back. Dan screamed. Shelley wedged the bottle in between Dan's lips.

"Your own good," Shelley said and squeezed the salt water down Dan's throat. "Fucking own good."

Dan held it down for a couple seconds and then vomited most of it onto his lap. Drool hung down his chin. He panted, "What're you... doing to... stop it."

"Say it again."

"Please..."

"Say the name again. The one you read. I can't decide which I like better."

"Stop..."

"Between the one you saw or Ben's. I can't decide. Say it again."

Dan said it again and screamed. He grasped his stomach and put his head between his knees. Through the tears he saw something next to his feet. Ben's glasses.

"Shelley?" Dan said. "Where's Ben?"

"Ben?" Shelley said. "Not here anymore. Could you, no, you know what? I think I like the name you saw better."

"Shelley!" Dan's eyes went wide. He looked around, terrified. "I can't see!

What... Shelley I can't see anything!"

"Yeah, same thing happened to Ben."

Dan cursed some more and cried and fell face first off the couch. He wheezed a minute then stopped breathing.

Shelley stared at Dan for a few moments, then said, "It's the most metal band name of all time. I'm certain it must be."

FREAKY PHALANGES

Tom Lucas

—

I t was my wife who first noticed.

We were on a lazy Sunday drive, the kind we like to take to purge our brains of the stresses of the week. It had been a particularly bad stretch. Back on Wednesday, she suffered a crippling injury at her job over at the gift card kiosk, losing her right hand to what can only be described as a biblically epic paper cut.

As we drove, she nursed her sore nub. She knew her bowling league days were finished and she was not feeling it. Meanwhile, I was coming off a tough week of auditing the financial records of a drive-through euthanasia clinic.

It was clear that we had a lot of negative energy to shake off so I made our drive considerably longer than usual. Unfortunately, the blur of the passing trees, the bright, smiling sunshine, and the sweet smell of farm country did little to level us out.

I should mention that we had also been fighting a bit because she had the nerve to point out that my hands didn't match. Can you imagine that? I assumed she was lashing out in jealous anger, as I still had both and she now only had one.

I was wrong.

I always drive with my hands at ten and two, so the evidence was right in front of me. Indeed, my hands didn't match. My left hand had become that of a baby's, the left of a man in his elder years. Smooth and small chubby fingers versus veiny, paper-thin skin. Neither hand was mine. Or maybe they were simultaneously what I once had and would one day possess.

No matter. As they were attached to my arms, they were mine.

I was going to need help fast. It took a few tries to get my baby hand to dial the phone but I was able to reach our family doctor, who cancelled his usual weekend bender after I explained that the rapid de/aging had moved past the hand and was already up to my elbows. My baby arm was now completely useless, and the grip of my geriatric right was rather feeble.

During the examination, I was having trouble breathing. Panic had set in. He just nodded and grunted as he examined my limbs. Cold and clinical, he jotted down a few notes and did his best to avoid making eye contact with me. Soon several other doctors arrived. Speaking in hushed tones, they carefully touched and manipulated my limbs.

They asked me stupid questions, such as:

"Does it hurt when I do this?"

"Do you crave milk?"

"Can you make a middle finger for me?"

"Do you feel the need to cry out of frustration? If not, why not?"

"Is true love real or just a movie thing?

The answer to all of their questions was yes. A thousand times yes. Except that last one.

The gaggle of doctors retreated to a corner of the room. They spoke in mutters and whispers and harrumphs and shouts. They waved their hands in dramatic, demonstrative gestures. They made points and counterpoints.

They returned to me. I sat on the edge of the table, fully nervous and concerned for my wellbeing. I was asked to look to the right as they shined a bright light into my eyes. I was struck in the head from behind with something dull and metallic.

I awoke in a padded room that had cameras in all the corners. I was told by a disembodied voice via loudspeaker that a small dimensional rift had formed in my chest. This is completely random and almost never happens, the voice said. I called shenanigans on that because how would they have a set-up for observing me if this doesn't happen regularly? It can't be cheap to keep a room with all this video equipment going. Stinking liars.

Now I've had a bit of time to live with this chest-mounted time-tear and the best anyone can tell is that it is causing time to swirl through my body at the cellular level. I am moving forward and back through the timeline with imperceptible speed. I am aging both forward and in reverse. I exist at every moment of my life simultaneously. This is how I can have a baby hand and an old fart's at the same time.

I haven't had the nerve to look in my pants.

I am not sure how long this has been going on. This has all happened before. This has never happened. This story is happening as I tell you. This story is an old memory. I don't know much but I know this:

One of three things will happen: I will become a baby and start anew. I will smell very nice. Or, I will age to brittle bone and dust and explode without warning. I will smell awful.

I can hear them placing bets while I wait. Old or young, fairly even odds at this point. I wonder what my wife would do with another baby. She already resents me. If I got all wrinkled and shriveled up will she still have sex with me? Am I still married at all? When was the last time I saw her? Did I ever marry?

Will I remember this? What happens next? What is the measure of a life lived in forward and reverse?

The third thing that's going to happen is that I am going to start soiling my diapers starting right frigging now. I'm scared as hell but I have to say that I am pretty excited about having a socially acceptable reason to ruin my drawers.

You do have to look for the silver lining, after all.

HOSTAGES

Michelle Ross

—

The hostages, though they can't speak through the fat strips of silver duct tape, nonetheless seem to communicate. I don't mean anything concrete, like an escape plan. One of them gets a scared look in her eyes, and another one mirrors the look back, like how Mom reflected my anger two days ago when I told her about how Kyra tripped me at recess, hence the scratches on my chin and palms. "That girl is a bully," Mom said. Then she softened. She said people who treat others like that aren't okay inside. She said Kyra probably has "a rough home life," and I pictured walls, floors, and furniture all scratchy as sandpaper.

The hostages are not strangers to each other the way the hostages in a movie I saw once were—random people who happened to be in the same place at the same time. These hostages are coworkers—Dad's coworkers. Ex-coworkers, since he was fired last week. There are twenty-seven of them, the number of kids in my fifth-grade class minus me. I make twenty-eight, but I'm not a hostage.

This isn't my first time at Dad's office, so I recognize a lot of the hostages. One of them I know by name. Judith keeps a stash of little toys in her purse for doling out to other people's children. She's a no-frills Santa Claus. On visits to Dad's office, Judith has given me the following toys: a pouch containing eight tiny, colored pencils; a calculator with neon-green buttons; a plastic cockroach that skitters forward on little wheels after you roll it backwards and let go.

Now Judith looks at me pleadingly as though I might help her. Or maybe she's feeling sorry for me because I'm a kid who is witness to her dad taking hostages.

The word "hostages" makes me think of the word "sausages." I think of those tiny pig-in-a-blanket sausages that come in shrink-wrapped packs, squeezed up against each other not unlike Dad's ex-coworkers are now. In the small conference room, only six chairs fit around the circular table. Of course, the hostages are not seated at the table. They're crammed in against each other around the perimeter of the room. They're also like a string of sausages, only side-to-side rather than end-to-end.

A hostage situation I didn't see on TV but heard about because I was up listening when my parents thought I was asleep involved Mom. A gunman entered an office where she'd worked, before I was born, and he'd taped her and her coworkers' mouths shut, too, just like Dad did to his ex-coworkers minutes ago. Mom didn't sound scared telling Dad about this. She sounded perplexed. "Do you know what scared me most? I was terrified that man was going to rape me in front of my coworkers. I worked in an office that was all men. I was the only woman. So it wasn't the fear of death or even rape itself that got to me. It was the humiliation of being raped in front of those guys."

Dad said, "Jesus."

Now Dad doesn't say anything. He stands in the doorway, his hunting rifle pointed at the wall a few feet above Judith's head. He scrunches up his shoulders like he's got an ache in his back or his neck. I look in at Judith and the others through the glass wall, warming that glass with my breath.

Dad isn't just mad at them, for still having jobs, or for being responsible somehow for his not having a job; he's mad at me, too, for having been on the floorboard in the back of his car without his knowing it, and on a school day; and for sneaking into the building, finding him in this situation. Of course, I hadn't known this was what I'd find. I'd hoped to get another toy out of Judith even though I'm too old for such things now, at the age of eleven. I'd hoped to feel comforted by Judith's eagerness to make me smile. I'd hoped to feel a little less worried about going back to school.

Most of all, I think Dad's mad I'm observing his poor role modeling.

That's a thing Mom is always saying to Dad—that he needs to be a better role model for me. Every time I ask for something—a glass of juice, a new tube of toothpaste—without saying, "please," he says, "How do you ask nicely?" Mom echoes his question when a few minutes later he inevitably asks, or tells, her to do something without asking nicely himself. Another thing that gets her going is when he says to me, "You're making me angry" or "If you do ____, I'm not going to be happy." Mom says, "She's not responsible for your feelings, Andy."

I try to think what Mom would say now. On top of everything else wrong with this picture, she wouldn't approve of the shirt he's wearing. She says it smells like sauerkraut; she says the smell is locked in and it's time to let that shirt go.

This is the same language Dad's boss, ex-boss, used with him. "I have to let you go, Andy." I wonder which one of these people is Dad's ex-boss. Four of the men wear long-sleeved shirts and ties as opposed to the polo shirts the other men wear, so I'm guessing one of them. Also, the tie men's eyes are a different kind of startled than everyone else's. Like Kyra yesterday when I cornered her in the girls' bathroom just as the bell that signaled the end of the school day rang, a rock in my hand triple the size of my fist.

I recognize the look in Dad's eyes, too. The realization that he's made a horrible mistake, that there will be repercussions, and those repercussions will find him no matter where he goes.

Artist: Paulaidan Minerva

OVERRIPE

Leslie Salas

—

This was not what Landry expected when her uncle said he was going to show her what "real Florida" looked like. She expected pastel sunrises on the seashore. The sand between her toes while she collected scallops where ocean met land. Maybe shaved ice and a hammock nap while the sun beat down. As the sun sunk below the horizon, perhaps she would help her aunt steam freshly-caught lobsters for dinner. But instead, there was this: a dirty field, dirty horses, dirty cows, even the dirty dog Benji at her ankles. Landry wrinkled her nose. It would take years to get the stink out of her hair.

When her aunt saw that all Landry had brought in her suitcase was a rainbow array of bikinis and floral loungewear, she tutted and dragged her niece to the second-hand store to select some dingy overalls and long-sleeved shirts to protect her skin from the sun and long, serrated grass. Landry begrudgingly wore those garments as she meandered the path between the stables and the cattle field. The dog dutifully followed.

"There are orchids in the swamp," her aunt had told her. "The most beautiful you'd ever seen." Landry was determined to find them. At least something in Florida should be beautiful.

Her uncle winked at her as she headed out on her mission. "Watch out for that swamp ape," he teased.

Landry rolled her eyes.

The bells around the cows' necks clanged as they munched under the afternoon sun. Landry kept her distance after having slipped and fell into a cowpie the day before. A horsefly buzzed by her ear and she swatted at it, sour-faced, as she trudged through the tall grass and toward where the prairie met water. The dog pranced in and out of the water, splashing and yapping. Landry watched the water's edge for alligators—her uncle had warned her that she should run away in a zig-zag if she saw any—but she figured a gator would rather get the dumb dog over her any day.

Cypress and mangrove trees held the earth to the water. Landry steered clear of the liminal space, clomping her aunt's boots in the mud as she searched the razorgrass for flower bulbs.

Benji growled at a figure kneeling at the water's edge.

"Benji!" Landry admonished the dog. He let out a huff before retreating to Landry's side.

The figure's skin, rough and cracked like papier-mâché, was the color of deep clay. They wore a skirt of woven palmetto leaves browned in the sun. Pleated long black hair ran down their back.

"Hello?" she asked.

The figure's hands, plunged wrist-deep into the slow-moving Okeechobee, remained still.

Landry approached slowly until she and the figure were close enough to share breath. The dog held back, offering a low growl. The figure's long eyelashes rested on their cheeks. Their mouth barely parted open. Landry couldn't tell if they were a boy or a girl—they were much younger than she was—and she marveled at their absolute stillness.

A blue heron took flight not far behind the statuesque figure. Landry watched its long wingspan skim the rippled surface of the large lake. It passed in front of another dark figure—this one wading waist-deep among the mangroves. This figure—with a flat chest and wide shoulders—wielded a harpoon spear, poised to strike. Red and white paint framed his face and forearms. A handful of feathers were tied into his black hair, which had been pulled up into a bun. Strings of shells coiled around his neck and wrists. The palmetto shift around his hips left nothing to the imagination. Landry felt a tightening in her chest and a stirring farther below as she studied his silhouette. Her cheeks flushed as the setting sun behind him cast the sky into vibrant pinks and oranges. A chorus of crickets started their evening song. His grip on the spear held strong.

Benji barked behind Landry. She spun, tripping over her own feet and landing butt-first into the muck behind the child figure. A third figure rested against a cypress tree.

"Benji, stop it," Landry said. The dog pushed his ears back and whined.

The figure's long, black hair hung in loose waves around her shoulders and covered her bare breasts. Her darkened skin held the same hard, papery texture as the other two figures, but her eyes were open—an inky void from lid to lid. The figure gazed down toward the knee of the cypress, where its roots spread out above the waterline. There sprouted several braided husks of leaves and a cluster of wild orchids. The flowers were surprisingly ugly with their ostentatious yellow petals splattered with brown like an overripe banana.

Her uncle's voice, brassy and loud, called from across prairie. "Laaaaandry," he called. "Supper!"

Benji's tail wagged at the familiar sound and he set off, running through the thicket at the promise of food.

The sky shifted to purples and the evening star shone bright on the horizon. The woman offered Landry her hand. Landry took it, impressed at the supple warmth of the figure's treebark skin. In the shadows of dusk, she couldn't make out if the figure changed her expression in response.

A splash at the water's edge split Laundry's attention. When she turned to bid the woman farewell, the figure was gone. In her place stood a tall oak. Landry's hand remained ensnared in its branches. She looked back at the other figures: tree stumps in the growing darkness. Treefrogs croaked. The water glittered around a dark lump on the shore.

"Benji?" Landry asked. But she knew better. The damn dog was gone, and now some Florida swamp ape was out to eat her.

The lump let out a deep, rumbling bellow.

In the rising moonlight, Landry got a better look. A crust of thick, armored scales. A long row of sharp teeth. Her shrill scream pierced the night.

At least some things in Florida could be beautiful.

ANDREA'S SENSES

Paul Beckman

—

Andrea poured herself a cup of black coffee and spit it out. She made another and had the same reaction. She's been making the same brand in the same way for over twenty years and couldn't understand it. She was a coffee snob. She smelled it and while it didn't smell bad it didn't smell like her regular coffee.

That night while she was sleeping her five senses got together to talk about their lives with Andrea and the possibility of forming a union.

Taste went first and told her story of the coffee and her Lean Cuisine dinner that she couldn't finish.

Nose shared how the smells she once loved had shifted, but yet, she didn't want a union.

Hearing complained about Andrea's habit of cranking her iPhone up to max volume to listen to her beloved operas, which was sure to bring on early deafness.

Vision was overall angry at Andrea who, since breaking up with her boyfriend six months ago, turned into a real slob and didn't seem to care anymore. Andrea, once a sharp dresser, now tossed her clothes in a pile on the bedroom floor and rummaged through the pile every day to find something to wear. Vision hated her non-planning of compatible clothes and accessories and the fact that she gave up on mani-pedis and beauty parlors and wasn't bothered by it, so she was a yes on union.

And Touch was a definite union vote. She couldn't even touch a man's arm without cringing these days.

The vote was 4 to 1 but it had to be unanimous. They others finally persuaded

Nose to join the others and if they couldn't help Andrea get back to her old self they would just shutdown their senses until she came to hers.

When Andrea got to work there was a vase with a dozen white roses waiting for her—the most beautiful she'd ever seen. There was also a card. *My Dearest Andrea, These past six months have been terrible. I miss you so much and want to try and rekindle our romance. Call me. Love, Alex.*

Andrea was touched and happy to hear from Alex. Unconsciously she smelled the roses and it was as if the room was filled with perfume. She twirled around taking in the scent and touching the velvet-like petals.

Next, she poured herself a cup of coffee, added a couple of sugar cubes, and it was the best tasting coffee she ever had. Taste did a happy dance on her tongue.

She called Alex and hearing his baritone voice made her smile and bang her knees together. They agreed to meet for drinks that evening.

When Andrea walked into the bar, she saw Alex across the room and walked over. They stood looking at each other and Andrea thought that Alex was not quite as good looking as she remembered but he was still okay. They hugged, lightly at first and then a lover's hug and she found his usual after shave a bit cloying. She broke from the hug and took his face in her hands and gave him a big kiss. Andrea felt uncomfortable touching him as they hugged but expected that because it'd been a while but then when she held his face to kiss him her palms sweated and she knew that all of her senses couldn't be wrong, so she said, "I just stopped in to say goodbye," and then turned and walked out into the welcoming evening breeze.

BREATH AND BLOOD

Juli C. Lasselle

—

T errell cut and coursed, full of his immortal youth, dogged, and Judson at the protest called his name, and he was always moving forward—nobody was ever going to touch him. Terrell was so far in front of him, seeming blind with his first full taste of manhood, swept between shadows of dust inside the storm of folks—a graceful, long-limbed man-boy, clever in his way, but oh, not nearly, not ever as clever as men with money and guns. Judson called out, *Terrell*, and he wanted to be there, to hold him back, but the swell of the angry folks at the protest, and the warm acrid scent of guns fired, and the hot dust he sucked down his lungs, and his boy's dark blood bubbling up from his perforated heart like the dust that rose unfettered was too stifling and too strong. The stampede of folks wouldn't stop for Judson that night, but he found his boy alive, briefly, staring up at the man with the gun—and time stood still, and the man was gunning and purposeful and mean—every look, every breath, was for him alone.

"Back up. Or else," the man said.

He was not afraid of the man, those words. Judson's bankrupt worker's back, the way he couldn't stop feeling it, imagining himself, a white-tailed deer shot through the spine, still alive, all his innards in one clean slice lightly lifted out of him. His hands, like two captive birds fluttering upwards out of harm's way, signaling to the man his intent was pure, and the bleeding boy mattered more than his hastily caged rage. Blood bubbles formed like corn kernels on the cob of his boy's parted lips. Each bubble a singular globe, a new world of breath and blood until it burst in unfulfilled man-dom. Kneeling at the side of his son, succumbing to enveloping ground, Judson kissed Terrell's wet lips—salty like parched earth, sticky like spilt seed. He lightly lifted the bloodied body of his firstborn son to his breast, and the barrel of the man's rifle shone in the fire-lit night, and he rose up from the swirls of dust, gun smoke, the cries of men a hailing of vacancy in his ears, the face of the man the only sound. The thing he remembered.

DEATH EVERY 3 SECONDS

Meg Tuite

—

S treets yawned thick with floundering old men, bellies tethered to slant.
Lips drooled and eyes, well they were askew, like there was sun to squint through. It was night and dogs were wailing at the wind.

Someone was going to die tonight. Maybe not someone known to go out, but men were watching porn on the Sabbath and nautical calendars were getting sloshed.

A man walked through streets wondering if his penis was impressionable because it had soared up and swept into another man's mouth, while his tightened wife was searching for parsley to layer on top of their pork roast. She did love the look of her greens. They rasped and scrambled for sky until she guillotined necessary overachievers into a rich lack of disparity.

Two instincts were recoiling when a girl was told the chemo was unsuccessful, when actually it had spent a year rolling her toward the tomb. Her estranged bowels had insisted that she quit her job and leaf through a buried life of broken clocks, toilets, and herself. Wasn't there another place to search?

He realized he was shaking more and his right hand wouldn't do what he said. Soon gravity called him by name and his body was underwater with rippling skin swaying on waterlogged feet. His dance was violin-shaped as the world bent under his weight. The hollow tracks of his bones loosened the streets. The sky was red and swollen. He was peopled with gestures that did not bury themselves.

The pork roast, satin in its pink skin, waited for the knife.

THE SHED

Dominic Lim

—

George hunches over his workbench piled high with rust-spotted tools. He takes a faded handkerchief from his pocket and rubs his heavy-lidded eyes, tries to wipe away the familiar images he has just seen on television: gunship helicopters, villages on fire, children hiding in rice fields. He came to his shed to forget about those things.

George reaches up to pull on the rope cord switch of the ceiling light bulb. An electric buzz fills the silence. He stares at the masses of spider webs clotting up the crevices of his shed. The corners in here are so damn deep, he thinks, as if somehow the edges of the room keep going on, falling away beyond what is really there.

In another time, in a war-torn country, he is in another room with dark, endless corners. Embroidered curtains seal in humid air, rank with the smell of fermented food. A shaft of noonday light illuminates a dirt floor. He is on top of a boy who opens wide a mouth full of crooked yellow teeth. George feels the boy's silent roar.

George swats at the air in the shed, waving something away. The musty air tickles his nostrils and he sneezes. He wipes his nose and turns towards the misshapen blocks of wood lying on his workbench. Earlier in the spring a cardinal resting on a crabapple branch in his backyard had sung such a sweet song that it moved him, gave him an unshakeable desire to shelter its tiny body. He went to his shed to make a birdhouse, but got only as far as gathering leftover wood from past projects before abandoning it.

He touches the pieces of wood. Too rough, he thinks. A pretty bird should have a pretty home. George takes a square of coarse sandpaper from his toolbox and smooths down the edges. His sparse graying hair splits into wet wedges against his scalp. Even though his arms are tight with arthritis, he feels the need to keep working and pushes past the exhaustion.

But as soon as one piece becomes the right size and shape, it no longer fits with the others, and so he must re-work everything else. He grips the wood tighter. Sawdust fills the air in front of him.

He is back in the other room. The curtains are letting in more light than before. A gust of chrysanthemum air wafts past. His short brown hair drips sweat onto the boy on the bed. No—surely it can't be a boy. A young man. His eyes are open, but blank, his lips dry and slightly parted. George stares, urging the corners of the young man's mouth to soften upwards. Move, dammit, smile for me. The room sharpens: he sees a small television affixed to a wall, a ceramic flower vase filled with wilting flowers, a silver tray on a table next to him with a dirty glass (completely empty), a bottle of whisky (half-empty), a holstered gun, and a serrated knife stained burnt copper.

That can't be right. He would never have left a knife out, let alone a gun, in a room with a stranger. He wills the things away, feels his brow burn. After several moments the images evaporate in the equatorial heat. He looks down again at the young man beneath him who is mouthing: "Take me." His face is concrete. "Take me to America."

George shoves the wood aside. A sliver drives deep into his middle finger. A sharp jab of pain shoots up his hand. He pulls back, cursing. He puts his finger close to his eyes and pulls a thick splinter out with a quick inhalation, leaving behind a bright, tiny dome of blood. He sucks on the tip of his finger and lingers on the iron tang before saying, "Enough."

He throws the shed's door open and breathes in the evening air. He takes a broom resting against the wall, reaches up to the corners of the shed and wipes away the webs. He sweeps the floors, pushing out clouds of dust. Scents of wood shavings fill his nose, but also fish grilled in banana leaves, French bread, and bowls of sticky rice.

George takes a rag and cleans the grimy windows. He notices a faint network of cracks in their surface. He continues to wipe. A band of orange light emerges, the fire of sunset in the sky, like a string of red lanterns in the night.

He stoops low and sees the signs of rot in the wood floor. Instead of removing the decaying pieces, George takes an oriental rug from the back of the shed and unrolls it on top of the planks. He strokes the worn fabric. The chestnut fibers feel like the placid smoothness of warm, brown skin. The rug's designs are roiling and black, the wispy whorls of a man's pupils. He is in a luxury hotel room with the man, engulfed in ivory sheets. The taste of honey and jasmine tea coat the back of his throat. The man whispers a few words to him, too soft to hear over the laughter clattering through the bedroom's open window. George leans in closer. The man smiles. His teeth are treasured pearls. His lips press warmly against George's ear.

"Take me," the man says.

George opens his eyes. The shed is clean now. He stands up and looms over it, fists on hips.

A flash of red catches his eye. A cardinal settles on the window sill. George stops dead still, not wanting to scare it away. It peers in as if staring at the pile of wood George had pushed to the side of his workbench. It chirps something shrill which sounds to George almost like a laugh before flying off into the night.

THE RATS

Jared Silvia

The rats are finally here, thank the broken sky. We have waited so long and the rats are finally here. We have bitten our fingernails bloody and chewed the skin from our fingertips in anticipation, but, at last, the rats are finally here, thank the broken sky.

Q. How long have you waited for the rats to come?

A. We have waited as long as we can comfortably remember, but the rats come in their own time. We have prepared the way, crafting a place for the rats with shredded cardboard, building up nooks for their hiding, passages for their scurrying. We have prepared offerings of canned fruits and memorized the recipes for breads and fragrant cheeses, all the best our civilization could offer the rats. We have waited so long for them to arrive.

Q. How did you know the rats had arrived?

A. We heard a lovely scratching inside the walls, which at first was soft and lonesome. We thought that we had imagined this scratching (it would not have been the first time), but those faint scuttles gave way to clear sounds we could hear and measure. We used our stethoscopes and knew their bodies through our walls, their beautiful claws scraping the old wood, their short fur blessing beds of cardboard, the pleased teeming of their mouths, moist for our offerings of canned fruits, breads, and fragrant cheeses. We praised the broken sky.

Q. What sort of rats have come?

A. When we have seen them crawling along the eaves at night, they have been brown, a lovely deep brown, and we think they are Norway rats, but whatever their type, they are here now, thank the broken sky. We have waited so long, and have tried so hard to be patient, but in truth our minds have wandered. We did our work, of course, as we all must, shredding the cardboard, the newspaper, opening cans of fruit, baking the bread, aging the fragrant cheese. Still, we would weep with fear that the rats might never come, and in our weeping, we found no sleep.

Q. Why have you so anticipated the coming of the rats?

A. When the sky was broken, what was left to us but waiting for the rats to come? We used to imagine generation after generation of descendants who look like us and put pictures of us on their walls, tell stories about us, in that way living forever, but life is short under the broken sky. We willingly devote ourselves to the rats, those who will live on. Their young, with their too-large heads, are already dancing in our walls. We pray for their persistence, a long line of rats, rats, rats, and that, for a while, they might remember us, might remember our canned fruits, remember our breads, remember our fragrant cheeses, remember our civilization that broke the sky, broke ourselves, and prepared a way for them, beloved rats.

Q. What will you do now that the rats have arrived?

A. We will wait in joy until the rats have grown strong and numerous. We will listen as they chew through the walls, and wait until they arrive inside. Then, once they have, we will watch as they come upon all the cans of fruit, all the bread, all the fragrant cheese. After, we shall prepare ourselves. We hope they will start with our toes so we can see the work of their beautiful teeth and know their truth. Then, as they chew through our flesh and organs, consuming our muscle and sinew, gnawing our bones clean, we shall praise their wisdom. When they have finished their work on us, we think, we hope, they will work upon this place, the material of it, chewing through the plaster and wires, through tiles and planks, through everything until all that remains is a pleasing rubble, a testament to their perfection. We have such joy at imagining this, the marker upon the place where we gave ourselves. We hope it will stay for a while, and then blow away, more dust for the kingdom of rats.

The rats are finally here, thank the broken sky. We have waited so long and the rats are finally here. We have bitten our fingernails bloody and chewed the skin from our fingertips in anticipation, but, at last, the rats are finally here, thank the broken sky.

EVEN AS AN AIRPLANE

Amanda Chiado

—

M y father was laughing when he was torn in half, and his mother rushed in with glue and his father—tragedy for hands—used his mouth and could only kiss him. I couldn't thread together my father's two distinctive parts. Our love squeezed them together until my father became two soft lumps of pulp.

His parents wept and lay around him through the night, as if they were rocks around a pyre. Night whirled around them in the cool cricket thick air. They prayed by wishing. Sometimes they were content in the grief that my father was torn in half before their eyes—and not in the streets of a city full of strangers who would never try to put a torn man back together.

My halved father laughed still, as a glob of shreds. The charm of his voice reached my grandparents, and they spread his remains of into a flat sheet that warmed in the glow of morning. My grandparents could watch a mending unending, could, by their blood alone, make a way into togetherness.

My grandfather clapped his hands like "I told you so," and my father folded himself into an airplane. My grandmother's smile was a landing strip, wide and welcome. My father ripped through the delicate morning away from the circle of stones and out of the waiting room. He slipped past my daughter's tangled hair, and wind blew against my face. My father laughed even as an airplane. The horizon spread its wings into the firelight.

WE WERE WAITING FOR BIG POLLY TO BRING US OUR COCAINE

Ephraim Scott Sommers

—

I farted around at the poker table in the back of Old Dog's Tavern with a bunch of sober old people, bored out of my eyes, trying to catch a good rum buzz and failing, the juke box zig-zagging between blues and country songs.

My buddy Knuckles was shooting pool for money instead of flipping cards with me because he hated being around old people, "grey heads" he called them, said they smelled like fear. When I took a break to grab another rum and meandered over to check his temperature, he met me at the bar.

"We burned the pot up to a hundred a game." He had one of those big furry Russian hats on. It was brown.

"Wow," I replied. "Is that the guy whose band played last night?" I pointed at the man across from us in a blue top hat and a leather jacket the color of wet redwood.

"Yeah," Knuckles whispered. "Lyle Cruz. Fucker's a legend on the guitar."

I studied the table, and it was all tied up, two balls left a piece, a pile of tens and twenties in a mess on the rail. Lyle Cruz leaned in, his straight black hair waterfalling down onto the felt, and missed.

After Lyle stood up and sighed, Knuckles clapped once and scanned the table.

"Damn," Lyle said, calmly. Underneath that blue top hat, he had a fuckable face if you know what I mean, real clear skin, symmetrical features, no five o'clock shadow, lean figure.

Knuckles sunk the nine-ball in the corner pocket, and Lyle still seemed mellow, drinking his golden beer directly from a big glass pitcher, no pint glass.

Then barely, by an ass hair, my friend Knuckles missed his next ball, the blue ten stalled ever so close to the center pocket. "Come on," Knuckles said, trying to will the ball in as if by magic.

Lyle crouched up to the table, then, called his pockets, and sunk two solids in one shot. Only the eight-ball was left for him to drop, and the cash would be all his.

"Fuck...okay...okay...nice shot, nice fucking shot," Knuckles conceded. It was all but over.

Lyle chalked his cue with a cube of blue then had another drink from his pitcher, taking his time. "All My Exes Live in Texas," shot out of a busted speaker in the ceiling above us, and then finally, after two hours of making us wait, finally, Big Polly stumbled in, but she was obliterated, absolutely shit-canned, but, somehow, yeah, there she was, still standing, in her usual uniform: the flip-flops with socks, the XXXL white t-shirt, the XXXL basketball shorts. The night had undone her long hair in a brunette hurricane around her.

"Is this the money you owe me, Knuckles?" Big Polly slurred, slamming her big paw down onto the pile of cash on the rail. When she did, she biffed her hip against the pool table. Knuckles' ten ball fell into the center pocket.

"Shit," I said. Knuckles had escaped.

Not so fucking easy for Lyle Cruz, however, who at that moment was taking off his blue top hat nonchalantly. Then, to everyone's surprise, Lyle slammed that big glass pitcher over the back of Big Polly's head so damn hard that it exploded.

With her paw still resting on the pile of money, Big Polly went down to one knee. Lyle had his pool stick above his head about to crack it over the back of her like an axe, but before he could, Big Polly got her free arm around his leg and ripped him down onto the shitty floor beside her.

It was a maelstrom of elbows and fists and hair then, Knuckles and I sitting next to each other on a couple of stools, smiling.

Lyle squirmed over onto his side, grabbed a handful of hair and put two big punches into Big Polly's face. It looked like it might go his way then, too, that is, until Big Polly started using her weight, shouldering her body over on top of the lean guitarist and never uttering a word while they wrestled it out, and Lyle, too, remained oddly, almost eerily quiet throughout the fight, that is, until someone, we weren't sure who, let out a pig-like squeal that stopped the whole bar where it was. Bartender Timmy cut the music. The crowd circled. Blood gathered in tiny red slicks on the ground around the two fighters as if from a bad transmission. I thought maybe Lyle had stabbed Big Polly with a knife made of glass.

But stumbling to her feet first was Big Polly, her massive cheeks and the chest of her shirt bloody, a purple mountain rising above her left eye. Out of her mouth and onto the green felt of the table came the pinky finger which had been, only moments ago, attached to Lyle Cruz's left hand, his fucking fret hand.

Big Polly started half-dancing, drunkenly, sprinkling the ten and twenty dollar bills all over Lyle who was sitting up by then and staring at the new space on his hand in disbelief.

Dropping Lyle's severed finger into the blue top hat like a gum wrapper into a trashcan, Big Polly scooped the blue top hat up, and walked out of the bar with it. No one followed.

Bartender Timmy produced a bucket of ice, but Lyle waved it off. He gathered himself for ten minutes or so, and then he limped outside too, leaving the money behind.

"Want a cigarette?" Knuckles smiled.

"Sure," I said.

When we got out to the sidewalk, we found Lyle Cruz with a red bandana stuffed into his pinky wound, his leather belt cinched crudely around his hand. He sat on the tailgate of a blue Toyota, feeding red shells into a double-barreled shotgun.

"She forgot our coke," I remembered.

"Well I'm up a hundred," Knuckles shrugged. The two of us walked back inside.

Artist: Brett J. Barr

SMOKING IN THE CITY

Jennifer Todhunter

—

You say you're in a relationship, that your apartment is the size of a closet, that you see the lights of the museum from your window. *It doesn't matter, you say, it doesn't matter how little space you have inside when the world is endless.*

Sometimes when we're messaging, you send me pictures of your city, of its different monuments, the random street vendors, of your hands in fingerless gloves fiddling, smoking. I think of your fingers threaded through mine, of them tracing the length of my spine, of them slipping inside me.

My partner thinks I quit, you say. She thinks I quit, but I walk around the city while she's sleeping, and the city begs for me to smoke.

It looks like that kind of city, I say, watching your cherry flame orange as you inhale.

Have you been? you ask, and when I say I haven't, you tell me I should come. *You can sleep on our couch, you say. We can eat wings, drink beer. We can fuck.*

When you talk about your partner, she can do no wrong. You tell me about the loft bed you share, of your galley kitchen, of all the spaces you squeeze in beside her–your front against her back, your forearm against her breast, your knee against her thigh.

That's not what marriage is like, I say.

It can be, you say, and I wonder what it feels like, to be so close to someone that the heat of their skin always wicks off yours, even when they're not around.

Do you think space is infinite? you ask one night. *Do you ever contemplate what it means to be truly endless?*

I don't know where I start, I say, *let alone where I end.*

Nobody does, you say. *Nobody.*

At night, my husband's feet avoid mine, his hands push me away. He has sharp edges. A start and a finish.

Do you think space is infinite? I ask in the dark, and he snorts and rolls over.

What is forever? I ask the next time we speak.

Forever is a fallacy, you say. *Nothing is forever.*

But you said the world is endless, I say, and I consider the weight of implied boundaries, the weight of my oxygen versus your oxygen, whether there is a difference of scale, whether I would be able to catch my breath if we were together. I consider how far a string, a rock, a thought would fall when weighted and dropped.

Forever isn't the same as endless, you say, your smoke blurring the screen.

IT'S NATURAL

Curtis Ippolito

—

Corduroys was a poor choice given the waterlogged quilt of multi-colored leaves. The air cold enough for snow intensified the throbbing of my knees. I'd been warned. Butted into my armpit, an unloaded rifle. Target practice completed days earlier. Could I pull the trigger when a buck filled my sights? My uncle said I should decide only after sleeping with the feeling.

A deer came along soon enough, our bellies hugging soggy eastern Ohio earth. Twenty yards out. Filled my crosshair. A young buck with few points. Ears flapping, his nose shoveled through the wet leaves. Moving to a tree trunk, his white tail danced in the stiff cold. I smiled at my uncle. He winked back. The odor of snuff embedded in his orange beard tingled my skin. We returned our eyes to the buck. It was doubled over. Convulsing. Thrusting. Grunting. Sounds foreign to my ears, widened my eyes. Hooves pawed. Antlers thrashed. Snot flew.

When it finished, it scampered off with delight and I sat bewildered. My uncle still smiled. It's natural, he said, explaining many male animals, including deer, masturbate. I would start doing the same in a year or two and that would be natural, too.

My mother's brother took custody of me after her death but not before my father abandoned me in a closet for months. I was six. I didn't see my father again until the day after the masturbating deer.

In the morning, I announced I wanted to bag my first buck. Later, packing our gear in the basement garage is when my paroled father showed unannounced. We spotted him a hundred yards out, strutting up the mountain's winding chalk-rock road, sun ablaze on his back. Walmart jeans. Worn-out red fleece. No-brand sneakers and the Indians cap with a broken red bill he kept in the closet on a hook.

"Go inside. Wait there," my uncle said.

I heard their argument through a floor vent and learned of the arrangement before being called down and informed. My father would spend the next day with us for the hunt and dinner afterwards.

The next morning, he returned in the same clothes. Shivering in the dark when we opened the garage. There wasn't enough light to examine his face without staring, so I didn't.

We pushed into the forest single-file. I led with my uncle behind me, our rifles aimed to the ground as safety dictated. My father started up immediately, his incessant blather drowning out the forest. Prison tales, wisecracks, glossed-over memories. I squeezed my rifle tighter with each. My uncle groaned every time his sister's name was taken in vain. The thick plume of condensation above the Indians hat lit my skin on fire. Shoulder taps returned my glare ahead.

At the blind, he wouldn't quit. Ignoring him failed. Nodding and smiling, same. He had no regard that the hunt's success hinged on silence. He blew off my uncle and got louder. Hours on and no deer sightings, we surrendered. I stowed the unused gear, unloaded our rifles. Backpacks shouldered, we retreated. I didn't want to bag my first deer with him anyway.

Halfway back, we stopped to pee at individual trees. Reassembling the line, my father took lead with me in the middle and my uncle behind me.

God, he wouldn't shut up. Hot air billowed above that stupid hat. My mother's name spilled from his lips. Her drug-induced death a convenient defense for his negligence.

I didn't plan what happened next. Maybe I did. After all, I unloaded only four of five bullets in my rifle before leaving the blind. Regardless, my rifle caught my attention swinging to the rhythm of my steps. Skin hot, I pulled back the bolt action as slow as possible to chamber the bullet with little noise. I lifted the rifle. No longer earth, the muzzle now aimed at my father's back. Sweat showered my body. My hand froze on the stock. Dread filled me visualizing my finger on the trigger. Then, my uncle grabbed my shoulder and squeezed. I grimaced, lowered the rifle.

"It's natural," he said. "But no."

"What?" said my father, spinning around.

"Nothing," my uncle growled.

Once my father started jabbering again, my uncle took the rifle with a stern look.

Back home, sunlight waned. I was sent inside to unpack the gear. My uncle said he's driving my father home. No dinner, no goodbye. Of course I approved.

My uncle returned hours later, said my father didn't deserve another chance and I never had to see him again.

I bagged my first buck a few weeks later and never hunted again. I also never saw my father again. Not another word. All these years later, I still don't know what happened to him. Sometimes I debate asking my uncle about that night. I wonder if he could have killed him. My father might have rotted away under a mat of soggy leaves more than a decade ago. Composted into something for a young buck to poke its nose through and gratify itself on. And that would be okay. After all, it's natural.

YOU'LL NEVER LEAVE

Steve Gergley

—

A t twenty-seven my body began to vanish. First it was small things I barely missed, like the runty little nail on my left pinky toe, or the shaggy coat of hair on my right calf, but after a while more important things started disappearing. Soon it was the disk of cartilage in my left knee, the pad of fat sheathed within my right heel. And as if that wasn't enough, each time something vanished, I would suddenly wake up on the concrete floor of my basement with no memory of how I got there.

It was summer. I was still living with my parents then, not sure of what to do with my life. In college I'd studied anthropology, and during those years I'd dreamed of someday traveling the world and immersing myself in the different cultures of mankind, but by the time I graduated I was already thirty grand in debt, so that never panned out. Instead I spent the next six years sliding gallons of milk into metal racks in the forty-degree dairy cooler of my hometown Value King supermarket.

Later, once my body started vanishing, I realized I'd had enough of that cooler, so I quit the next day.

My parents went to London for vacation that August. At the time I hadn't yet told them about my vanishing body, so they let me stay behind and house sit.

While they were gone I looked for a new job. I was so sick of living at home and feeling like a failure, so I scoured the internet for something full-time and sustainable, something that would finally let me escape the prison that was my parents' house.

A few days later I got called in for an interview at the Topine Free Library. The interview was for a full-time library assistant job, and it was the only paid position available that didn't require a Master's degree, so for once I was actually qualified for the job I was applying for. By then my entire right leg was gone except for the skin, but I didn't care about that for the moment. The only thing that mattered was my interview. So, to help me get around my buddy Colin let me borrow a pair of crutches from the hospital where he worked.

Around eight-thirty on the morning of my interview, I crutched into the kitchen to grab some milk from the fridge. Moments later I woke up in the basement. When I tried to stand up, I discovered a bag of empty skin piled in the place where my left leg used to be.

Now the severity of my situation finally set in. I tore through my flattened pockets in a panic, searching for my phone. Then I remembered: I'd left it on the dresser in my bedroom upstairs.

From here I tried to calm myself with some deep breaths. When that didn't work, I lay back on the cold concrete and stared up at the ceiling. There I saw the bones of my missing toes bracing the sagging pipes above. I saw the fibrous ropes of my tendons holding the furnace's tube in place. I saw the pad of fat from my heel jammed into a leaky crack in the wood.

For the next hour I looked around for the rest of me. I wasn't able to find everything I'd lost, but by then it didn't matter because I finally understood. This place would never let me leave.

flippin, arkansas

Lauren Suchenski

—

We arkansas moonshined down the freeway – signs following us like ghosts, ancestor stories lurking in the hills. we pulled at memories we didn't have, like teeth splayed out; like ozark rock shining in the glint. we arrowhead aimed for places in time lost, horseback travelers, abandonment and gap-toothed storefronts. ghost towns ship-wrecked by time, by poverty, by an anchor pulling somewhere deeper than rock – sedimentary and solitary and sedentary.

   i thought about typhoid fever taking old aunt lena, my great-grandmother flossie riding bareback in her dress down the middle of the town. i thought about the flu taking grandma without a name. i thought about old grandpa medlock buried in the cemetery; riding on one solitary horse to Flippin, Arkansas; tending the grocery store in town at the turn of the century. i thought about racism embedded in the rocks, the silt of magic baked into the earth's crust. i thought about the rainbow trout splayed out in the White River. i dipped my hands into the river, imagined the wheel of time spinning my great-grandmother in a cotton dress, on a summer's day, hands fresh in the water – 7 years old, dripping ghost-fire. brave, strong, full of meadowlight and beauty. i thought about my great-great-grandfather getting dragged for miles by a pack of runaway farm horses; the public hanging in the town square of a cowboy for raping the sheriff's daughter. i felt the ghosts in the air, or the ancestor stories still flowing in the White River. i greeted the strange gravel of time, walked its planks, hurled its seasons onto my back. tried to imagine the bodies, the lives they lived, the stories they breathed. when i silted my hands into the enormous body of the clear river, i tried to feel her hands inside of mine. tried to feel the endless grace of a century or two wrapping around me. the playful stream of lives gone by still swimming in the waters all around us. embedded in the crust of the earth. storied earth, oh wise-old grass; blowing. always knowing things that i will never know. the way my great-grandmother's hair looked like in the august light of autumn. twirling around ghosts even then. the vision of her dead sister walking up the lane towards her, vanishing at the eaves of the porch. the distant memories of dna laced into our bones. like the silted crevices of the earth encrusted/entrusted with our stories. like rib cages splayed wide in rock teeth/gulping/chomping/keeping our secrets safe, keeping our stories safe, silting out like erosion. the strange ghosts we don't remember/the old bodies we cannot unearth/the unmarked graves we cannot find/the ancestor songs still swimming in the streams; rainbow trout, or golden oxygen named chemistry. or has the river kept flowing? or has the river kept flowing. and do the rocks dream only to forget?

HALF-WHITE, HALF-CHARRED

Tara Isabel Zambrano

—

I n the distance, along the hazy horizon, you see a settlement. *That's where the gypsies live*, your wife says and curls her fingers on your arm. Her hand smells of cleaning agents—she's a clean freak— rushes to shower and makes you change the sheets, after you make love to her. Every time. *The gypsies kidnap children; steal husbands*, your wife whispers—her chin resting on your shoulder. This is your second marriage and you aren't sure if this'll work too. Maybe you misread everything. Took all that organized shit as a sign of something proper. In any case, she hasn't yet complained of lint-infested corners or dusty fan blades and you haven't yet found an excuse to clear your throat to drown her words and walk away. You sip your tea, let the warmth stay in your mouth a bit longer than usual, and think of the gypsy girl you saw standing on the roadside. Her bare toes digging the dirt, her big forehead marked by sparkling dots, her dark curls escaping from the bun like baby snakes emerging from a hole.

When your wife is away, surfing on the coast of Andaman, she sends text messages to you. *Miss you, Sweetie*, followed by a sparkling, throbbing heart emoji. Your fingers fumble over the text and then close the app. Outside the window, the overgrown grass sways in full sun. You decide to visit the settlement the next day, look for the girl. In the thin strains of dawn, the smoke billows up from a circle of tents. A woman, dressed in black, is about to duck into one of the canvas structures. *Hey*, you call out, and she turns around, her kohl-rimmed eyes, little moons. You follow her into the dwelling with a wispy peach curtain. Inside, it feels as if you've entered another universe—broken dolls and ripped scarves, sea-shell necklaces, metal bangles and anklets on the scattered pieces of rugs. She points you to a wooden stool and asks you to remove your wedding ring, your wristwatch. Then she sits across from you, pulls out a deck of cards. You open your mouth to say you aren't here for a tarot reading. Instead, you exhale and stare at her, completely still.

A few minutes later, the girl walks in—a raised pink in her cheeks and her neck, her gaze slippery. Maybe she saw you walking into the tent. You get up with a strong urge to touch her and she approaches you, a sly smile. Her fingers are dusted with soot, her chin tiny. She comes close, you can feel her breath on your nose: the loamy air that has left her and now wants to enter you. It's still so early in the day and there is a violent flutter in your stomach as she places her hand on your crotch. Gaseous, explosive. You allow her to unbutton your khakis, push you towards the floor, her skirt hitched up, her tan, tattooed legs straddling your pelvis. You bring your lips closer to the girl's mouth—it feels like the edge of a waterfall. The old woman shuffles the cards and starts cursing, her sharp voice dissecting the humidity. The curtain sways in a mild breeze and from the opening you catch a glimpse of a dipping clothesline touching the monsoon slick earth, the simmering coals on an angidhi cooking a bird— its feathers half-white, half-charred. And you continue to slow dance inside the girl, still trying to believe that this is happening-your hand moving away from the girl's hips to her shoulders, reaching out to the dirty tassels of a nearby lamp, your palms laced in a shimmering cobweb, finding comfort. The air roils white. The dust rushes and settles on your skin, as if it has been waiting.

INSOMNIA

Dan Kennedy

—

S asha cannot sleep because she is thinking about Chris, on whom she has a crush. Chris cannot sleep since he likes Jessica, who does not like him. He stares at the lone lit window of his neighbor's house, where one of his classmates, Sasha, lives with her family.

Jessica cannot sleep. She twirls a pink phone cord around her finger and contemplates calling Zach, telling herself that she'll hang up as soon as she hears his voice. Ultimately, she decides against it and falls back to her pillow, resolving to tell her friend, Chris, about how she likes his friend, Zach.

Zach rips another sheet of paper from his notebook, balls it up, and drops it on the ground, where it joins the others. He cannot find the words to describe Lindsey. Their elusion keeps him awake. A train whistle cuts through the night. In a burst of inspiration, Zach thinks he can do something with it. He fervently pens a quatrain. If Jessica were to read Zach's verse, which makes no mention of Lindsey's name, she'd be able to sleep.

Lindsey reads the label on the pill bottle for the thousandth time. Since she can never sleep, her parents brought her to a doctor, who prescribed a drug called Ambien. A train whistle cries in the distance. Lindsey feels an affinity with its sound. She is in love with a girl in her English class, Sasha, but of course she cannot tell anyone, least of all her parents. Plus, this guy, Zach, who is also in English class, writes cryptic poetry, which Lindsey believes is about Sasha. In all likelihood, Sasha reciprocates Zach's feelings. Lindsey hates him for it. She tugs at the silver crucifix around her neck. Her mother bought it for her last Christmas and gave it to her after midnight mass. Lindsey tries to decide if she should take no pills, or all of them. She lies awake on the hammock of her indecision.

Lindsey's parents drink cocktails before bed and pretend that their daughter is fine. They sleep deeply.

FUNERAL ARRANGEMENTS

Racquel Henry

—

Alice walked into the church in her best black dress. A veiled vetting hung over her eyes from her pillbox hat. Some people were chatting while others loomed around the casket saying prayers. Many waited for the service to begin with their eyes as dead as the corpse. Alice sat in the first row. She wanted to be close to Will.

She put her purse on the seat and moved closer to the casket. Will looked plastic, like the cakes on display in the bakery section at the grocery store. He was perfect, but stiff and unreal. *It isn't fair*, she thought. He was right in front of her and she couldn't hold him.

*

She remembered their first date: dinner, moonlight, water flowing not far away, the way Will kissed the chocolate frosting from the cake off her lips. She'd gone home that night, kicked off her high heels, and stared at the ceiling from her bed. She envisioned her future with Will: the white dress, the house (preferably one with a pool), the two perfect kids. As she stared at the ceiling she could see each of the fantasies play out like scenes from a movie. She sighed and closed her eyes.

*

They were supposed to get married.

But Will already had a wife. Out of nowhere he had told Alice that he was married to the love of his life. He wanted to sort things out—had to *stop* seeing Alice.

She begged him for one last date, pressed her chest close to his and kissed his earlobe. Sung the word *please*, like it was a song on repeat. Will couldn't resist.

When the day came, she lit the candles, and when the timer sounded took the soufflé out of the oven. It was her third attempt. It was still a little sunken in the middle, but it would have to do. She was out of time. She set the table. She'd made a salad, honey glazed carrots with mushrooms, and bought a bottle of wine, too. She studied the tiny shadows that the items on the table cast on the walls of the dining room. She loved the house this way, dark with just enough light to create the shadows that often kept her company.

Alice wore the tightest black dress in her closet. The only thing she regretted was that it didn't have a lower neckline. She fixed her makeup one more time before taking a seat on the couch with a glass of wine and waited for Will's knock.

*

Alice was asleep when Will arrived two hours later. In fact, his thunderous fist against the door startled her out of her dreamlike haze so much so that she almost knocked her glass of wine off the coffee table. She stood at attention, pulled her dress down and smoothed her hair. She flung the door wide open ready to throw her arms around him but stopped short when she took in his appearance. He wore a faded Yankees t-shirt and basketball shorts. He used to dress up for their secret dates. Now, he couldn't be bothered with looking good. *He couldn't even fucking put on real pants*, she thought.

He smiled and she stepped aside so he could come inside.

"Sorry I'm late," he said, shoving his hands in his pockets.

"It's fine," she said. She was upset, but as always, seeing his smile made her lose her will to argue. Plus, she didn't want him to spend those last few moments arguing.

She pulled his arms around her. There was a time when they would greet each other and would change from solids to liquid, the two of them pouring into each other. But that night, hugging him was like stacking bricks. She blinked to stop her eyes from stinging, then pulled away.

"Dinner's probably cold, but I can zap our plates in the microwave," Alice said.

"Listen, Alice, I can't stay too long..." Will said.

"I know," she called from the kitchen. "I won't let this take too long."

Will ate in silence. It was up to Alice to make small talk, which was something they never had to do before. It proved things were different, that things were final. She pushed her carrots around with her fork until Will stood up.

"I'm sorry, Alice. I'm not feeling so well and I better get home. Sheila's probably wondering where I am."

Alice nodded. It would only be a few hours before the Destroying Angels mushrooms launched their attack on his kidneys and liver.

*

Alice did a lot of digging to find out about the funeral, but it didn't bother her. After following Sheila to the Bayer Funeral Home, money was all it took for the receptionist at the funeral parlor to give her the time and date. She had leaned over the counter in her best low cut top and slid the envelope with money over.

*

Shame it had to end this way, Alice thought during the service. She would have given Will her world, everything in it. But he wanted Sheila. Sheila was always in the way.

When the service was over, Sheila got up and gazed at Will one more time.

Alice placed her hand on Sheila's back and Sheila jumped.

"Sorry for your loss," Alice said.

"Thank you," Sheila said, dabbing her eyes with a handkerchief. She tilted her head at Alice. "I don't believe we've met. How did you know my husband?"

"I was a friend," Alice said.

THE GOOD BOOK

Lynn Mundell

——

The man had said to live by The Good Book and all of our problems would be solved. How to not lose our entire group, but grow it like our ancestors had—Sarah, Abraham, Ishmael, Isaac, Rebecca, Jacob. Each named by another, unlike us, who recently re-named ourselves, and some would say badly. How to identify sins, such as envy, greed, and gluttony, like when we killed a wild boar and ate until we were sick. How to stay positive through war, plague, pestilence, all that we'd survived before but might succumb to the next time around, like Teacher Julie finally had. The man on the record player had started to say where to get The Good Book, but then the battery died and that was our last double A.

The Good Book would tell us How to Live and that was all we wanted, even Beatrix Potter, the youngest and most despondent among the five of us. So, we began moving from town to town, each as empty and dusty as an abandoned bird's nest, the cold whistling through the bones of our forefathers seated in stalled cars and caught mid-stride along sidewalks, their phones dead in their hands. There were words everywhere—on billboards, old fliers, posters. Most of them concerned how to avoid the end, where to hide from the latest conflict (meat lockers, bank vaults, basements, like the one where we'd been napping). There were so many words, but nothing any of us would call good.

Walking gave us purpose, that and looking for the book. We never met anyone else. At each new town, Beatrix Potter would call, "Wassup, beautiful? 517-2936"—something he'd found on a napkin on a café counter, in front of a smiling skeleton holding a coffee pot. Sometimes his words would echo, which was even worse than silence. We began to pick through vacant buildings and read many interesting and irrelevant things. How to set a table properly. That a premiere happens but once. If you prick holes in the bottom of a check, it takes longer to clear at the bank. That a man named Elvis was once king. Slowly we were learning about our past, what it had meant to be the human race. The many small things that together showed you were alive.

According to our old paper calendar, we'd been searching for one year, two months, and five days when we found The Good Book. It was buried under a pile of clothes in a kid's bedroom up north. We recognized it right away by its heavy black cover and gold lettering that said, "Charging into the Future". It was by far the finest book we'd ever seen. Beatrix Potter did his strange ululation, but this time it sounded joyful. In the book, row upon row of faces looked out—hundreds, in fact. They wore earrings and hairbands, braces and braids. One girl even had a big flower behind her ear. Underneath each picture was a wonderful name: Bethany Goldstein, Billy Tsang, Michael Woods Jr., Nikisha Holmes. We sat in a circle and took turns reading about these people and their accomplishments: Best Legs, First Chair, Biggest Flirt, Most Likely to Succeed. Then we read the handwriting we could decipher, with advice about summer, friends, enemies, love, and life. We read until the sun set and then we made beds among the clothes in the room. It felt like a new beginning. We could see what we were supposed to look like—smiling and clean. The pictures showed even a tribe as small as ours could be champions. That if you had an entire book of good words to live by, like the man on the record said, you might just stand a chance of being saved.

THE MAGIC OF HANGING UPSIDE DOWN

Gabrielle Griffis

—

Anya could hear the wrecking ball smash the theater down. Moisture and mold eroded the internal structures of the building. Icy New England winters gave way to humid summers. Aspergillus blossomed over audience seats, slowly devouring water warped boards. There were three kinds of people in the world, Anya thought. Those who make things worse, those who try to keep things in stasis, and those who try to improve things.

Anya hung another bunch of lavender upside down. Inverting a form meant to retain water kept microbes from devouring its cellular structures. Herbs hung from the ceiling, lemon balm, borage, feverfew. She enjoyed hanging plants upside down, stalling the state of decay long enough to make a tea or salve from dehydrated leaves.

It was like cheating time.

The city had fallen into a regressive state of entropy. Inspired by department stores sucking capital out of local commerce. Empty storefronts and condemned symbols lined the once lively downtown. A strip mall pulled customers from locally owned restaurants into its franchises. Money floated out of the city.

Empty yellowed windows expressed a collective death. The former industrial town never seemed to recover from the download of inanimate things. Plastic ceaselessly being pumped into their psyches from other realms.

In the back of the building, seedpods shook on hollow stalks. In the summer, bee balm and catmint overflowed from garden beds. Sunchokes and nasturtium fed hungry pollinators.

Anya boiled bayberries over a hotplate. The wax would be separated and poured into a candle. She dipped a mullein stalk in tallow.

***

There was a time when Anya wanted nothing. Her spirit had been stripped of joy. Plans for development went on behind closed doors. The people never had a chance. At the city meeting, Anya stood before the town and made her case. She begged the mayor to delay the project. No one listened.

Before the strip mall was built, Anya sat in the field where it would be placed. She watched warblers and robins forage for grubs amid goldenrod and milkweed. She apologized to the hairstreaks and snails for the destruction of their home. She wiped her eyes on her sleeve as the wind blew through the field. They had nowhere to go.

Anya uprooted plants from the meadow. She wiped her hands on her pants, which were covered in dirt. She placed the perennials in the back of her car. Stars emerged as the sun set over open earth for the last time.

She watched the people grow sicker. Emaciated and bloated forms, opposite ends of an unwell extreme. Land was parceled and unshared. Communication occurred in bisected lines, stymied by bureaucracy.

Former factories eroded into the earth. As a teenager, Anya walked the halls of the city's abandoned asylum. Beds with restraint straps turned over in the gloom. Wire cages rusted over broken windows. She didn't think much had changed. Society's solution for masking madness took the form of isolation.

Leaves littered the asylum floor. Violets grew from broken porcelain sinks. As vines overtook the building, it occurred to Anya, that the only way to fix her soul was to align with nonverbal entities. They spoke languages of neurons and synapses, poisons and fragrance. They redeemed rigid architecture, crumbled walls into small mountains.

She could never grow too close to people, perpetually caught in love-hate relationships. She loved a dancer once, but his parents moved him to pursue a professional career. They spent their final afternoon collecting flowers and berries. She took him to the asylum. He wove her a flower crown. They sat under the decaying architecture squishing the juice out of fruit and smearing it on each others faces. They laughed, and then cried, and then he left.

Anya grew tired of watching her feelings die. She walked the city and gathered wild geraniums for a poultice. Magenta flowers grew throughout fractured asphalt. Dead love felt like cut stems, withering.

***

Years elapsed. She opened the shop downtown. Rain flooded the drains. Brides entered the boutique across the street. For sale signs replaced window mannequins. She poured vinegar into mason jars stuffed with mugwort. Used fennel to ward off evil spirits.

People drifted through the door, absorbed in their stories. Each head had its own mental tempo, Anya thought. It was a wonder anyone could converse, that thoughts could be comprehended. She imagined conversations were like butterflies, meeting and departing in air. There was a certain rhythm everything fell into, impossibly.

She wondered if her sorrow arose from a constant state of dying interactions. In the same way she got sad when blossoms turned to husks.

Anya let the plants rebuild her soul. It had been filled with loss and cobwebs. She pressed flowers, arranged them around old portraits. Her Great Aunt once walked the asylum, stuffed moths in her mouth.

Anya wondered if the dancer would return. She was used to being forgotten. It was easier to get lost in floral time, when the tinkling doorbell led only to disappointment. She hung everything upside down. Everything was better upside down. She imagined tipping the city and shaking it out of its husk.

CPSIA information can be obtained
at www.ICGtesting.com
Printed in the USA
LVHW080724080122
708017LV00021B/207